Amy Cross is the author of more than 100 horror, paranormal, fantasy and thriller novels.

Battlefield

Nykolas Freeman book 2

AMY CROSS

First published by Dark Season Books,
United Kingdom, 2017

ISBN: 9781521184547

Also available in e-book format.

www.amycross.com

CONTENTS

BATTLEFIELD

PROLOGUE

January 17th, 1644

AT FIRST LIGHT, THICK fog hung in the air. Everything was a haze of white, save for the land itself. Muddy, uneven soil was still partially frozen from the cold night, with wisps and curls of fog drifting languidly past. The scene was silent, too, save for occasional coughs in the distance.

The two vast armies were unable to see one another as they waited for the fog to clear.

As morning wore on, voices began to call out from time to time. Royalists and Parliamentarians taunted one another, yet neither side was willing to make the first move and charge into the white unknown. For so long as the fog remained, the battle was forestalled and the ground was left unbloodied.

Only around midday did the fog lift enough for

the two sides to start seeing one another. Faint, shadowy figures began to emerge from the white thrall, although still no-one made a move. As the fog lifted a little more, more figures came into view, on the flanks of two opposing hills and with a stretch of moorland spread between them. Thus emboldened, the Parliamentarians start flinging stronger and stronger insults in the direction of their enemy, hoping to goad them into attacking first. The Royalists, on the other hand, were wise to such tricks and stood their ground.

"Where's the coward Villiers?" a voice yelled from the Parliamentarian infantry. "Let him lead you into battle!"

"Villiers is here!" another voice shouted back. "His sword awaits your watery blood!"

Still the fog withdrew, lifting gradually and at its own pace, showing no regard for the two armies that itched to get their battle underway. Finally, however, by 2pm the front lines could see each other well enough, and the men of each side stared into the eyes of their opponents. All through the valley, thousands of chests tensed in anticipation, and the fog drew back further, revealing ever great masses waiting for battle to begin. Every man knew that most would be killed, but every man also believed in his heart that he would survive.

It was the Parliamentarians, under Thomas Ledgemore, who finally broke first.

Infantry charge was met with infantry charge, and there was time for only one volley of musket-fire to ring out before the two sides met on the battlefield. Swords swung at limbs and cries ran out, and blood began to flow into the mud. Now the fog began to intensify again, although it was too late for either side to withdraw now. Fresh waves came from either side, swarming the scene and quickly taking the places of their fallen comrades, crying out angry threats against their opponents. To the south, Royalists on horseback began to make their first charge, countered swiftly by musket-fire and then by Parliamentarian foot soldiers. The remainder of the two armies hung back, uncommitted, as the furious battle raged. When Captain John Villiers of the Royalist unit was mortally wounded by musket-fire, his body was quickly trampled into the mud as the soldiers continued their battle, and his solid gold standard fell to the ground. Boots quickly hurried past, pushing the gold out of sight beneath the blood-soaked soil.

The stench of death filled the air, and the fog grew thicker and thicker.

***

Crying out, Michael Appendon swung his sword at the man ahead, striking his armor but failing to deliver a convincing blow. Swinging around, he narrowly missed getting his waist sliced open, and then he tried once again to bring his enemy down. This time he aimed at the fellow's neck, hoping to cut through the gap beneath the man's helmet and chest-plate, but once again his sword simply glanced against the metal.

"By God," the Royalist soldier sneered, raising his own sword high above his head, "you shall -"

Suddenly a volley of musket-fire struck the man square in the chest, blasting him back several feet until he slumped down against the muddy ground.

All around, men roared and screamed.

Cries of victory and death.

"For the king!" a voice shouted.

"He'll hang yet!" countered another.

Wasting no time, Michael stumbled forward and drove his sword into a gap between the armor plates that secured the chest-plate of another Royalist soldier. He heard a grunt of pain from the man's lips, but this only emboldened him to twist the blade, then to pull it out and strike again, this time driving it straight through the eye of his enemy until he felt the tip hitting the inside of the back of the man's helmet. Pulling his bloodied sword clear, Michael stepped over his vanquished enemy and hurried onward, already searching for the next opponent. He counted two kills by his own hand so far, but he was thirsty for more. After just a few seconds, another Royalist came charging toward him, swinging a sword that missed Michael's face by inches as it came crashing down.

"Traitor!" the man hissed.

"I fight for the freedom of this country," Michael shouted, adjusting the grip on his sword. "There are traitors on this battlefield, but they are not among my side."

"You would kill the king!"

"Aye, I would that!"

Their swords clashed, but neither man was able to land a blow.

"Your blood will flow into the ground," the Royalist sneered. "Mark my word on that!"

Raising his sword again, Michael saw that his new foe was already wounded from some earlier encounter, and that the man's left arm was hanging loose. Only a string of flesh kept the limb attached to the shoulder, so Michael threw his weight against the man, knocking him to the ground and battering his face with his hands. Having weakened his enemy further, he then slammed the handle of his sword against the man's face before slicing the blade through his neck. As soon as he saw blood erupting from the wound, he stumbled to his feet and staggered onward, filled with the knowledge that there were hundreds, perhaps thousands more Royalists still to be slain.

All around him, Englishmen were fighting Englishmen, pushing the brunt of civil war ever onward.

Spotting another Cavalier stumbling toward him through the fog, Michael raised his sword and prepared to bring it crashing down against the man's head, before hesitating as he suddenly realized all had fallen still. As if the world had frozen, Cavaliers and Roundheads alike had ceased to battle, and instead were looking toward one particular spot ahead. Glancing around, Michael saw that everyone seemed dazed, so he slipped through the crowd, desperate to see what vision had brought the entire battle to a sudden standstill. In all his time fighting, he had never before seen two opposing armies suddenly cease their combat in such a manner, yet bitter enemies now stood shoulder-to-shoulder, sharing a sense of abject horror.

In the distance, fresh cries rang out. Although he had fought in many battles already, Michael felt he had never heard the sound of men in quite so much pain.

As he continued to make his way forward, fog seemed to move back in with great speed, making it increasingly difficult for him to see what was up ahead. With each step, however, he began to make out the scene a little more clearly, until he realized there were several bodies huddled together on the ground, already leaking blood into the mud. Such a sight was far from unusual in the heart of battle, of course, but nearby soldiers from both armies were dropping to their knees, as if they had seen something so terrible that their hearts and souls were starting to crack.

"Run men!" a voice cried out nearby. "It's some form of witchcraft!"

Michael saw a shape in the fog up ahead, something unfamiliar. Running forward, he began to make out some kind of large metal casing, but a moment later he stopped when he saw scores of soldiers lumbering forward through the fog with their swords raised. He braced himself for an attack by the Royalists, before realizing that there were already Royalists all around him, and that they seemed just as terrified as the Parliamentarians. Watching the approaching army approaching through the fog, Michael began to notice that these soldiers seemed different somehow. The closer they came, the clearer their features became, and finally he realized that their skulls were visible through the rotten flesh that hung from their faces.

"May God have mercy on our souls," muttered

someone nearby.

"What are they?" another soldier asked, taking a cautious step back.

"What manner of witchcraft..." Next to him, a Royalist stood with a drained and pale face, as if he might be about to faint. "It looks like... It can't be true! It can't be!"

As a soldier up ahead was hacked to pieces by the undead army, the rest of the men – both Parliamentarians and Royalists – turned and ran together. Scrambling past one another, they cried out, some in pain and some in madness. All were desperate to get away, filled with the kind of pure horror that can tear a man's mind apart. Voices cried out, and even Michael himself found himself unable to stand his ground. Running with the rest, he raced across the moorland, as agonized screams rang out from the heart of the battlefield.

***

Several hours later, once darkness had fallen, the remains of the Parliamentarian unit made their way home along a barren road. Not one man dared speak; instead, each of them considered his own private torment, and the horrors he had witnessed. Their commander had told them that the Battle of Sharpeton must never be spoken of again, and all had agreed. The Royalists, they were all assured, had agreed the same.

Still, Michael Appendon couldn't help glancing over his shoulder every few steps, to make sure they weren't being followed. He half expected to see the nightmarish creatures lumbering through the night, dragging their rotten bodies and their rusty weapons with them. Freezing rain was falling, and as hard as he tried, he couldn't stop thinking about the horrific sights that had appeared in the fog. He'd seen some of his dearest friends cut down by creatures he couldn't even begin to decide. When he glanced at his surviving comrades, he saw the same shock in their eyes. All that was left was for him to mutter a few words to God, praying that whatever had happened during the battle, it would never be seen again.

In the distance, high up on a hill, a lone woman watched as the soldiers walked away from Sharpeton.

CHAPTER ONE

Today

BECCA WINCED AS SHE heard another bump from downstairs. Sitting on the corner of her bed, with her back against the wall, she listened to the sound of her father stumbling about in the front room below. His footsteps sounded uneven, as if he couldn't quite control himself. In the darkness of her bedroom, the little girl's eyes were wide with fear. The storm outside didn't bother her at all, but she was terrified of her father's drunken rage.

A moment later there was another bump from below, and this time the sound of breaking glass, followed swiftly by her father's muffled voice cursing and complaining.

Outside, wind swirled the rain around, sending it crashing against the window.

Swallowing hard, Becca listened to the sound of

her father banging about as he headed into the kitchen, no doubt to get the dustpan and brush. Some variation of this situation occurred almost nightly, and she knew what to expect. Sure enough, a moment later she heard her father opening the closet in the corner of the kitchen, then she heard him pulling the broom out, and then some more curses. A moment later she heard the sound of broken glass being swept across the floor, then a bump.

Then nothing.

Silence followed, and for several minutes the house remained completely quiet. The sound of the storm was almost soothing now. As tempted as she felt to relax, however, Becca knew that her father had most likely just passed out for a few minutes. Glancing over at the Winnie the Pooh clock next to her bed, she saw that it was almost 1am, which meant that with luck her father might well be done for the night. A moment later, her gaze settled on the framed photo of her mother and sister. She only dared take the photo out of the drawer after bedtime, when it was less likely to be spotted and confiscated.

Outside, rain still lashed the window and a strong gale could be heard blowing across the moor. A moment later, there was a rumble of thunder. She liked thunder. Thunder meant that sometimes she couldn't hear her father at all.

"Becca!" she heard him calling out suddenly. "Becca, get down here!"

She flinched and then waited, hoping that he'd simply pass out again, like most nights.

"Becca!"

Still she waited. Two cries was a bad sign, but if he called a third time, that would mean she'd definitely have to -

"Becca!"

Realizing that she had no choice, the little girl clambered off the bed and made her way cautiously across the darkened bedroom. Just eleven years old, she'd learned long ago that her father's drunken rages couldn't be ignored, not once they passed a certain point of no return. If she stayed upstairs, he'd only come storming up in an even worse mood. There had been nights like that in the past, nights when she'd tried to stay in her room, and she'd always ended up being dragged out and forced to go downstairs, down into the front room where her father's whiskey bottles littered the floor. And the angrier he got, the more his hands began to wander, especially if he'd been mixing spirits. Better to keep him calm as much as possible.

Cautiously, she opened her bedroom door and looked out at the brightly-lit landing.

"Becca!" her father's slurred voice called out from downstairs. "Get down here, you little... Becca!"

CHAPTER TWO

"THIS," THE ELDERLY MAN muttered darkly, as he climbed out of the cramped taxi and adjusted his glasses, "had better not be a waste of my bloody time!"

"Doctor Clarke!" a voice called out, as a dark figure hurried through the rain. Silhouetted against the arc lights in the distance, she quickly reached him and held her umbrella out for them to share. Already, her feet were starting to sink into the boggy ground. "My name is -"

"Mary Baker," he replied, squinting a little as he peered across the rain-lashed moor. The lights in the distance were blinding, illuminating the rain-lashed dig site. "I know who you are, young lady, and I know what you do. You're another meddlesome upstart who thinks she's smarter than everyone else. What I *don't* know, Miss Baker -"

"Doctor Baker."

"*Doctor* Baker..." He sighed. "What I *don't*

know, is why you've called me out to the middle of nowhere on a Saturday night at..." He checked his watch, and then he sighed again. "Christ, it's gone midnight. I'm getting too old for this sort of rubbish."

"We found something you really have to see," she told him. "I couldn't explain it over the phone, you'd think I was insane. What we've found here..." She paused for a moment, trying to find the right words. "You just have to see it for yourself."

"I know you *claim* to have found something," he muttered, watching as several figures in the distance moved through the mud while stepping carefully around patches of dirt that had been roped off. "I read your initial report into the dig you've been carrying out here."

"And what did you think?" Mary asked.

He glanced at her. "I thought it was baseless, meandering garbage," he said calmly, "and I honestly began to wonder what kind of mind could possibly come up with such trash. You might have a future as an author of wild fantasies, *Miss* Baker, but your abilities as an archaeologist are very much in question! I can only imagine that you're trying to compensate for some deep-seated and extremely justified sense of inadequacy. I also took the time to look up your doctoral work. Jesus Christ, you're a hack!"

Before Mary could answer that barrage of insults, Doctor Clarke stepped forward and opened his own, larger umbrella, and then he set out across the mud, squelching through thick, watery puddles that slowed his pace. He muttered a few obscenities under his breath as he felt cold water seeping into his shoes and through his socks. All around, rain was still crashing down, blown through the air by a high wind that continually changed its direction, whipping first this way and then that across the moor. Doctor Clarke let out a few more curse words under his breath, frustrated that the muddy ground kept him from going faster, while up ahead he saw dark figures still hurrying through the night, darting between high-standing arc lights that had been weighed down at their bases by piles of sandbags. Already, half the equipment looked to be sinking into the mud.

"I think you're going to change your mind when you see what we've found!" Mary called out as she struggled to keep pace. "Doctor Clarke, I've always been a huge admirer of your work, ever since..." She hesitated for a moment. "Well, anyway, your reputation is immense. I've read all your books, I quoted your work extensively in my doctoral thesis, and that's why I knew we had to get you out to look at this. I mean, more than anyone else in the country, you're probably the leading expert when it comes to this period of history."

"Probably?" he asked.

"Well, *definitely*, but -"

"I'm going to want an apology," he continued, still squelching through the mud. "When this is over and I've debunked your ridiculous claims, I'm going to want one hell of a groveling apology for dragging me out here to the arse-end of nowhere!"

"But Doctor -"

Above, a loud clap of thunder rumbled across the sky, causing Mary to look up in shock. The weather forecast had predicted rain, but not a full storm.

"If word of this palaver gets out," Doctor Clarke continued with a long-suffering sigh, "and I end the evening in a particularly bad mood, I might decide to destroy your career. Do you understand that?" Receiving no reply, he glanced back at her for a moment. "You could be laughed out of the profession for this. If I tell my colleagues about your mindless stupidity, word will quickly spread and you'll become unemployable. Seriously, *Miss* Baker, that's how much weight my opinion carries. You'll have to give up your dreams of a career in archeology and start flipping burgers with the rest of the lower middle-class graduates."

"Please, Doctor -"

"This is what happens when any Tom, Dick or Sally is allowed to go to university," he added, clearly warming to his theme. "We end up with idiots in the academic system, pumped up with a sense of their own importance and desperately trying to make names for themselves. Judging by your youth, Miss Baker, I assume you are a product of the Blair generation. I don't know who to dislike more. The Labour government for opening the floodgates, or the Tories for not shutting them again!"

"I know my claims are pretty crazy," she replied, forcing herself to ignore his rant, "but I promise you, I wouldn't have asked you to come here tonight if I wasn't sure of my findings. Really, *really* sure."

"Oh Christ," he replied, "do you know what I hate the most?"

"Rain?" she asked, forcing a smile. "Mud?"

"Young people," he groaned. "You lot never

know your place, do you?"

Again he muttered some curse words, but this time he turned and focused on getting to the dig site as quickly as possible. Cold and tired, he wanted merely to disprove her claims and then get back to his hotel room in town, and maybe sneak in a Guinness or two. As he got closer to the roped-off area, he saw several dark objects glistening in the mud, while a little further off there was a large white tent, its sides billowing in the relentless wind and rain. Nearby, one of the arc lights was swaying dangerously in the wind, as if it might get blown over at any moment.

"So what do we have here?" he asked with a contemptuous sigh as he stopped and looked down at the objects on the ground. "Mud, mud and more mud?"

***

"This is a Cavalier helmet from the English Civil War," Mary said a few minutes later, as they stood in the tent. Holding up the battered, cracked helmet, she turned it around in the light for him to see properly, just as another rumble of thunder filled the night sky outside. "Typical lobster-tailed pot type, most likely from a Royalist harquebusier. Judging by the area around the rear, and this section of -"

"Late 1644, possibly early 1645 construction," he snapped, interrupting her.

"I was thinking it might be from as early as 1642," she replied, turning the helmet around to show him the front. "Based on this patterning here, and also -"

"Completely impossible," he continued, snatching the helmet from her hands and tilting it to examine the inside. "This detailing here was never used before the middle of 1644, and combined with the joins here and here..." His voice trailed off as he examined the helmet for a moment longer. The sides of the tent was flapping in the wind, and rain could be heard pounding down outside. "No, Miss Clarke, 1642 is impossible. This is a typical seven-shilling cheapie from late 1644. In fact -" He shoved it back into her hands. "I'm surprised that someone with your *supposed* level of education could make such a mistake. This is rudimentary stuff, my dear, first-year undergraduate level. Where did you get your doctorate, anyway? A modern polytechnic?"

Biting her tongue, Mary set the helmet down. She'd expected Doctor Clarke to be difficult, but his ill-tempered aggression was starting to make her want to scream. "There's also -"

"So you found a helmet in the mud," he continued, interrupting her yet again. Reaching out, he gave her a pat on the head, and she was too shocked to pull away before he was finished. "How thrilling. Aren't you a clever little thing? Can I go now?"

"We found more than *one* helmet."

"How wonderful. A passing group of infantrymen ended up getting ambushed here, and for whatever reason their equipment was left to rust. Hardly a staggering discovery of -"

"Three hundred and twenty," she added.

He opened his mouth to reply, before hesitating

for a moment. For this first time since his arrival, he seemed a little taken aback.

"Three hundred and twenty Cavalier helmets and assorted piece of armor," she continued, "and almost the same again from the Roundhead side. We've also found a huge quantity of bones, many of them damaged in a manner consistent with battle wounds. Muskets, swords, the remains of horses, cavalry standards and infantry equipment, plus -"

"Impossible," he said firmly. "Out of the question."

"We've *found* them, Doctor Clarke," she replied. "My team and I have dug all of those things and more from the mud over the past couple of weeks, and we're still finding new items every day, every *hour* even. This is quite possibly the most significant archaeological discovery in England for decades. Don't you see what must have happened here? It's already absolutely clear that this moor was the sign of a major battle in the -"

"Don't be ridiculous," he muttered, shaking his head.

"Doctor Clarke, the evidence -"

"We're three miles from the village of Sharpeton," he continued. "There are absolutely no records of a battle having taken place anywhere in this vicinity during the English Civil War."

"Clearly one *did* take place."

He shook his head.

"This was a battlefield!" she added.

"And then everyone conveniently forgot to mention it?" he asked, unable to stifle a faint smile.

"Miss Baker -"

"*Doctor* Baker," she reminded him.

"The English Civil War has been extensively studied," he continued, with the tone of someone explaining a simple topic to a child. "We know everything that happened. We know the people who were involved, the groups, the events that took place. I myself have extensively studied troop movements, and I can assure you that there are very few gaps in our knowledge. We can pick any period during the entire conflict and say with a high degree of certainty that we know what was happening throughout the country and -"

"Sure, but -"

"We know all the major battles. Edgehill, Newbury, Naseby... We know the turning points, we have all the pieces of the story and -"

"I know, but -"

"And now here you are," he added, steamrollering her attempt to answer, "trying to claim that there was *another* significant battle that took place at the height of the conflict, with hundreds of casualties on either side..." He sighed, seemingly a little breathless now and definitely red in the face. "And somehow we knew nothing of this event until today. Think carefully before you say another word, Miss Baker, because you're on the verge of losing what little reputation you have left."

"I admit that it's extremely unlikely, but -"

"It's more than *unlikely*," he blustered, making his way over to a table in the corner and taking a look at several more battered old helmets that had been laid out.

"It's impossible. There was no Battle of Sharpeton during the English Civil War! That is simply a fact."

Mary paused for a moment, watching as the old man picked up one of the helmets and turned it around in his hands.

"Then explain what we've found here," she said finally, forcing herself to stay calm, and still hopeful of changing his mind. "I'm not an idiot, Doctor Clarke. I know that the odds of uncovering a key battlefield like this, one that was somehow lost to history... I know it beggars belief. I know there's no conceivable way this could be happening. There should be records of this battle if it happened, contemporary accounts, but the fact remains that we've uncovered a battlefield right here, just outside Sharpeton, one we knew nothing about. Judging by the size of the discovery so far, and the fact that we're still making new finds every day, I think it's clear that this was one of the biggest battles of the entire English Civil War period."

"And then after it was over," he muttered, "what happened? Did both sides just agree to pretend it had never happened?"

"I..." She paused, aware that the idea was preposterous. "I can't conceive of a reason why they would do something like that, but... I know it sounds crazy, but for some reason, the battle seems to have been covered up. No-one wanted to admit that it happened. It's as if the survivors all agreed to pretend that there had never been a battle here at all. Why would they do that?"

Still examining one of the helmets, Doctor Clarke seemed lost in thought for a moment, before finally turning back to her. He seemed on the verge of telling her once again that she was mistaken, but there was just a trace of doubt in his eyes, as if he couldn't quite summon the same blustering energy that had emboldened him such a few minutes earlier.

"Okay," he said finally, "show me *exactly* what you've got here. Don't editorialize, don't give me your opinion, just show me and let me form my own view. I still don't believe for one second that you've discovered proof of a lost battlefield from the English Civil War, but..." He paused, before looking back down at the battered helmet in his hands, and then at the others arranged on the table. "You certainly appear to have found *something* of note."

CHAPTER THREE

"DON'T MISS ANY BITS," Becca's father muttered, slumped in the armchair and struggling to focus his eyes as he watched her working. The TV was flashing in the corner, with the sound muted. "I don't want to -" He let out another hiccup. "I don't want to step on bits of glass in the morning. You don't want me cutting my feet, do you?"

With all the big pieces from the broken bottle now swept up, Becca leaned down to start searching the carpet for smaller shards. Running her fingers through the fibers, she quickly found a few thin pieces, which she gathered together and placed in the dustpan. She knew, however, that she wasn't done yet. There had been one night, just a few months ago, when she'd missed a large piece of a broken wine glass, and her father had ended up cutting his toe on the edge. Not only had he raged at her for hours, but he'd also bled all over the floor and she'd been the one who'd had to clean up the mess. She didn't want to have to get the First Aid tin out again.

"Get it all," he continued, his voice more slurred than ever. He took another swig of whiskey straight from the bottle, followed by another hiccup. "Check if -"

And *another*.

"Check if some went under the chairs."

Reaching under the sofa, Becca felt about for stray shards. There were old tissues and pens, and staples, and plenty of dust bunnies that looked like strands of solid fog when she pulled them out. After a few more minutes, however, she felt certain that there were no more pieces of glass. Taking the sections of broken bottle from the dustpan, she tried to piece them back together, and she quickly found that apart from one or two tiny slivers, she had pretty much everything. Carefully making sure not to spill, she got to her feet and then began to carry the dustpan to the kitchen. As she passed her father's armchair, she held her breath, desperately hoping that he wouldn't -

"Hey," he said suddenly, reaching out and grabbing her wrist, almost making her spill the broken glass. "Come back and sit with me when you're done in there, okay?"

"I'm tired," she told him. "Can I go to bed?"

He shook his head, before hiccuping again. "Come sit with me."

She paused, trying to think of another excuse, before finally nodding.

"Okay," she said. "I'll come back."

Please pass out, she thought to herself. *Please,*

just fall asleep.

Once her wrist was free, she made her way into the kitchen and tipped the broken glass into the bin, which was already overflowing with cigarette butts and pieces of burned pizza. After making a mental note to change the bin-bag in the morning, she spent a couple of minutes tidying the dirty plates that had been left by the sink, before realizing that she was just delaying the inevitable. A shiver of fear and revulsion passed through her chest as she thought of previous nights like this one. Ninety-nine times out of a hundred she could more or less control her father, but then were the nights when he just wouldn't fall asleep...

Turning, she looked back through to the front room and listened for her father's snores, but finally she heard him shifting in the chair and she knew he was still somehow awake. Still not wanting to go back through yet, she sniffed her hands and then went to the sink, where she took a moment to wash the smell of red wine from her fingers. Then she took a couple of minute to dry her hands thoroughly, while still playing for time, still hoping that he'd nod off. Glancing at the clock, she saw that it was half one now.

Finally she stopped and stood in silence for a moment, listening to the silence of the house.

Was he asleep?

She held her breath.

Please...

Suddenly she heard another hiccup.

"Have you seen the remote?" he called out a moment later.

She sighed. Making her way through to the front room and stopping in the doorway, she saw that her father was searching for the remote control, although he hesitated when he saw her and fixed her with an intense, drunken gaze.

"Can I... Can I go back to bed now?" she asked. "Please?"

"Which bed?"

She felt a shiver pass through her chest. "I'm tired and -"

"Come here," he continued, patting his knees. "Come sit with Daddy."

"I'm tired."

"No, you're not. Not yet."

She swallowed hard.

"Come over here, Becca."

Refusing would just anger him more, so she edged toward him while making sure not to get too close.

"Daddy misses Mummy," he told her, swaying so much in his chair that he could barely keep his head up straight. "Do you ever think about that? You're not the only one she left behind. Daddy loved Mummy very much, and when Mummy left, Daddy ended up all alone." He hiccuped. "Mummy was a very good Mummy, but to Daddy she..." He paused, staring at his daughter and having to refocus his drunken gaze every few seconds. "Do you want Daddy to feel sad?" he asked finally, before patting his knee again. "Becca? Do you?"

Yet another hiccup.

She hesitated, trying to work out *exactly* how much her father had drunk so far. If he was just slightly tipsy, he'd only want a hug. A horrible, tight hug, but still just a hug, and he'd probably pass out soon enough. Then she'd be able to slip free and go upstairs. The problem, though, was that the broken bottle made it hard to tell whether he'd drunk more than usual, in which case the hug would be more than a hug. She watched, trying to buy herself time, as her father leaned across the armchair's side and tried to reach out to her, and finally – as his fingers brushed against her arm – she took a cautious step back.

"Becca," he slurred, "come on, just -"

Before he could finish, he leaned too far and the entire chair tipped on its side. Becca immediately leaped back as her father tumbled to the floor.

"Jesus Christ," he muttered, half grimacing and half laughing as he struggled to get up. "Becca, help -"

Turning, she hurried through to the hallway.

"Becca, get back here!" he screamed. "Rebecca Jameson, that is an order! Get back in here and help me up!"

Realizing finally that he was too drunk to be trusted, Becca hurried to the front door and pulled it open. Rain and wind immediately crashed against her, almost blowing her back into the house, but she stood her ground. She could hear her father rolling around on the floor in a drunken stupor, hiccuping every few seconds, and she knew that he was past the point at which he'd ever be able to remember the night's events. All she had to do was keep out of his way until morning, and then he'd have forgotten everything and she'd be safe for another day.

Figuring that anything was better than being in the house, she decided she'd have to do what she did every time he was like this, and stay out for the night. She slipped out onto the cold porch and pulled the door shut, and then she looked out at the vast, stormy scene ahead of her. There was no moonlight, but for a moment she thought about the dark moors stretching out all around the desolate, remote house. One good thing about living so far from town was that there was never any danger of running into anyone, even late at night.

This was becoming a habit. Several times a week, Becca had to leave the house at night in order to avoid her father. Fortunately, she knew exactly where to go, thanks to a strange crack in the ground that she'd discovered a few nights earlier.

CHAPTER FOUR

"THIS WOUND WAS CLEARLY inflicted by a sword," Mary explained, holding up one of the many skulls that had been recovered from the mud. "See the way the bone is shattered around the temple? A glancing blow from a sword, probably basket-hilted. The way the bone has been -"

"Let me see!"

Grabbing the skull, Doctor Clarke turned it around in his hands for a moment, examining the broken section before running a fingertip against the damaged edges.

"Careful with that," said Daniel, one of the other archaeologists working the site. "It's hundreds of years old!"

"I'm aware of that," Clarke muttered dourly, rolling his eyes. "Thank you all the same."

Daniel glanced at Mary, but she simply shrugged.

"This proves nothing," Clarke said finally. "This country, indeed this entire world, is littered with old bones. If there's one thing this over-populated planet will never run out of, it's bones!"

"It proves that there was a battle here," Mary replied.

He sighed. "One skull does not a battle make."

"Jackass," Daniel muttered under his breath.

"But two *hundred* skulls?" Mary continued. She lifted a sheet that was covering a nearby table, revealing several more skulls, some of them complete and some badly damaged. There were several jawbones, too, along with a couple of random fragments. "At first it occurred to me that this could be some kind of burial site," she explained, "but the Royalists and Parliamentarians wouldn't have shared a cemetery like this. The distribution of body parts and weapons, the topography of the area with two hills almost adjacent to one another, *everything* points to this having been the site of a battle. The bones you see here are just a small sub-set of the overall find, these are just the ones we found today."

"We're still digging new discoveries out all the time," Daniel added.

"Fine," Doctor Clarke replied with a sigh, glancing at Mary, "but you still haven't explained why this battle is in none of the history books. Rather puts a damper on the whole idea, eh?"

"I'm working on that."

"Do you have a theory?"

"I have some ideas."

Chuckling, he made his way to the table and

looked down at the other skulls.

"I've heard some wild claims in my time, Miss Baker," he muttered finally, "but no-one has ever been quite so brazen as to attempt a rewrite of English history. I know that young people like to challenge the orthodox, but there must be limits. Proper archaeological procedures must be adhered to, or did they not teach you that at whatever state-funded institution you attended?" He glanced at her with a faint, superior smirk. "How old are you, by the way?"

"I don't see that it's -"

"Humor me."

She hesitated for a moment. "Thirty-one."

"Thirty-one?" He smiled. "A mere child. Christ, when I was starting out in my career, you hadn't even been conceived. At the age of thirty-one, I was already learning at the knee of some of this country's finest minds, and I spent my time listening to them and take their wisdom onboard. I certainly didn't challenge and provoke them in such a crude manner. And now here you are, at the tender age of thirty-one, trying to convince *me* that my entire body of work has been based on an incomplete reading of history? Your temerity is breathtaking."

"You seem to be taking this kinda personally," Daniel pointed out.

Holding up another skull, Doctor Clarke seemed lost in thought for a moment. He turned the skull around roughly in his hands, handling it with no real care.

"I told you not to bother with this guy," Daniel continued, turning to Mary. "He's got a reputation as an arrogant jerk, and he's only proving that tonight. We don't need him or his stuck-up opinions, we can call the _"

"Maybe you could go outside and see how the others are doing," she replied, interrupting him.

He opened his mouth to reply, but the words seemed to catch.

"Please, Daniel," she added. "Just let me talk to Doctor Clarke alone."

Sighing, Daniel grabbed a set of gloves from the counter and – without saying another word – headed out into the rainy night. He was muttering to himself as he left, though, and his displeasure was evident in the way he slouched through the door.

"I didn't believe it at first either," Mary continued after a moment, watching as Doctor Clarke examined another damaged skull. "When we started the dig and found the first few helmets, I assumed it was an anomaly, I assumed that by sheer chance they'd ended up buried here. Then we found more, and more, and they just kept coming the further we dug. I told myself it wasn't possible, I went over the original accounts of the period dozens of times, searching for something I'd missed, but eventually I realized that what we'd found here..."

Her voice trailed off for a moment, and she watched as Doctor Clarke set the skull down. Somehow, in the space of just a few minutes, he seemed to have begun to handle the skulls with a little extra care, as if their value and importance was becoming more apparent.

"I didn't ask you to come here tonight so that I could lecture you on what I've found," Mary added. "I asked you to come because I honestly don't know *what* this all means. You're the expert in this kind of -"

"Am I?" he asked, raising a skeptical eyebrow.

"Of course you are! Everyone knows that!" She waited for him to reply. "If I'm wrong, then *show me* why I'm wrong. If I'm missing something huge and vital, then please, for God's sake, *point it out!*" Again she waited, exasperated by his continued silence. "I don't have as much experience as you, not by a long way, but I have enough to know that discoveries like this don't happen every day. They don't even happen every *century*. If this is truly a lost and forgotten English Civil War battle -"

He smirked, as if the idea was amusing.

"If that's what it is," she said firmly, "then it's a huge find! I just don't want to announce anything until I'm sure! The last thing I want is to look like a fool."

"The Battle of Sharpeton," he replied, heading over to the tent's door and looking out at the dark field, where several men were still working in the mud. He paused for a moment. "The Battle of Sharpeton," he said again, as if he was testing the words, trying them out to see if they sounded right. "Two great armies presumably came together, Royalists and Parliamentarians, just outside a dull little town. And then..."

His voice trailed off.

"And then what?" she asked cautiously.

"Exactly," he muttered. "A battle ends either with victory for one side, or with a tactical disengagement. Either way, Miss Baker, *someone somewhere* makes a note of the damn thing. For it not to appear in any history books, in any contemporary accounts or records..." He paused, before turning to her. "There would have had to have been a very conscious, very deliberate and very well-planned effort, agreed by both sides, to forget that such a battle ever happened."

"Why would they do that?"

"Why indeed?" he asked with a shrug. "They wouldn't, Miss Baker, so obviously that can't be the explanation. Just because the facts are not apparent, that's no excuse for us to retreat into the realm of fantasy. Let's not be so immature that we start believing in the impossible, else we might end up losing our minds entirely. There was no Battle of Sharpeton here, it's simply impossible."

She waited for him to continue. "Fine," she muttered finally, too exhausted to keep arguing. "Thank you for your time, Doctor Clarke. I'm sorry you feel you had a wasted trip."

"Are you dispensing with me so quickly?"

"We'll carry on working," she told him, "but obviously you -"

"I didn't say I was *leaving*," he replied, interrupting her. "I might not believe in your hypothesis, my dear, but I can certainly see that you've got a conundrum on your hands. Now that I've come all this way, I might as well help you get to the truth. I believe you mentioned on the telephone that you'd secured a room for me nearby?"

"The King's Head," she replied. "The whole

team is staying there."

"An apt name, considering what happened to the King's head at the end of the war." Sighing, he looked out at the rain for a moment longer before turning back to her again. "I've never been one for crawling about in the mud, Miss Baker. I prefer a nice dry desk, some books, and perhaps a pint of the local ale. So why don't we retire to the King's Head and see if we can nip this whole mess in the bud? Let us put our heads together and work out what really happened here."

CHAPTER FIVE

A FAINT PATCH OF moonlight shone down, lighting patches of moorland with an ethereal blue glow as Becca made her way toward the horizon. All around, more rain battered the ground and strong winds rustled across the land, and Becca's dress was already soaking wet and heavy. She glanced over her shoulder a couple of times, looking back toward her house in the distance, but she knew deep down that her father couldn't possibly be following her. At some point he'd simply pass out in his chair and then he'd sleep until morning, and she'd be back long before then. And then she'd have a relatively normal day, because days were usually okay. Her father only drank at night.

Before all of that, however, she had to visit the crack in the ground.

It took almost half an hour before she reached the ridge near the top of the moor. Stopping for a moment, she stared at the dark crack up ahead. Almost half a mile long, the crack ran straight through the ground, as if some force had reached down and torn the land apart. Becca had no idea what had happened, but she knew the crack hadn't existed when she was younger. She remembered coming for walks with her mother, when they were both trying to get out of the house, and there had been no crack back then. Even just a couple of weeks ago, this patch of land had been smooth and undamaged.

Now there was a crack, as if the ground itself had begun to split open.

Slowly, Becca made her way forward until she reached the edge of the crack. Shivering in the rain, she stared into the darkness, trying to imagine how deep the crack ran and what might be at the bottom. Since she'd never heard her father mention the crack, and since she knew no-one else to ask, she felt as if somehow this part of the moor was hers, as if maybe she was the only one who'd noticed its existence. Sometimes, when her imagination was running overtime, she even wondered if it had opened up *for* her, offering a means of escape. She daydreamed occasionally about a beautiful, happy world that might exist down there, far from the misery of her life at the house, although she also knew that such things weren't really possible outside the confines of a storybook.

The crack was just a crack in the ground, a geological anomaly.

"What do you want to read tonight?" she remembered her mother asking every bedtime.

"*Alice in Wonderland*!" Becca had invariably

replied.

"Again? You don't want to try something else?"

"Please! *Alice in Wonderland*!"

Her mother had read the book to her again and again. It had been their story, their moment alone at the end of the day. Sometimes, she felt her mother liked reading to her because it was an excuse to be upstairs, away from her father's drinking. Other times, however, she truly believed that her mother enjoyed the book just as much. At first, Becca had liked *Alice in Wonderland* for its silly story and strange creatures. Later, after things got really bad, she'd become more interested in the idea of escaping, of traveling to some other world.

She'd always known that was impossible, of course.

She'd told herself that people didn't really get to run away from home and go somewhere new.

But then the crack had appeared.

Taking care not to slip on the wet grass, she edged closer through the rain and wind, finally crouching down as she reached the edge of the crack. As always, she took a moment to peer into the darkness, imagining what might be down there. Sometimes she liked to think there was a monster, something vile and terrifying, or maybe someone kind who could take her away from the misery of life with her father. At other times, she imagined a vast nothingness down there, as if she could slip into the darkness and cease to exist. On a night like tonight, when her father had been particularly angry and particularly forceful, the idea of simply vanishing from the world was more enticing than ever.

In the back of her mind, she even wondered if her mother had fallen into the crack, and was waiting for her at the bottom.

"Can you read for me?" she remembered asking her mother in the hospital one day, sliding the book onto the bed.

Her mother had tried, but she'd been too weak after all her hair had fallen out, and after her gums had become so sore. In the end, Becca had ended up reading the story out loud, and her mother had listened. Their roles had reversed in those final few weeks.

And now her mother was gone.

She inched a little further forward, while reaching out and putting a hand on the edge of the crack, to support herself. This was usually as far as she dared go, although there had been one night when she'd been a little braver and had gone a few centimeters further.

Tonight, however, she had an advantage.

She'd been clever.

Reaching into her pocket, she took out the flashlight she'd borrowed from her father's toolbox. It took a moment for her to find the switch on the side, but finally she shone a bright, strong beam of light down into the depths, picking out the rough rocky walls that led down into darkness. For the first time, she saw how the crack extended deep through the soil.

A sudden gust of wind blew up behind her, as if it was encouraging her to go further, almost trying to push her all the way in. Reaching out, she grabbed the edge of the crack and steadied herself.

Staying in place for a moment, she continued to

shine the light down into the depths, trying to see as far as possible. A sloping ledge extended for several meters before stopping abruptly. Becca had never dared go that far, although she'd often wondered what she'd see if she could peer all the way to the bottom. Tonight, with rain falling harder than ever, she told herself that there would be no harm in just inching forward and *trying* to take a better look. She stayed in place for several minutes, debating the possibilities and hoping to find some extra reserves of courage, before realizing that there would be other nights, better nights, and that she wasn't quite brave enough just yet.

And then she spotted it.

Something small and metallic was glinting in the dirt, right down at the tip of the ledge. Leaning a little further forward, she tried to make out what she'd found, and after a moment she realized it was a coin. Dented and battered, and not like any coin she'd ever seen before, but definitely a coin. The torchlight made the coin's surface shine bright, but she couldn't shake the feeling that it was made of gold. Reaching out, she tried to grab the coin, only to find that she wasn't quite close enough. She looked down at the rocky ledge and, figuring that she'd be okay so long as she was careful, she began to make her way deeper into the crack than ever before.

"You're my brave little girl," her mother's voice whispered in the back of her mind.

She reached out again, but her fingers were just a few millimeters too short.

Taking care to hold onto the rocks, she wriggled

a little deeper.

Finally she reached the coin and pulled it out from the dirt. Sure enough, as she turned it over in her hands, she found that it was dented and twisted, and clearly very old. Holding it up, she saw unfamiliar words on either side, and an image of someone who definitely wasn't Queen Elizabeth II. She tried to imagine how old the coin might be, and how it had ended up wedged in a crack that had opened in the ground, but finally she realized she'd need to find someone she could ask. Not her father, though. It would have to be someone smart, maybe someone in Sharpeton or one of the other towns nearby.

Slipping the coin into her pocket, she turned to crawl back out of the crack. At that moment, however, the ledge crumbled beneath her and gave way. She immediately dropped the torch as she turned and tried to steady herself. For a brief moment she felt she was safe, but then more of the dirt came loose in her hands.

Crying out, she tumbled into the darkness below.

CHAPTER SIX

"HELP YOURSELF TO ANYTHING from behind the bar," the landlord muttered groggily as he made his way to the door behind the bar. "Just leave money on the plate next to the till and I'll ring it up tomorrow. Whatever you do, keep the door locked. That's the whole point of a lock-in. And don't make too much noise."

Muttering something else under his breath, he headed upstairs.

"I'd forgotten about the tragedy in Sharpeton," Mary muttered, taking a closer look at the old framed school photo next to the jukebox. The faces of seventeen smiling children stared back at her, and the image showed them standing next to a school bus. The same school bus, she assumed, that had been found all those years ago, after the children had vanished on the moor. "Such an awful thing," she continued. "The villages around here are so small, almost everyone must have been affected. I can't imagine anything sadder than for so

43

many children to be lost in one night. It must have been like a whole generation suddenly vanishing into thin air."

"Guinness?" Doctor Clarke asked.

Turning, Mary saw to her surprise that Doctor Clarke was already making himself at home and pouring a pint.

"It's 2am," she pointed out.

"Guinness helps me think," he muttered, tilting the glass as he continued to pour. "That's what I tell myself, anyway. It also makes me more agreeable, and I've got a bad – no, *horrible* – feeling that you're going to keep peddling your crazy theories. Trust me, it'll be to your benefit if I'm a little loosened up."

"You still think I'm wrong, don't you?"

"I *know* you're wrong. I'm just waiting to prove it."

"You saw what we dug up," she continued. "There's more coming out of the ground every day, it's not just a theory, it's -"

"A dumping ground," he said with a self-satisfied smile, as he carefully finished pouring the Guinness.

She frowned. "A dumping ground?"

"Someone dumped a load of old pieces of equipment there after the war was over. A kind of seventeenth century landfill, if you like."

"Along with hundreds of bodies?"

"Stranger things have happened."

"Both Cavaliers *and* Roundheads?" she continued. "Who would put them in the same spot? I mean, the idea crossed my mind at first, but it doesn't make any sense."

At this, Doctor Clarke paused for a moment, before taking a sip of Guinness and making his way around the bar. Heading to the slot machine in the corner, he reached down and switched it on, causing the main display to light up and start flashing.

"Are we allowed to turn that thing on?" Mary asked.

"I have absolutely no idea, but it might help me think." He paused for a moment, fishing through his pockets for some money. "The landfill idea is just a working theory, that's all, but it's better than anything *you've* come up with so far. Got any change I can borrow?"

Sighing, she handed him some coins, and then she watched for a moment as he slipped them into the slot and the machine whirred into action. Lights flashed and bells whistled, and an LED screen came to life, casting a red glow on the old man's face.

"You don't remember me, do you?" she asked finally.

"Of course I do."

"Really?"

"You're that annoying woman who dragged me out into the rain a couple of hours ago to look at a bunch of relics. My memory isn't *that* bad, dearie."

"I mean from before," she continued, sighing again. "Doctor Clarke, I used to take your class at the University of Westchester. Several of your classes, actually. I took my undergraduate degree there before moving on to Cambridge."

Glancing at her, he raised a skeptical eyebrow.

"I had tutorial sessions with you sometimes," she added. "You even graded a few of my second year papers. I guess a lot of students pass through that place, and it *was* almost a decade ago."

"*You* were a student of mine?"

She nodded.

He frowned. "Well, there's a surprise."

"Given that I'm apparently so inept?" she asked, raising a skeptical eyebrow.

"I rarely remember any of the people who attend my classes," he muttered, hitting some buttons on the front of the machine and causing the wheels to start spinning. He glanced at her again, as if he was briefly trying to remember her face, before turning back to study the machine. "I've been teaching the same subjects at the same university for twenty years, Miss Baker, and in all that time there has not been *one* student who truly impressed me. Everyone just goes through on rails, trying to get a decent degree that they can toss aside as soon as they score an office job. The Blair dream of university education for all, eh?" He jabbed at the buttons again, clearly unhappy with the machine so far. "I don't blame any of you, though. The modern education system is broken and it seems to spew out... unsatisfactory specimens."

"I didn't get an office job," she told him, struggling more than ever to hold her tongue. "I got a scholarship and I went on to do post-graduate research, and then I managed to finance doctoral study while waiting tables at a restaurant. And now I'm here, working in the field!"

"I've seen the field you're working in," he replied, before letting out another muttered curse as the machine denied him victory. He quickly jabbed at the buttons, to get them spinning again. "Digging up a patch of land in the middle of nowhere is not a particularly great achievement. Who's sponsoring the project, anyway? Let me guess, you persuaded someone to give you some money by -"

He caught himself just in time.

"In this politically correct world," he added with another sigh, "I should probably redact the rest of that idea."

"There's a company that wants to drill on the moor," she replied. "As part of their deal with the local authority, they agreed to sponsor a limited archaeological survey of the area. Obviously they were just paying lip-service to the idea of checking the land, but now we've actually found something so I've applied for an extension of the program. I don't really see how they can turn me down, not when this site is clearly of such great -"

"Ah," he said with a grin, "I think I'm starting to understand. You want to claim some grand discovery, just so you can block the drilling project. Funny, I didn't have you pegged as some kind of environmental activist. Tell me, did you plant those helmets and bones up there as part of some con job?"

She opened her mouth to tell him to go to hell, but she managed to hold back at the last moment.

"I'm an archaeologist!" she said firmly. "I'm just like you! And the only thing I care about right now is the fact that we've made a huge discovery that could revolutionize our understanding of the English Civil War! If a major battle really *did* take place here on the edge of Sharpeton, and if it really *was* covered up by both sides, we need to find out why. Something like that would be unprecedented, it'd change our understanding of the entire war!"

"We already know everything about the period," he muttered, before letting out a gasp of frustration. The machine had once again denied him, but he quickly dropped more coins into the slot.

"You can't really believe that," she told him.

"We know everything about the past."

"Seriously+"

"You've entered the profession at an inopportune moment," he continued. "There's no more history left to discover. I'm afraid it was all gobbled up by those who went before you." He reached out to hit another button, before hesitating as he waited for the flashing lights to line up. "All the grand discoveries have been made," he added, studying the flashing lights carefully, trying to pick his next move. "All the important books have been written, by men such as myself. All the puzzles have been solved. There's nothing left except a few scraps of dirt here and there, maybe some loose ends to tie up."

Frustrated, Mary leaned across him and randomly hit a button on the machine.

"Hey!" he hissed, pushing her hand away. "*I'm* playing here, not *you*! Get your -"

Before he could finish, a series of bells rang deep inside the machine, and a moment later a small flurry of coins came rushing out into the tray near the underside. Shocked, Doctor Clarke reached in and pulled the coins out.

"Thank me later," Mary said dourly. "I know you think this is a fool's errand, but I'm not just hoping for luck from a bunch of random bones and helmets. I've been following the procedures that *you* taught me in class a decade ago, I've been self-critical at every stage." She paused, watching as he counted his winnings. "You're a busy man, Doctor Clarke. You lecture all around the country, sometimes abroad."

"Damn straight," he replied, clearly paying more attention to the coins than to her.

"You command high fees."

"You'd better believe it."

"It's said you won't even get out of bed if there isn't money on offer."

"Jealous?"

"So why did you come tonight?"

He paused for a moment, before turning to her.

"If my theory is so insane," she continued, "and if it's so completely impossible that I'm right, then why did you agree to come out here, hundreds of miles from your home, in the middle of a storm? When I invited you, I gave you the gist of what I was proposing. I never actually thought you'd agree, I thought you'd blow me off, but here you are. And you're *still* here, wasting your oh-so-valuable time talking to me, when you could have turned right around and gone straight back to

Westchester." She waited for a reply. "So what gives? Obviously something here has caught your interest."

He stared at her for a moment, before glancing at the photo on the wall.

"How many children disappeared here?" he asked. "Seventeen?"

She nodded.

"And that was, what, ten years ago now?"

She nodded again.

Handing her some of the coins, he made his way back over to the bar and took another sip of his Guinness. This time he seemed lost in thought, as if his bubble of pomposity had finally begun to deflate.

"Sharpeton isn't far from Wyvern," he said finally, turning to her. "Knarlesford, Retcham, Sporrington... The Baxendale house. As a student of the period, I'm sure those names, when put together, remind you of something very specific."

"Nykolas Freeman," she replied.

He nodded with a faint, sad smile. "Very good. Yes, you're right. Nykolas Freeman."

"You're the expert on Freeman," she continued. "Your entire career is built on your study of the man."

"Don't remind me," he muttered darkly.

"Your first book on Freeman's life is one of the key texts that got me interested in this period of history," she told him. "The lectures you gave at Westchester were fascinating, you really brought the man to life in those classrooms. The barbarity, the cruelty..." She paused. "I still remember the day you taught us about what happened at the Baxendale house, the way

Freeman slaughtered that family. A ninety minute lecture ended up lasting three hours, and by the end of it everyone was exhausted but we all went straight to the library! You brought the whole thing to life, even though it was such a horrible incident! You made the study of history seem vibrant and important again."

He swallowed hard, clearly feeling uncomfortable.

"You probably know this part of the world better than anyone," she added. "Is that why you're so against my discovery? Are you worried I'll use it to make you look foolish? Doctor Clarke, I swear, nothing could be further from the truth. I simply want to -"

"Nykolas Freeman wasn't real," he said suddenly, interrupting her.

"I -" She paused, staring at him with an expression of shock. "I'm sorry? What did you just say?"

Carrying his Guinness to the window, he stopped for a moment and looked out at the dark street before taking another sip. Somehow he seemed a little older now, more frail, as if the lines on his face had become even deeper over the course of just a few seconds.

"During the past year," he continued finally, "I have begun to look at the documents in a new light. I threw away everything I thought I knew about Nykolas Freeman, and I focused on the facts. *Just* the facts, you understand. I really pared it to the bone and went back to basics. I even re-read the sources that described the man's ax and silver ring." He paused, still staring out the window, before turning to her. "As it turns out, I had been fooling myself all along. Somehow, to my great chagrin, the rest of the academic world went along with me and no-one pointed out my errors. How I wish they had, but..." He paused again "So next month," he continued, "with the heaviest of hearts, I shall present a conference paper in which the entire basis of my academic career will be torn apart. I shall prove to the world that Nykolas Freeman never existed."

She opened her mouth to argue with him, but his words were so shocking, she felt that perhaps he was trying to play some kind of trick.

"So now you understand why I want to deflate your ludicrous theory about a battle near Sharpeton," he added. "Miss Baker, I'm merely trying to save you the kind of embarrassment that I myself am about to endure. Trust me on this. Nykolas Freeman was a myth. He was never real. And the Battle of Sharpeton never happened."

CHAPTER SEVEN

SITTING UP IN THE gloomy depths of the crack, Becca felt a stinging sensation on the palms of her hands. There was barely enough light to see anything at all, but as she held her hands up she was just about able to make out thick, grit-filled scrapes that had lacerated her flesh down to the wrists. Wincing, she brushed the worst of the dirt out of the wounds and tore away a few loose scraps of skin, and then she took a moment to suck dirt from the wounds. As she did so, she looked around and saw that she'd fallen into some kind of narrow groove that had split the rocks apart.

Glancing up, she realized with a flash of relief that the crack was only a few meters above her, and that the sloping wall would be easy enough to climb. As she stumbled to her feet, she already felt her sense of panic starting to fade. Her left knee hurt a lot, and when she took a step forward she realized it was more than a graze; looking down at her leg, she saw various cuts and bruises but she also felt a tight sensation around the kneecap, which made it hard to walk. Still, she knew she was lucky that she hadn't been more seriously hurt in the fall, and that climbing out wouldn't be difficult. There had been a moment, before hitting the bottom, when she'd worried she might fall forever.

Spotting the gold coin nearby, she limped over and picked it up. She knew she was being dumb, but at the same time she liked the coin and it was the first new thing she'd found in a long, long time. Slipping it into her pocket, she resolved to take better care of it from now on, and above all to not let her father see it.

Ever.

He'd only take it away.

Nearby, the torch had rolled all the way to the wall, with the light-beam still shining. Becca picked that up, too, and swung it around to get a better look at the chamber.

The space itself was long but not wide, and more than ever it seemed as if the ground had literally been torn open, creating a deep crack that ran down into the depths. Taking a step forward, and ignoring the pain in her knee as best she could, Becca saw a vast, empty darkness up ahead, and she couldn't help wondering whether the crack ran all the way to the center of the planet. Reaching out, she steadied herself against the cold, damp rocky wall, and she squinted slightly in an attempt to see a little better. She knew full well that no-one sensible would go exploring the place, but at the same time she also figured that she could get out fairly quickly. Besides, in all the books her mother had read to her in the past, the heroes had *always* gone exploring, and they'd always survived just fine. She felt certain her mother wouldn't have read those stories to her if they weren't true.

Her mother would never have lied to her.

Turning, she looked up toward the crack and reassured herself once again that she'd be able to scramble up the sloping wall easily enough. Besides, the storm sounded worse than ever outside, and she couldn't go home for several more hours. She needed to wait until dawn, so that she could be sure her father would have passed out.

With the torch in her right hand, she made her way along the passageway. She had to clamber over several rocks that blocked the way, and the passageway was almost too narrow at some points, but she managed to pick her way along, sometimes slipping sideways between the sloping walls. With every step, she began to wonder more and more whether she might find her way to some magical world. She told herself that such things were impossible, of course, and that only silly little girls believed in fairy-tales. At the same time, some deeper part of her soul couldn't shrug off the idea of finding somewhere new and magical, and she was already imagining a whole new world that might turn out to be hers and hers alone. Or maybe, just maybe, she'd find her mother there. The nagging sense of hope just wouldn't go away.

"Read me a story!" she remembered begging her mother.

"Another one?"

Her mother had always acquiesced. Every time, she'd taken yet another book from the shelf and begun reading another bedtime story. And in every one of those stories, a brave little girl or boy explored somewhere new. That was simply how the world worked in stories, so why not in real life too?

Just as she felt the passageway was going to become too narrow, she found that it began to open out again instead, and the torch's beam of light shone across a much wider area with a curved wall far ahead. Stopping for a moment, Becca looked around, and she began to realize that she'd found some kind of large chamber tucked deep underground. There were dark rocks strewn across the ground, but the more she looked, the more she realized that there seemed to be no more tunnels, no more passages or doorways, nothing to indicate a chance to go deeper. She scrambled over a pile of rocks, still hoping against hope that she might have discovered something magical, but finally she stopped and sighed.

There was no gateway to another world.

No chance to escape.

Just a hole in the ground, dark and cold.

Trying to fight against the disappointment, she turned and shone the torch over toward the far wall. This was at least a place her father didn't know about, a secret and -

Suddenly she froze.

On the very far side of the chamber, there sat a man.

Becca kept the torch-beam trained on him,

convinced that at any moment she'd find that *he* wasn't a *he* at all, that the man was merely a deceptive arrangement of rocks and shadow. As the seconds ticked past, however, she became more and more certain that there really *was* a man sitting on the ground, with his back against the wall and his head tilted down, almost as if he was resting or even asleep. His features were covered by a tall, wide-brimmed hat, and he was sitting completely still, as if he hadn't even noticed that Becca had come to disturb his rest.

He wasn't a white rabbit with a stopwatch.

Or a little cricket wearing a top-hat.

Just a man.

She waited, but all she heard was the sound of the storm far above, still battering the ground with rain.

"Never talk to strangers," she remembered her mother telling her. "Do you understand? Be polite, but always, *always* be careful around people you don't know. Promise you understand that."

"I promise," she remembered replying.

But she also remembered her mother being kind to people, especially the homeless men and women who sometimes begged at the train station. Strangers weren't *always* dangerous.

And now here she was, down in a hole in the ground, shining her torch at the strangest stranger she'd ever seen.

She opened her mouth, wondering whether to be polite and say hello before leaving, but somehow the words caught in her throat. She tried to imagine what her mother would want her to do in this kind of situation, and it wasn't hard to hear her mother's voice telling her to leave immediately. Then again, she knew her mother would also have told her not to go into the crack in the first place. Her mother always knew what to do in any situation, her mother was wise and smart, and yet...

Her mother had left her alone.

Because of her mother, she was living with her father now.

So clearly her mother hadn't been right about *everything*.

Slowly, cautiously, Becca took a few steps forward toward the figure. Less than six months ago, before her father had taken her out of school to be home-tutored, she'd come second in an egg-and-spoon race at Sports Day, so she felt confident she could run fast enough if necessary. The hunched man still hadn't moved an inch, at least not as far as she could tell, so she figured that he probably wasn't going to suddenly jump up and attack her. In fact, as she edged closer and closer, she was starting to wonder if the man was alive at all. She figured he might be dead, or a statue.

She swallowed hard, and finally she stopped just a couple of meters from the man.

Close enough, she told herself.

Any closer, and he might be able to grab her.

Like her father in his arm chair.

She opened her mouth again, and this time she knew she had to say *something*. She tried to imagine the most polite way to start a conversation, and finally she settled on a few words.

"Are you okay?" she asked, her voice sounding

frail and terrified.

So frail and terrified, in fact, that she immediately felt she'd been too quiet to be heard.

"Are you okay?" she asked again, making sure to speak more loudly this time.

She waited.

No reply.

Still unable to see the man's face, since his head was tilted down and his hat's wide brim covered his features, Becca looked at his boots and saw that they were big, running almost up to his knees, and that they had large metal buckles. They looked like nothing she'd ever seen before, and she couldn't help wondering whether they were old. Shining her torch at the man's hands, she saw a silver ring on one of his fingers, and a moment later she noticed that the cuffs of his white shirt were slightly frilled and torn. The man looked like someone from one of her history books, which made no sense since she knew people didn't dress like that anymore.

Glancing around, she suddenly realized that there was no sign of food or water, and that the man didn't seem to have any possessions at all. She turned back to him, but somehow she felt certain that he wasn't dead and he wasn't a statue.

"Are you hungry?" she asked cautiously. "Do you have something to eat?"

High above, beyond the chamber, the storm still raged.

"What are you doing down here?" she continued. "Are you homeless? Is this where you live?"

She waited, but the man remained perfectly still.

"My name is..." She paused, wondering whether it was wise to tell him, before realizing that there couldn't be any harm. "My name is Becca... I mean, *Rebecca*. Rebecca Jameson, but I prefer to be called Becca. What's *your* name?"

She waited. The light from her torch glinted against the man's silver ring, picking out the edges of a simple cross etched into the metal. Becca tilted the torch slightly, aiming the beam toward the man's hat, before suddenly realizing that it would be rude to shine so much light near his face.

"Sorry," she said, lowering the beam. She waited, but still there was no response. "I live nearby," she continued. "My father and I live in a house on the side of the next valley. It used to be a farm, but it's not anymore. It's just us now. There aren't even any animals, 'cause my father says they smell bad and that they're too much trouble. He won't even let us get cows or llamas. So we live there and..."

Her voice trailed off as she realized that the man didn't seem to be listening.

Forcing herself to be brave, she took a step closer. This, she figured, was what her mother would do in such a situation. She kept the torch shining slightly to one side, so that she could see the man a little better while not aiming the beam straight at him. She wanted to see his face, to find out if he was okay, but at the same time she was wary of getting *too* close. One of his hands could suddenly reach out at any moment and grab her arm. Still, she was closer now than she ever dared to get to her father when he was drinking, and now she could smell something rotten in the air.

"Do you want some food?" she asked.

Silence.

"Are you all by yourself down here? Are you just..." She paused. "Are you just sitting here?"

Again, silence.

Worrying that the man might be hurt, Becca slowly reached out with her left hand, telling herself that it wouldn't hurt to just give him a gentle nudge on the elbow. Her heart was racing, but finally her fingertips brushed against the fabric of the man's shirt and she pushed with as little pressure as possible, just to see if he'd respond.

Nothing. The fabric was bone dry, though, so clearly the man had been down in the crack since before the rain started.

Stepping to one side, Becca leaned around to see if she could see the man's face. With his head tilted down, it was almost impossible to make out his features at all, but now she realized that he had matted, graying hair that hung down to cover his features. She could just about see his cheeks, which seemed impossibly hollow and stringy, almost as if there was barely any flesh left clinging to the bones. When she tilted the torch, she realized that his eyes were closed, as if he was asleep.

"Hello?" she whispered.

No reply.

Taking another step to the side, in an attempt to see the man's face better, she suddenly felt her foot bumping against something on the ground. Looking down, she saw a large ax resting on the rocks, with cuts and dents all over the edge of the blade. She reached out to grab the ax's handle, before hesitating for a moment and then telling herself that it might be better not to interfere. Taking a deep breath, she crouched down and took a closer look at the ax, and she couldn't help wondering how it had come to get so battered. Thick scratches had been carved through the metal, and the leading edge was ragged, as if it had repeatedly struck something hard. Finally, unable to help herself, she reached down and ran a fingertip against the blade, feeling all the dents.

And then, slowly, she realized she could hear a very faint creaking sound. She froze, absolutely certain that the sound had come from the man, but the chamber was quiet again and she didn't dare look up. Instead, she kept her eyes focused on the ax. Terrified that the man might have moved, she took a deep breath, trying to calm her pounding heart. Finally she asked herself what her mother would do, or what the hero would do in one of her bedtime stories, and she immediately knew that the answer would be the same in either case. Slowly, she looked up at the man's face.

Sure enough, his eyes were slightly open now, watery and black, staring down at her.

CHAPTER EIGHT

"OF COURSE NYKOLAS FREEMAN was real!" Mary said as she followed Doctor Clarke up the stairs to their rooms above the pub. "How can you possibly suggest otherwise?"

At the end of the landing, rain was battering the window with more force than ever.

"The man was a specter," Clarke replied as he reached his door and fished the key from his pocket. "He was like Robin Hood, he was an imaginary figure who was conjured up in an attempt to scare and entertain people throughout the country. An extremely effective figure, one who expertly tapped into the fears of people in the mid-seventeenth century, but fiction nonetheless." He sighed. "And I fell for it."

"But the incident at the Baxendale house, when Freeman killed an entire family..." She paused. "There are multiple contemporary accounts of that night! It happened!"

"*Someone* carried out that heinous act," he muttered, opening the door and then turning to her. "Not Freeman."

"And the raids on the Offingham Arms -"

"Again, someone else." He sighed. "All these acts were ascribed to a single individual, creating a kind of bogeyman figure, when in fact they were the work of multiple, lesser priest hunters. When you actually start digging deep into the stories, you realize there's no evidence whatsoever for Freeman's role. There's not even a body! In my original book, I tried to explain why his grave had never been found, but only now can I see the obvious answer. There's no grave, because there was no man! And his infamous ax and silver ring? Don't you think they would have shown up by now if Freeman really existed?"

She stared at him for a moment, clearly shocked.

"The royal court," she stammered finally, "the... Freeman is mentioned by name!"

"Oh, I'm sure there was a grain of truth at the root of it all," he said with another sigh. "There was a man named Nykolas Freeman, or something similar, perhaps he even set off to hunt priests, but he most certainly didn't commit all the acts that have been ascribed to him. The idea's ludicrous, if you think about it sensibly. Freeman would have had to have been some kind of monster, a figure of almost mythic evil and power. I know the human heart is capable of great barbarity, Miss Baker, but I see the situation very clearly now. Nykolas Freeman, at least the version recorded in history books, was just a story." He shrugged. "I suppose my reputation is going to take rather a knock, isn't it? My books might well have to be pulped."

"Nykolas Freeman was real," she replied.

He shook his head.

"You wrote so many books and papers about him! You addressed conferences!"

"And I got my facts spectacularly wrong!" He leaned against the doorjamb for a moment, his eyes red and tired. Two pints of Guinness, downed in quick succession, had taken their toll. "The reason I'm admitting this to you now, Miss Baker, is that I want you to see that it's okay to be wrong. Sometimes we *have* to be wrong before we can be right, but we must always recognize our errors as quickly as possible, so that they don't consume us." He sighed again. "Your theory about a great battle that was subsequently hushed up... It's preposterous. Please, don't make the same mistake that I made. Don't ignore the reality of the situation and allow yourself to believe in a fantasy. If you do, you'll only end up like me. A tired, discredited old fool whose career has been built on a lie."

She shook her head.

"Think about it," he continued. "The stories of Nykolas Freeman are so grandiose and barbaric, so grotesque! *Nobody* could be so utterly cruel. I'm sure you've heard about how he's supposed to have beheaded little Jessica Baxendale in front of her parents. That's just one of many tales that were spread far and wide throughout the land, as part of an effort to terrify the populace. I just wish I hadn't propagated the myth further with my work, but at least I can put that right now."

They stood in silence for a moment, as Mary tried to work out how to respond. She felt certain that Doctor Clarke was wrong, although she also felt she wasn't in a position to question him, not on such a vast and important subject. Despite his irascible nature, he was the historian she respected more than any other. She couldn't deny that, deep down, she craved his professional approval.

"My advice," he continued wearily, "is to get some sleep. In the morning, we shall take another look at your discovery and we shall find out what it *really* means. Just because there's no obvious explanation right now, that doesn't mean we should go leaping to extremes. The world is riddled with people who embrace the easy answer, Miss Baker. If you're serious about your career, and if you really want to make a name for yourself, I would suggest that you proceed with extreme caution and accept my help. Issuing absurd claims about some hitherto-unknown battle is a sure way to become a laughing stock."

"But -"

"And tomorrow," he added, as he stepped into his room and headed over to the desk, "we shall find out what really happened out there in that muddy field."

She sighed. "Doctor Clarke -"

Before she could finish, she watched in horror as he took a gun from his suitcase. Dark brown and a little over a foot long, the pistol had clean silver sides.

"A replica seventeenth century flintlock pistol," Clarke said proudly, aiming the gun directly at her. Too drunk to keep his hand steady, he chuckled at the shock in her eyes as he turned and waved the gun around. "A simplified snaphaunce or, if you like, an early doglock. Remarkable thing, I had it made for me by a fellow in East Grinstead, based on specifications that I supplied." Closing one eye, he attempted to aim toward the open window. "I'm quite sure this is the most accurate replica in the world."

"I think we should call it a night," Mary said cautiously, realizing that he was way too drunk. "A replica pistol is lovely, but -"

Suddenly the gun went off, grazing the window-frame before hitting a lamp-post outside.

"Jesus!" Mary shouted, running forward and taking the weapon from Doctor Clarke's cold, clammy hands. "Is this thing real?"

He laughed as he turned to her. "Can't live in a world without real things, my dear. What's the fun of a dummy, when one can hold a working example in one's hands?"

"I'm confiscating this 'til morning," she told him.

"I beg your pardon?"

Sighing, she headed out of the room and then turned back to look at him. "You could kill someone with this!" she pointed out. "Twenty seconds ago, you had it aimed at my face!"

"I was just joshing with you," he replied. "Come on, be a good sport and hand it back. I promise I'll put it away and go straight to sleep." Stepping toward her, he stumbled against the corner of the bed and almost fell to the floor, before steadying himself against the wardrobe.

For a moment he seemed quite unable to continue, as if he was having trouble keeping the room from spinning. "I'm not even drunk! Christ, I'm just... not as sober as I could be, that's all!"

"You can have it back tomorrow," she told him firmly. "Good night, Doctor Clarke."

Pulling the door shut, she took a step back and a moment later she heard a bump from inside the room, followed by the low groan of a man who had fallen over and now faced the immense task of righting himself.

"What was that noise?" the landlord asked suddenly, hurrying through from his room.

"Nothing," Mary said quickly, hiding the pistol behind her back. "I heard it too, but I think it was just a car backfiring outside."

He stared at her for a moment, clearly suspicious.

"Right, then," he muttered, "I guess... Back to bed. I'll see you all for breakfast in the morning." He seemed poised to ask something else, before turning and heading back into his room.

With that, Mary was left standing alone in the corridor, feeling as if the wind had just been snatched from her sails. Her heart was pounding and she couldn't help reliving the moment when the pistol had been aimed at her head. She wanted to bang on Doctor Clarke's door and tell him what she really thought of him, but she felt she didn't have the right. After all, she was still just a lowly post-grad trying to make her name, and he was the great, revered Doctor Alistair Clarke of Westchester University, one of the country's leading experts on the English Civil War and the man to whom all others deferred. His word, in the academic community, was highly respected. Even just arguing against his opinion had felt wrong somehow, as if she'd been overstepping her rank.

After a moment, she heard snores coming from inside his room, as if he'd fallen asleep on the floor.

Hearing footsteps nearby, she turned and saw Daniel making his way up the stairs.

"Were there raised voices up here?" he asked wearily. "And some kind of loud bang?"

"We were discussing a few things," she muttered, as Doctor Clarke's snores became louder.

"I know you respect this guy, Mary," he continued, "but he seems like -"

"Not here," she said hurriedly, grabbing his arm and leading him to one of the other doors. Once they were inside her room, she pushed the door shut. "I know he can be abrasive -"

"Abrasive?" Daniel smiled. "He's the rudest guy I've ever met in my life! I mean, I'd heard the stories about him, so I was prepared for him to be *crotchety*, but..." He paused for a moment. "Why didn't you stand up to him more? Why didn't you tell just tell him he was wrong? Mary, I've seen you give hell to people in the past, you're one of the toughest people I know. And then suddenly tonight you hold back and act all deferential around this complete asshole."

"Maybe he's *not* wrong," she replied.

"Jesus, you need to believe in yourself more..."

"No, I need to focus on the work," she said

firmly. "No-one's ego matters in this, Daniel. I brought Doctor Clarke here specifically so that he could poke holes in my theories. I knew he'd be critical, and that's what I want! If the work we're doing here can survive *his* analysis, along with all the barbs and brickbats that come at the same time, then we can start to think about showing it to other people. Clarke's the litmus test."

Daniel stared at her for a moment, but he knew better than to argue. "Fine. Which room should I sleep in tonight? My own or..."

"I think I just need to get some rest," she told him. "I'm tired and we all need to be up early in the morning."

Daniel turned to leave, before spotting the pistol in her hand.

"It's Doctor Clarke's," she said with a tired sigh. "I confiscated it."

"Mary..."

"Just leave it. Everything's under control."

Nodding, he pulled the door open. "I know you respect this guy, Mary, but some day you're gonna have to stand up to him and tell him he's an asshole. Maybe if someone had done that a little sooner, his head wouldn't be so far up his ass." He waited for a reply. "I mean it, you have to stick to your guns. You and I both know that what you've found out there in that field is extraordinary. Don't let Alistair Clarke or anyone else take it away from you."

Once he was gone, she locked the door and then set the gun down before grabbing her laptop. Sitting on her single bed in the corner, she quickly brought up a website about the feared, notorious Nykolas Freeman, the man who was said to have tormented the citizens of several counties with his unending witch-hunts. Freeman had been a notorious figure and had come to dominate historical discussions of the mid-seventeenth century, so to hear Doctor Clarke suggesting he hadn't been a real man at all was something of a surprise. Finally, dismissing that notion entirely, she began to look up old references to the town of Sharpeton, logging into academic databases that she hoped would help her find the truth.

"It has to be here somewhere," she muttered under her breath, scrolling down the first page as she searched for any hint of the town being mentioned in contemporary literature. "An entire battle can't have been forgotten. It doesn't make sense."

CHAPTER NINE

A BOLT OF LIGHTNING crackled through the air, briefly lighting the moor as rain continued to fall. Scrambling up the sloping rock wall, Becca finally spilled out into the stormy night air, tumbling onto the grass and rolling before getting to her feet. Turning breathlessly, she looked back into the darkness, but to her relief she saw that the man hadn't followed her. All the way from the chamber up to the crack's entrance she'd been terrified he was chasing her, but now she realized there was no sign of him.

She waited, but the only sound was the constant rain, still hissing all around as it battered the moor. Strong winds rushed through the void and rippled against her wet dress, but she kept her eyes fixed on the crack, determined to make sure that she was alone. In her mind, she could still see the man's eyes, black and watery, staring straight down at her.

Finally, with her heart still pounding in her

chest, she got to her feet and began to hurry home. Thunder rumbled above and the sky flashed with lightning, but every time she looked over her shoulder she saw only the vast, rolling moors all around. She tripped and fell several times, landing in pools of muddy water, but on each occasion she forced herself to get to her feet and keep walking. When she reached the house, she could hear her father crashing about in the front room, so she went and curled up in the wood-shed, waiting for dawn and silence. Her wet dress clung to her skin, chilling her to the bone, but she didn't dare go inside, not yet. Shivering, with chattering teeth, she hugged herself tighter and closed her eyes, just as another boom of thunder rattled the shed's wooden walls.

"There's no reason to be scared," she imagined her mother telling her. "Don't be a silly sausage, Becca. Everything's okay."

"Why did you leave me here with *him*?" she heard herself asking.

"Becca -"

"Where are you?"

She waited, but she couldn't imagine what her mother would say in response. What could make someone disappear like that and leave her loved ones behind? She understood that maybe her mother didn't love her father anymore, but she still wished she hadn't been left behind. One day she'd gone to visit her mother in the hospital as usual, the next day she'd been told they'd never be going again. Her sister had left just hours after that, and Becca had been left alone with her father.

The walls of the wood-shed shook as a strong

gust of wind rushed across the valley.

Becca hugged her knees tighter, trying to stay warm as the gust died down.

Sitting in silence, she took slow, deep breaths and told herself not to be so sad. At the same time, she couldn't help remembering a day several years earlier when she and her mother had gone to the supermarket and a homeless man had been sitting outside with a polystyrene coffee cup in front of his crossed legs.

"Put this in the man's cup," she remembered her mother telling her, pressing a 50p coin into her hands.

She remembered being scared and shaking her head.

"It's okay," her mother had told her. "Don't be scared. I'm right here."

She'd been terrified, convinced that the scary man would hurt her if she dared go close. Finally her mother had taken her by the hand and walked with her, leading her toward the man and then crouching down and pointing at the cup.

"Go on, honey," she remembered her mother saying. "There's no reason in the whole world to be scared."

It had taken all Becca's courage to toss the coin into the cup, and then she'd immediately taken a step back.

The man, meanwhile, had murmured a few words.

"That's better," her mother had said, as they'd headed into the supermarket. "I'm proud of you."

And that, she realized, was why she'd dared go

so close to the man in the crack. She'd been hoping that maybe her mother would give her a sign, would somehow let her know that she was watching and that she was proud.

There had been no sign.

A few minutes later, she heard a faint bumping sound nearby, coming from outside the wood-shed.

She tensed, telling herself it was just the wind, but after a few seconds the bump returned, this time hitting the outside of the wood-shed with more force. Looking toward the open doorway, Becca told herself that there was no-one out there, but finally she saw a shadow moving through the moonlight. Terrified that the man from the crack had found her, she squeezed her eyes tight shut, even as she heard footsteps shuffling into the shed. She imagined the battered ax glinting in the low light, and the man's dark, watery eyes staring down at her. With each passing second, another footstep edged closer, no matter how tightly she squeezed her eyes.

"Be brave," she imagined her mother telling her. "Becca, be -"

Suddenly she heard a hiccup, and then her father's drowsy voice.

"Becca?"

Looking up, she saw him standing over her, swaying slightly.

"Is that you?" he continued, reaching down and grabbing her by the collar, before pulling her out and sending her slamming into the shelves opposite, with enough force to crack the wall.

CHAPTER TEN

FLAMES ROARED HIGH INTO the night sky, bursting from every window in the house as screams continued from inside. Forming a circle around the building, scores of armored men held long wooden poles, each with a sharp metal tip, and they used those poles to stab at anyone who tried to climb out of the burning house.

"Don't let any of them escape!" a voice sneered from nearby. "The sinners must burn for their cowardly actions! Let all in England hear the tale of the conspirators who sought to hide a Catholic priest! Let everyone know that, for their efforts, they were burned alive!"

A moment later there was the sound of breaking glass, as one of the upstairs windows was smashed from within. A woman appeared, her nightdress and hair already burning, but one of the armored men used his pole to reach up and stab her repeatedly, forcing her back into the flames. She screamed as she fought, but the pole's metal tip dug into her belly and finally broke straight through her chest, skewering her. As she began to vomit blood, the woman gripped the frames of the broken window, as if she was still trying to haul herself out. Still impaled, she was powerless to get free as the flames consumed her body, and finally the man twisted his metal pole and pulled it free, sending her corpse slumping back into the flames.

"Excellent work," said the man on horseback. "The Lord sees our work today, and he recognizes that we are virtuous in his name. These Catholic sympathizers deserve no better, and they shall face far worse torment in the depths of Hell!" Turning, he looked down at the corpse of a man whose throat he had slit just a few moments earlier. With contempt in his eyes, he spat at the body. "These priests will be rooted out," he said darkly, "wherever they might hide. This, and this alone, is my purpose in this world."

Watching from nearby, cowering in the bushes, Doctor Mary Baker stared in wide-eyed horror as the man guided his horse gently around the burning house. Silhouetted against the flames, the rider seemed utterly calm and imperious as he watched the inferno, and he didn't even flinch when a fresh set of screams emerged from the other side of the building. Holding her breath, Mary waited for him to leave, so that she could break from her hiding place and run to safety, but suddenly she saw the silhouetted figure turning to look straight toward her, and finally their eyes met.

"No," she stammered, getting to her feet and running across the clearing, desperately trying to reach the trees. "Please -"

Before she could take another step, she felt something slamming into her back, and she looked down at her chest just in time to see a metal-tipped pole bursting out through her ribs. Stumbling, she dropped to her knees as blood began to soak the front of her shirt, rushing from the wound. The pole's metal tip twisted, and then was used to start dragging her back across the grass until she came to a stop next to the dead priest. After a moment, looking down at the grass, she saw the shadow of a man on horseback getting closer, coming up behind her as if to revel in her suffering.

"And what have we here?" Freeman asked. "A collaborator? A Catholic sympathizer, perhaps? Or a witch!"

Mary opened her mouth to beg for mercy, but no words emerged from her lips. Instead she remained in place as she saw the man's shadow dismounting from the horse, and a moment later she felt the blade of a knife pressing against her throat.

"May the Lord have mercy on those who have sinned," Freeman said calmly, towering above her from behind, "and may they burn forever in the fires of eternal suffering."

With that, he sliced the blade across the throat, bringing blood bursting from the wound and erupting from her mouth. She fell forward and -

"No!" Mary shouted, sitting up suddenly in bed.

Cool morning light was shining through the window, but she instinctively reached up to feel her throat. The dream had been so vivid, and had seemed so real, she still couldn't shake the feeling that Freeman might be around somewhere. She glanced across the room, seeing only her suitcase on the desk, and finally she managed to calm her nerves just a little. A moment later, however, she spotted Doctor Clarke's flintlock pistol resting on the table, and she remembered his drunken antics from the previous night. Taking slow, deep breaths, she got to her feet and headed over to the window. Her knees were trembling, and she could still feel the sensation of a blade slicing through her throat.

It had just been a dream, she told herself, even though it had felt impossibly real.

Reaching under her t-shirt, she felt the spot on her chest where the blade had burst through. The flesh was smooth and undamaged now, though the dream remained vivid and her heart was racing.

Outside, the village of Sharpeton was already awake, with several people going about their business in the early morning sunshine. Still feeling shaken from her dream, Mary checked her phone and then began to get dressed. Today had to be the day when she finally proved that the Battle of Sharpeton had taken place. She had to stay focused.

CHAPTER ELEVEN

"IT WAS IN HERE yesterday. Becca, are you sure you haven't touched my torch?"

Pulling another drawer out, Becca's father tipped the contents onto the counter and then began sorting through the various knives, hammers, saws and other tools. His hands were trembling slightly, and he was making plenty of noise as he continued his search. Finally he started tossing the tools back into the drawer, a process that was somehow even noisier.

"Becca? Come on, if you took my torch, just admit it. I promise I won't get mad."

Watching him cautiously, she tried to work out how much he already knew. After dragging her into the house during the night, her father had made a few vague comments about pneumonia and about mistaking her for a fox, and then he'd grabbed some towels so he could dry her, only to suddenly pass out halfway up the stairs. She'd dried herself and then finally she'd gone up to bed at around 5am, but now just a few hours later she was awake again, having not slept at all. Her father, clearly hungover and bad-tempered, seemed to have forgotten the night's events entirely.

"What happened to your face?" he asked as he rooted through another drawer.

She flinched, remembering the moment he'd slammed her into the wall. As usual, she simply told herself that it had been an accident, that *of course* he hadn't meant to be so rough. Or that he'd been telling the truth when he'd claimed, drunkenly, to have mistaken her for some kind of animal.

"I fell over."

He stared at her for a moment. "Huh."

She looked down at the potato salad he'd given her for breakfast.

"I must have left the stupid torch outside," he said with a sigh, grabbing a fork and using it to pull two burned pieces of bread from the toaster. "I'll need it later, though. I want to work on the other car. You should have heard how much the bastards in town wanted to fix the alternator. I can do it myself." He sighed again. "Becca, I'll need you to drive the old yellow car from the garage to the front of the house. It's just a few meters. You can do that for me, can't you?"

She nodded.

"The keys are on the side," he added wearily. "I'll take the other car into town."

Scooping some smelly potato salad from the tub, Becca thought back to the moment when she'd run from the underground chamber during the night. She remembered dropping the torch and then turning to grab it, only to see that it had rolled back toward the man. Apart from slightly opening his eyes, the man hadn't moved at all, but she'd still been too scared to go back to fetch the torch so she'd decided to just leave it behind. Now she felt as if she'd made a mistake, and she was even starting to question whether the man's eyes had *really* opened at all. Deep down, she wondered whether she'd just been so jumpy, she might have imagined the whole thing.

Maybe there hadn't even been a man at all. Maybe, she figured, she was going crazy. She was only eleven, but she supposed it was possible.

"Do you want to come to the store with me," her father asked, "or do you want to stay here? I'll only be a couple of hours."

"I'll stay here," she replied, preferring that to another Sunday morning getting dragged around the shops.

"Sure?"

She nodded.

"I guess I'll have to buy another bloody torch," he muttered, clearly annoyed as he started searching for his keys and wallet. "That'll be more money down the drain. I don't know where these things disappear to, Becca. There's only the two of us out here, but nothing's ever where I leave it." He looked around for a moment, before sighing. "Have you seen my -"

"Your car keys are in the hallway."

"I already looked there."

"They're in the bowl by the door," she

continued. "I put them there after I found them on the floor."

"What were they doing on the floor?" he muttered, heading over and kissing the top of her head.

She flinched.

"I'll be back soon," he added, heading to the door. "Don't do anything naughty while I'm out." He stopped to slip his shoes on, and then he turned and watched for a moment as she ate. "Everything's okay, right? Are you sure you're not mad at me for anything?"

She glanced at him and shook her head.

"Okay," he continued, clearly a little worried about another black-out from the night before. "Back soon. I'll pick up something special for tea." Another pause. "How did you get that bruise on the side of your face, again?"

She hesitated. "I told you. I fell."

"When?"

"This morning."

She waited, hoping that he wouldn't ask any more questions. The last thing she wanted was for him to realize that *he'd* been the one who'd caused the bruise, that he'd pushed her against the wall of the wood-shed in his drunken attempt to get her back into the house. She hated his alcohol-fueled rages, but she hated his attempts to make up for them even more. She knew it was wrong to hate her father so much, but all she wanted was for him to leave her alone.

"Is it possible for someone to go mad when they're little?" she asked finally, hoping to change the subject.

He frowned. "Huh?"

"I was just wondering."

"I don't know, Becca," he muttered, turning and heading out of the room. "Jesus, you can be weird sometimes."

For the next few minutes, he bumbled about in the hallway, taking forever to gather whatever he needed for the trip to town.

Becca sat silently at the table, willing him to leave while taking a few mouthfuls of the potato salad. Once her father had *finally* left the house, she sat in the kitchen and waited until she heard the car's engine starting. Heading to the window, she peered out and watched as the car drove away along the bumpy muddy road that led toward town. She waited a few more minutes, until her father was completely out of view, and then she reached into her pocket and pulled out the gold coin she'd found during the night.

That, at least, was real. But the man in the chamber, he had to have been imaginary. And she was going to prove it.

CHAPTER TWELVE

"WE NEED TO START digging right here," Mary explained, pointing at the edge of the map as she and Daniel sat at a breakfast table in the corner of the pub's main room. "If you look at the hill *here*, you can see it would have offered a good vantage point for an infantry maneuver during the battle, which means there should be more bodies along here..."

She ran a fingertip along a line.

"And up to here."

"The soil's going to be a lot tougher to get through around the ridge," Daniel pointed out. "It'll take longer."

"That's fine," she continued, "but we need to find something that really proves beyond all doubt that there was a battle. I've already put in a request to extend the dig and there's no way they can turn me down, but we'll also need more funding and that's only going to happen if we have cast-iron proof. I know it means rushing things, but this is the most practical approach." She pointed at another spot on the map. "We need to look at this area, too. If I'd been a general in a battle here, that's where I'd have put my infantry troops. They must have left something behind."

"There's no point standing around, then," Daniel replied. "Let's get out there and -"

They both turned as they heard a bump outside, and they watched through the window as Doctor Alistair Clarke steadied himself against a table in the pub's courtyard. Seemingly unaware that he was being observed, the older man focused on not spilling his pint of Guinness as he stumbled toward a nearby table and sat down. A strong wind was blowing through town, and Clarke struggled to light his cigarette. After a moment, a brief gust not only killed the flame from his lighter, but also blew his tie into his face. Finally, giving up for a moment, he took a sip of Guinness.

"Liquid breakfast?" Daniel whispered with a smile. "Jesus, the man never stops. No wonder he's so angry all the time."

"Get out to the site," Mary replied. "I'll catch up."

"Mary..."

"I just want to talk to him for a moment!"

"The man's a drunk! You're wasting your time with him!"

"He's a drunk with an outstanding reputation," she pointed out. "If I can get him on our side, there's no way our application for a deadline extension can be ignored." She watched for a moment longer as Clarke continued to struggle with the cigarette, almost setting his tie on fire in the process. "Believe it or not, that man has one of the finest academic brains in the country."

As Daniel headed through to the pub's car-park, Mary made her way cautiously to the door and then out into the courtyard, where the wind was strong enough to blow old chocolate bar wrappers from the ashtrays. Tucking a loose strand of hair behind her ear, Mary made her way over to Clarke's table. Even as she got closer, she realized he hadn't noticed her, and that he was too busy unfolding the newspaper on his lap, searching for the crossword even though the wind was doing its best to tear the pages from his hands. Finally she set the flintlock pistol down in front of him, and this at least attracted his attention.

"Ah," he said archly, "I see you've finally decide to return my property."

"You were drunk."

"I was playful."

"You could have blown my -" Catching herself just in time, she realized she didn't want to say those words out loud. "Would you like to come out to the dig with us this morning, Doctor Clarke?" she asked, trying to steer the conversation back to more normal matters. "I was thinking it might help if you could actually see us at work."

Glancing at her, he seemed distinctly unimpressed.

"I shall be quite alright here," he said finally. "This crossword won't complete itself, will it?"

"Are you at least staying in town for a little

while longer?"

"As I believe I told you last night," he continued, "I have some work of my own to complete in the area, and *that* will be the focus of my attention. I might as well make this trip useful. I've been up since the crack of dawn. While you were doubtless still rolling around in bed, I was planning my itinerary for today." He reached into his pocket and took out out a pen. "I'm sure you won't hesitate to tell me all about your latest findings this evening, and then I can point out where you're going wrong." He muttered something else under his breath. Whatever it was, he sounded distinctly unenthusiastic.

"What will it take to convince you?" she asked.

"A lot more than some skulls and helmets."

"More military equipment?" She waited for a reply, but after a moment she watched as he filled in the crossword's first answer. "Muskets? We already have muskets, Doctor Clarke. And swords, and various other weapons. I'm already in a position to prove that there as a cavalry unit, and infantry and -"

"Five across," he replied, interrupting her as he read a clue out loud. "A serpent's bidding comes to mean nothing for a man holding the car keys. Any idea what that could be?"

"You're not taking this seriously."

"The crossword? I assure you, I always take the *Times* crossword extremely seriously. There's nothing wrong with my priorities."

"I'm doing exactly what you told us to do," she continued. "All those years ago in your lectures, when I was a student, you told us to never let ourselves become slaves to dogma or received opinion. You told us it was okay to risk making a mistake, because at least then there was a chance we might learn something new." She waited for a reply, but after a moment she began to wonder if he was even listening. "You specifically told us that we should challenge the opinions of others, so long as we had good reason."

"Did I really say all that?" he asked, taking another sip of Guinness. "How frightful. I was a frightful bore back then, wasn't I?"

She watched him for a moment longer, before realizing that he was clearly never going to take her seriously until she had actual proof to show him.

"You used to care about the truth," she continued finally. "You used to say that reputations didn't mean a thing, and that only the truth was important."

"I rather believe the reverse now."

"You don't mean that."

"Don't I?" He smiled as he glanced at her. "Run along, Miss Baker. Clearly I can't persuade you that you're wrong, so you'll just have to find that out for yourself. You know where to find me when you're ready to admit it. I shall take a little drive this morning, but I'll be back after lunch." With that, he took another sip of Guinness and then wrote an answer into the crossword.

Turning, Mary headed across the courtyard, fighting the urge to tell the great Doctor Clarke exactly what she thought of him. There had been a time, long ago, when she'd respected him a great deal, when she'd wanted to model her career after his own, but now she was starting to feel the opposite. Clarke was a close-minded old grump, the kind of person she never wanted to be. She briefly regretted inviting him at all, before reminding herself that he might still be useful.

Once she reached the car park, she remembered with a sigh that Daniel had already taken the jeep, which meant she'd have to walk to the dig site. At least the rain had stopped for now, although when she turned and looked toward the moor, she shivered at the thought of fighting her way through the gale.

CHAPTER THIRTEEN

THE NIGHT'S RAINFALL HAD left mud everywhere, and the morning sun had barely begun to dry the land. Squelching through boggy fields, Becca at least had her mother's old pair of Wellington boots to keep her feet dry, although they slowed her down and made it much harder to walk. By the time she reached the crack in the ground, several miles from her father's house, her legs ached worse than ever.

Above, the cloudy gray sky was still recovering from the storm.

Becca stopped for a moment, staring down into the gloom. Remembering the sight of the man down there, she told herself that the whole thing had clearly been in her head. Her mother had always told her that she had an over-active imagination, and it seemed hard to believe that there might *actually* be a strange man living down in a crack beneath the moor. Still, the idea was enough to send a shiver of anticipation through her chest, and she remembered another piece of advice her mother had given her once.

"The only thing to fear is fear itself. If you're scared of something, face it and you'll quickly find that it's not so terrifying after all."

Easy to say, Becca felt, but not so easy to put into practice.

"If I do this," she said out loud, hoping her mother could somehow hear her, "then in return, you have to give me a sign that you're watching, okay?"

She waited.

"Okay," she added, even though she knew she was lying to herself. "It's a deal."

Crouching down at the edge of the crack, she began to make her way into the darkness. She moved slowly and carefully, keen to make sure that she didn't fall again, and this time she managed to maneuver herself to the very edge and drop down, landing cleanly on the rocky surface below. Looking along the passageway, she saw the darkness up ahead, but she was pretty sure she'd dropped the torch at the chamber's entrance. There was no way she was willing to go into the chamber *without* the torch, but as she made her way forward she quickly spotted something glinting on the ground, near the wall.

Reaching down, she picked up the torch and switched it on.

"Hello?" she called out.

Silence.

She made her way through the narrowest part of the passageway and then into the chamber itself, at which point she shone the torch toward the spot where she'd seen the man during the previous night.

She gasped as soon as she saw that he was still there, still leaning back against the wall. It was as if he hadn't moved at all.

Reaching into her pocket, Becca pulled out the slightly-squashed, clingfilm-wrapped sandwich she'd made at home. It was just a couple of slices of white bread, with some mayonnaise and pickles in-between, but she figured a man living in a hole in the ground probably wasn't *too* fussy, and besides her father never kept the fridge properly stocked. Stepping forward cautiously, she approached the man and then leaned down, setting the sandwich on the ground. She wasn't quite sure what to say, but she felt that she needed to at least let him know that she'd brought him some food. After all, he seemed to be asleep.

"I hope you like mayonnaise," she said finally. "It's not much, but... We didn't have anything else in the fridge."

She waited, but the man remained completely still and silent, almost like a statue.

"I brought you something to drink, too," she continued, taking a carton of juice from her pocket and setting it next to the sandwich. "It's a got a straw and..."

Her voice trailed off as she waited again for the man to move.

Looking at his hands, she saw that they were dirty and old. She didn't dare get too close, but when she squinted she realized that some of the man's fingers seemed to have large patches of flesh missing, and she could see dried veins stuck to bare sections of bone.

Reaching down, she took the straw from the side of the juice carton and stuck it through the foil hole on top, and then she gently pulled the clingfilm from the sandwich, in case the man's hands hurt too much to do it himself.

"I hope you like them. I'm sorry there's not more."

Again she waited, hoping for a reply.

Hearing the howling wind outside, she looked up and listened for a moment. The wind seemed almost to be moaning as it blew down through the crack, and she couldn't help but think about the long walk home.

"I should go now," she said finally, turning back to look at the man. "I only came to bring you these, and to get Dad's torch. He gets really mad sometimes if he loses things, and when he gets mad -"

Suddenly she realized the man's head was moving, and she could hear a low creaking sound coming from his neck. His head was lifting slowly, as if he could barely summon the energy. Becca watched with open-mouthed shock as his face finally came into view. Taking care not to shine the torch directly at his features, Becca was nevertheless able to see now that he was an old man, older than she'd realized, with deep wrinkles in his leathery flesh and large, watery eyes. He was thin, almost gaunt, with a scruffy gray and white beard covering his jawline, and there were several old scars etched into his flesh, most notably around his left eye. His gaze, intense and fixed, seemed to almost burn with furious power.

"I..." Becca froze, unable to shake the feeling that the man was unlike anyone she'd ever seen before. "Are you okay?" she asked finally.

Slowly, the man tilted his head to one side, reminding Becca of a dog she'd met once in the park. She couldn't help but notice patches on his face where the flesh had dried up, even wearing thin in some places so that parts of his skull were revealed. There were holes, too, in his skin, as if worms and maggots had made their home there for a while, although the man looked too dry now for anything to live in his body.

"I brought you some food," she continued, hoping against hope that the man might at least smile. When he simply stared at her, however, she took an instinctive step back, ready to run. "I'm sorry if I disturbed you," she told him, trying not to offend him by looking too upset. "I didn't meant to wake you up, not if you were sleeping. I just thought you might be hungry down here, but we only had mayonnaise. I'm sorry if you don't like that, but... We don't have so much money, and mayonnaise is cheap and..."

Her voice trailed off, and she realized the homeless guy probably didn't care too much about the price of mayonnaise. Reaching into her pocket, she took out the gold coin from the night before. She wanted to keep it for herself, of course, but she felt that maybe she was being greedy. The old man, she told herself, probably needed it more.

"Here you go," she remembered her mother saying to a homeless woman one day in the center of town, tossing money into a cup. "I hope it helps."

And that had been it. Just a few simple words.

"Here you go," Becca said out loud finally, her voice trembling with fear as she tossed the gold coin toward the old man. "I hope it helps!"

With that, she turned and hurried back across the chamber. When she reached the passageway, she quickly slipped between the rocks, not daring to look back in case she saw that she was being followed. She didn't want to run, in case the man realized she was scared and felt offended, but at the same time she wanted to get away as quickly as possible. When she reached the slope that led up to the edge of the crack, she peered over her shoulder, but there was no sign of him following so she turned and quickly clambered up until she was able to slip out onto the wet grass above.

Taking a deep breath, she sat back and tried to calm her nerves. She knew her father would be furious if he found out that she'd given food and money to a complete stranger, but she also knew that her mother would approve, and that was more important. After wiping some fresh mud from her boots, Becca set off on the long traipse home. At first she walked slowly, but eventually she broke into a run, worried in case her father got back to the house too soon.

The wind picked up, blasting across the moor even though the storm had passed now. In the distance, unseen by anyone, a solitary figure stood on one of the ridges, watching as Becca ran home.

***

Down in the chamber, a faint creaking sound broke the silence. There was no light in the chamber now, but slowly a withered, partially skinless hand reached down and took the gold coin.

CHAPTER FOURTEEN

THE VOICES OF TOURISTS echoed all around as Doctor Alistair Clarke made his way along the aisle. Up ahead, the altar of St. Martin's Church awaited in all its splendor, and this was where most of the tourists had gathered, their phones flashing as they took photos. Rather than joining them, however, Doctor Clarke made his way around to one side, heading further back toward a part of the church that remained neglected by most visitors.

"Keep your voices down!" he hissed at a group of particularly excitable girls, who'd begun giggling as he passed. "This is a church, not a social club!"

"Whatever," one of the girls muttered, but Clarke ignored her.

Heading away from the hordes of visitors, he finally reached the far end of the church and stopped in front of a life-sized black statue that stood tucked away, set back slightly in an alcove. For a moment he stared up at the statue's face, admiring the smooth features, and then he looked down at the inscription beneath the figure's feet. He'd stood in the exact same spot many times before, having turned the journey into something of a pilgrimage during the writing of his many books on the subject of the English Civil War. On this occasion, however, things felt different. Instead of a sense of awe and wonder, he was filled with regret.

Looking up at the statue's face again, Clarke felt a shiver pass through his chest.

"Nykolas Freeman," a voice said suddenly. "Scourge of the five counties."

Turning, Clarke saw the local priest ambling over.

"I know who he was," Clarke muttered, glancing back at the statue. "Or at least I *thought* I did. Once."

"There's a lot of opposition to this statue remaining here," the priest continued. "There are those in our community who would rather forget that Freeman ever existed. They see him as a bad omen, as a reminder of much darker times, but that's precisely why I insist on having the statue remain here. We cannot simply tidy away the past and pretend it didn't happen. It's better to face the truth about what our ancestors did, no matter how ugly that might seem. If we forget the past, we risk repeating it." He paused for a moment, looked up at the statue. "Besides, it's said that Freeman was a good, God-fearing man once, before he turned to such barbarity."

"He's said to have committed the most atrocious acts," Clarke pointed out, his gaze still fixed on the statue's face. "There are even those who doubt that such a man could have existed."

"Oh, he existed," the priest replied. "I think we can put that question to rest."

"Maybe," Clarke muttered, lost in thought for a moment.

"If you have any concerns in that regard," the priest continued, "I'd advise you to read a book called *The Priest Killer* by an eminent historian named Alistair Clarke. He wrote several volumes about the period, actually, and they're all highly entertaining. In fact, we have copies in the church gift shop."

"I'm sure you do," Clarke replied, suppressing a sigh.

"Some of the stories about Freeman are utterly ghastly," the priest muttered. "It's said that he took one poor woman and boiled her alive, and then before she died he began to peel her skin away."

Clarke nodded. He remembered mentioning that incident in one of his books.

"He also had a predilection for feeding live victims to his pigs," the priest continued. "They say the screams could be heard for miles. Pigs are vicious beasts, you know. They can crunch through bone!"

"So I believe."

"Another famous story about Freeman," the priest added, with a hint of fascination in his voice now, "is that he used to cut off the genitals of his male victims and -"

"That's fine," Clarke replied, interrupting him. "I know the stories."

"Are you sure you don't want to hear more?" the

priest asked. "Some of the tales are extremely shocking. Awful, awful things, to be sure." He leaned closer. "Apparently, one time, Freeman dragged a young maiden to his farm and smeared oil over her bare body, and then he took red-hot metal tongs and -"

"That's quite enough of that, I think," Clarke said firmly. "We wouldn't want to discuss such awful things in a house of the Lord, would we?"

The priest opened his mouth to continue, before nodding and adjusting his collar, as if he'd briefly started to enjoy the stories a little too much. Glancing over his shoulder, he made sure no-one could overhear them, and then he turned to Clarke again.

"You heard about the incident last year, I assume?" he asked.

"What incident?"

"A young girl whose family had moved into Baxendale House," the priest continued. "Miss Laura Woodley, I believe was her name. She made some rather startling claims regarding Nykolas Freeman, and the whole thing became a minor sensation in these parts for a few days. I believed she went around telling people that she'd encountered Freeman himself as some form of apparition, that he'd somehow come back from the dead. The newspapers were full of her claims."

"I recall reading about it," Clarke muttered, nodding sagely. "She ended up in a psychiatric institution."

"For a while," the priest continued. "Obviously no-one of sound mind would believe her claims, although I'm told there *are* some in the area who think she might have been telling the truth about her encounter. People can be rather superstitious around these parts."

"Childish rubbish," Clarke replied. "She was obviously some hysterical teenager who thought she could gain attention by making outlandish claims. Or she was on drugs, or mentally ill. What was it that she said again? Nykolas Freeman was alive and well, and stalking the countryside once more? That she'd seen him with her own two eyes?"

"A tad melodramatic," the priest muttered.

"And of course," Clarke continued, "even in this age of cellphones and cameras all over the place, she offered not one shred of evidence. I don't know what's more remarkable, the idea that someone would make such a claim, or the idea that there are idiots out there who'd believe it. The whole thing sounds like a grotesque farce from beginning to end."

"The human mind is a -"

Before the priest could finish, both men flinched at the sound of schoolgirls running along the aisle.

"Excuse me," the priest continued, clearly unimpressed. "I think I shall have to go and restore a little order." He turned to hurry away, before seemingly remembering one more thing. "Take a word of advice. When you exit through the church's gift shop, pick up a copy of *The Priest Killer* by Alistair Clarke. That's the one with the most detailed descriptions of Freeman's horrific acts." He adjusted his collar again, as if it felt too tight. "Not that anyone enjoys reading such things, of course, but one cannot hide from the barbarity of the world. It's all true history! Why, if you think about it, as a priest myself, I might have been hunted by Freeman back in the day. I'd have ended up getting..."

His voice trailed off as he stared at the statue for a moment, and then he frowned as he turned to Clarke.

"What was I talking about, again?"

"You were going to go and deal with those loud-mouthed girls."

"Of course," the priest stammered, adjust his collar yet again. "Of course, absolutely."

With that, clearly a little hot and bothered, he turned and hurried along the aisle.

Left alone next to the statue of Nykolas Freeman, Clarke stared up for a moment longer at the face of the man he'd spent his entire life studying. He'd come to the church because he wanted to remind himself that Freeman had been a real person, to somehow calm his doubts, but instead he was increasingly convinced of the opposite. The priest's mention of the previous year's incident, and of the bizarre claims made by the girl from the Baxendale house, only seemed to reinforce the idea that Freeman had become a joke, a kind of bogeyman. In the depths of his soul, Clarke was starting to realize that Nykolas Freeman had been no more real than Robin Hood.

"I've wasted my career on a phantom," he muttered finally, with a hint of anger in his voice. "I've been a goddamn fool."

On his way out, he stopped by the gift shop and saw copies of his own books, laid out in a display. He grimaced at the sight of one in particular, bearing the title *The Priest Killer* and with a painting of the Freeman's ax on its cover. Somehow that book in particular, of which he'd once been so proud and which had apparently so enthralled the priest, now served as a reminder of his foolishness.

CHAPTER FIFTEEN

ALTHOUGH THE RAIN HAD passed several hours ago, Mary still found that the ground was extremely muddy as she made her way across the moor. Every footstep briefly squelched down into the boggy ground, and her legs were already a little tired from the trek, but at least she was halfway to the site now. Reaching a stone wall that ran over the crest of the hill, she stopped for a moment to get her breath back, while reminding herself to get in better shape some time. Maybe join a gym.

Glancing over her shoulder, she saw the town in the distance, and she imagined Doctor Clarke still sitting at a table in the pub's courtyard, probably starting on another Guinness.

"Arrogant asshole," she muttered under her breath, feeling a renewed determination to prove him wrong. "I've been up since the crack of dawn," she added, mimicking his pompous voice, "planning my itinerary." She rolled her eyes. "Whatever."

Turning to look ahead, she was about to set off again when she realized that a thick bank of fog had come rolling across the moor, having seemingly materialized out of nowhere. She quickly zipped her coat up as the fog began to fill the air all around her, and for a moment all she could do was wait as the horizon disappeared in every direction. Looking over her shoulder, she saw that the town was already out of sight. Pulling her phone from her pocket, she brought up Daniel's number and tried to call him to let him know that she'd be a little late, but she found that she had no coverage.

"Great," she said with a sigh, looking around but seeing only thick fog. Leaning back against the stone wall, she figured her best bet was just to stay put and wait for the worst of the fog to pass. Despite her earlier mockery of Doctor Clarke's drinking habits, the cold air was enough to make her wish she was the kind of person who carried a hip-flask.

"Nanny!" a voice called out suddenly. "Nanny, where are you?"

Startled, Mary looked around, but there was no sign of anyone.

"Nanny?" another voice shouted. "Mr. Bronson? Are you still here?"

She waited for someone to come into view, but the fog was thick enough to reduce visibility to just a few meters. Still, the moors had been clear a few minutes ago and she'd seen no sign of anyone nearby.

"Nanny, please!" the first voice shouted, this

time with a hint of fear. "Nanny, say something! Nanny, we're scared!"

"Nanny!" another voice called out, and then another.

Children, she realized. They sounded like children.

Turning, Mary realized the voices seemed to be coming from all around. She knew there was no reason to be concerned, but at the same time she didn't like the idea of people being out there in the fog, close but unseen. She waited for some hint of movement, perhaps a faint outline of someone in the white haze, but there was no-one. Finally the voices faded for a moment, leaving her alone in the white silence.

"Nanny!" a girl shouted suddenly, right behind Mary.

Spinning around, she expected to see someone, but instead she found herself facing another wall of fog. She could hear footsteps, though, crunching nearby through the cold grass.

More voices rang out in the distance.

Figuring that she couldn't get lost if she kept the wall in sight, Mary began to make her way forward.

"Nanny!" a girl's voice sobbed, sounding as if she was close to tears. "Nanny, please!"

The voices were causing Mary to start panicking now, even though she told herself over and over that there was no need. She almost tripped in the mud, but she quickly steadied herself against the wall and kept walking, while all around the fog seemed to be getting thicker. No matter how hard she tried to stay calm, she couldn't shake the growing feeling that something was wrong. It was as if some unseen force was reaching through the fog and into her chest, slipping its fingers between her ribs and trying to draw her away from the wall. For a moment, she felt certain that if she lost the wall, she'd never find her way out of the fog and -

Suddenly a scream rang out. Mary stopped and looked back the way she'd come. The scream had sounded like a young girl, her voice filled with pain, and a moment later there were more screams, filling the air.

"Hello?" Mary called out, taking a step back. "What's wrong? Are you -"

Before she could finish, she tripped in the mud and landed hard. Stumbling to her feet, she looked around, only to find that she could no longer see the stone wall. She stumbled back the way she'd come, but the wall seemed to have disappeared entirely. Figuring that she'd simply become disorientated, she tried a different direction, still with no luck. Her sense of panic was growing now, and she quickly realized that she had no idea which way to go. The screams were still calling out, seemingly coming from every possible direction, and after a moment Mary stumbled back and fell again, this time landing in a particularly boggy puddle of mud. Turning, she tried to get up, but the screams were too loud now and she felt as if they were almost on top of her.

Suddenly something bumped against the back of her head, sending her crashing forward. She let out a gasp of pain, but the screams had stopped again, as abruptly as they'd started. Looking over her shoulder, she was shocked to see that the fog was starting to lift, and within a few seconds the white haze had begun to drift away across the moor. Mary turned, looking for the source of the screams, but gradually she realized that there was once again no sign of anyone nearby. She could see the wall again, though, about twenty feet away. Stumbling to her feet, she made her way back over, gratefully pressing her hands against the wall's damp stones as if to reassure herself that they were real. Her heart was pounding and she kept looking around, but the fog was gone now and the moor was once again empty.

Glancing down, she spotted a rectangular metal plate set into the stone wall. She crouched down and took a closer look at the lettering engraved on the surface:

In memory of the
17 students and 2 teachers
who disappeared near this spot

17th January 2010

She read the plate a couple more times, to make sure she wasn't misunderstanding, before realizing that she must be near the site where the schoolchildren had vanished several years earlier. Everyone in the country knew the heart-breaking story of the old school bus that had been found abandoned, but exhaustive searches of the area had never yielded any clues as to the fate of the missing children. The story still popped up in the media periodically, usually around the anniversary, but no answers had ever been forthcoming.

For a moment, she allowed herself to consider the possibility that the voices had somehow come from the children themselves, although she quickly dismissed that idea. She told herself instead that the fog had simply disorientated her, and that the rest had been the product of some hyper-active thoughts. After all, she'd already experienced a nightmare about Nykolas Freeman, so she figured her thoughts were a little unsettled. The explanation wasn't entirely convincing, but it felt better than -

Suddenly she felt a vibration in her pocket. Slipping her phone out, Mary saw that not only did she now have coverage again, but Daniel was calling. Somehow the real world had found her again.

"Hey," she stammered as she answered. "I'm -"

"We found something," he replied breathlessly, interrupting her. "Mary, this is big."

"What did you find?" she asked, getting to her feet. Her heart was still racing, but she felt she couldn't tell him about her strange encounter with the fog, at least not until she'd understood it herself. Besides, news from the dig site was far more important.

"Where are you?" he replied.

"I'm on my way. I'm about half an hour from the site."

"Get here fast," he continued. "That hunch you had about digging near the ridge? It's paid off more than you could ever dream."

"What did you find?" she asked again.

"Just get here, Mary. If I told you over the phone, I don't think you'd believe me! You have to see this for yourself!"

CHAPTER SIXTEEN

"SHOW ME!" MARY CALLED out as she reached the site. Stumbling through the mud, she made her way past the tent and toward the spot where Daniel and two other workers were carefully setting pieces of metal out on a white sheet. "What have you got?"

"Jesus Christ," Daniel replied, staring at her in shock. "What happened to you?"

Looking down at the front of her coat, Mary realized she was covered in mud.

"It's nothing," she muttered, "I'll tell you later. Just show me what you found." Making her way around to the other side of the sheet, she looked down and saw various muddy, rusted chunks of metal that had obviously been dug up during the morning. There was a sword-tip, and what looked like the side of a battered helmet, and several sections of a musket. After a moment, however, her eyes settled on part of an old metal standard, complete with a rusted tip that seemed to contain some kind of crest or emblem. "Is that..."

"The battle standard of Captain John Villiers," Daniel replied, his voice filled with a sense of awe. "Mary, do you have any idea what this means? We haven't just found the site of a lost battle. We've also solved one of the biggest mysteries of the English Civil War!"

Crouching down, Mary stared in shock at the emblem. Her mind was racing, but she already recognized the design from several textbooks and her natural caution was already fading, replaced by a sense of excitement. John Villiers had been a Royalist soldier who was famous for having displayed exemplary bravery in the heart of battle, but he was also known for having disappeared without a trace some time in early 1644. Reaching out, she carefully picked up the fragment of metal and wiped some more mud from its surface, but she already knew without a shadow of doubt what she was holding.

"Villiers must have fought in the Battle of Sharpeton," she whispered. "This must be where he died."

"And when the battle was forgotten, or covered up," Daniel continued excitedly, "the circumstances of Villiers' death were lost to history!"

"This is incredible," she replied, unable to stop staring at the piece of metal in her hands. "It's *more* than incredible, it's..." She paused for a moment. "It's proof! No-one can possibly argue with us anymore! Even Doctor Clarke's going to have to admit that we've stumbled across something important. We can get the dig extended, we can get more funding, we can find out what really happened here!"

"If there was a Nobel prize for archeology," Daniel continued, "I think you'd have it in the bag right now."

"Not just me," she replied, still unable to take her eyes off the discovery. "All of us."

"It was your idea to dig here," he reminded her. "You're the one who pushed the council to let us get our hands dirty. Mary, this is going to make your name! You're gonna be a way, *way* bigger deal than Alistair bloody Clarke."

"It's not a competition," she muttered, turning the metal over to check the other side. "Even Clarke is going to be amazed by this. The man might be cynical and critical as hell, but he's not going to deny what's right in front of his eyes." She paused, before finally setting the object down. Her hands were trembling, and she felt as if she couldn't quite comprehend the magnitude of the latest discovery. "What else did you find? More bodies?"

"*Several* more," he replied, "and that's without even digging too deep. It's pretty clear that the Battle of Sharpeton was a major event."

"Of course it was. Captain John Villiers wouldn't have been here if it was just a skirmish. This must have been a battle the size of Naseby or Edgehill."

"Which makes it all the more surprising that it was covered up," Daniel pointed out. "I mean, there are really *two* miracles here. The first is that anyone would even *try* to cover it up in the first place. The second is that they could have succeeded. The Royalists and Parliamentarians were at each other's throats, so why would they come together and both agree to pretend this battle never happened?"

"They wouldn't," she replied, getting to her feet. "It's inconceivable, but... Clearly it happened." She paused for a moment, trying to figure out the best approach. "Keep working. Get everything cataloged and numbered, and wrap the standard up so I can take it with me. I need to get photos and start inspecting it properly, but I won't do that here at the site, I'll take it back to my room. And don't let anyone else know about this, not yet. I want to be absolutely, 100% positive about what we've got here before we start telling the world."

"And then will you tell me what happened to you on the way here?" he asked.

"What do you mean?"

"You took twice as long as you should," he continued, "and you're covered in mud, and something clearly spooked you."

She opened her mouth to tell him about the fog and the screams, but after a moment she realized she'd only be inviting ridicule. It would be better, she figured, to focus on the work and just write off her earlier experience as some kind of panic attack.

"Nothing happened," she said finally. "Come on, don't get distracted. We're on the verge of the most significant discovery of modern times, and I'm not going to let superstition derail our work."

CHAPTER SEVENTEEN

"HAVE YOU SEEN DOCTOR Clarke this afternoon?"

Turning to her, the barman rolled his eyes.

"Not for a few hours," he told her, clearly a little unimpressed, "but I reckon he's in the Clarendon. It's the only other pub in town, so that's probably where he's set himself down since I turfed him out of here."

"You threw him out?"

"Not permanently, but..." He sighed. "The man seems nice enough, but he'd downed three pints of Guinness by lunchtime and I'm not having drunks in my pub. I told him to get lost 'til this evening. He didn't take too kindly to that, but he buggered off without putting up too much of a fight. Took his car, as well. He's lucky I didn't call the cops and report him for driving under the influence."

"I'd better go and sober him up," Mary replied, turning to head back out. "Thanks for -"

Stopping suddenly, she spotted the photo of the

116

schoolchildren on the wall, next to the bingo machine. She paused for a moment, thinking back to the voices on the moor, and then she turned to find that she was being watched by the barman.

"The disappearance a few years ago," she said cautiously, "was it -"

"My son was one of them," he replied, interrupting her. Stepping around the bar, he made his way over to join her, before tapping on the picture to indicate one of the smiling faces. "Robert Swanson. Thirteen years old." He paused for a moment, as if just looking at the photo was enough to bring him to the verge of tears. "I still remember the morning they set off on that trip. Seventeen of them, and two teachers. He so nearly didn't go. He'd just got out of hospital after having a metal brace put in his knee, but he begged us and we gave in. It was only supposed to be a jaunt out to the moor, something to do with getting closer to nature."

"And then what happened?" Mary asked.

"And then they were gone," he continued. "Just like it said in the papers. When they didn't come back, the police started looking for them. We all figured their bus had either crashed or got a puncture, something like that. As it started getting dark and the night turned cold, we all headed out to help with the search, and eventually someone spotted the bus parked up out Clifton way. The kids' bags were still inside, but there was no sign of them. No damage to the bus, either." He paused again. "That was several years ago now, and no-one's found so much as a hair of any of them since. It's like they vanished from the world."

"I'm so sorry," Mary replied. "It must be hard, not knowing."

He nodded, while still staring at the photo.

"What do *you* think happened?" she asked cautiously.

"You wouldn't believe the crackpot theories some people come up with," he continued. "There was one guy came here, reckoned he could prove aliens had come down and taken them off in a UFO. I threw him out so fast, his feet couldn't touch the ground. Other people think they were murdered and the bodies were hidden somewhere, and they'll be found one day. I don't know about that. Monsters, fairies, ghosts... You name it, someone somewhere's made the suggestion. There are some bloody idiots in the world."

"Do you still have hope that they might turn up?"

He opened his mouth to reply, but something seemed to hold him back.

"I'm sorry," she continued, "I didn't mean to..."

"Robert'd be in his early twenties now," he replied after a moment. "I'm not a fool, I know he's gone for good." He stared at the photo for a moment longer, before turning to her. "I reckon they just vanished into thin air. I know it sounds crazy, but I reckon God just decided it was their time and he took them. All of them, just like that. No pain, no fear, just vanishing in the blink of an eye." He clicked his fingers together. "Gone."

"I'm not sure the world works like that," she pointed out.

"Seventeen kids disappeared that day," he

continued. "I don't think there's *any* explanation that could make sense. The truth is, even though I told you just now that I know Robert's gone for good, there's still a part of me that thinks he might show up. Impossible things happen, right? It was an impossible thing that took them all away, so why can't another impossible thing bring them back? That's why I'm still here, still in Sharpeton, waiting around just in case he shows up. Imagine if he came to the door one day and found we'd given up and left?" He paused. "My wife couldn't handle it, she moved away, but..."

His voice trailed off for a moment, then finally he sighed and headed back over to the bar.

"Nan Gold and John Bronson were good people," he added. "They'd never have let anything happen to the kids, not if they could've helped it."

"Nan?" She paused, thinking back to the plaintive voices crying out for someone named Nanny on the moor. She told herself that she'd imagined the whole thing, that she'd subliminally stored that information from some old news report and regurgitated it as part of a panic attack. The last thing she wanted was to start worrying people by claiming to have heard ghosts, or to cause offense with tasteless theories.

"Are you and the others going to be in for supper this evening?" the landlord asked, clearly keen to change the subject. "I can reserve a table for you, if you like. Believe it or not, we actually get busy round these parts sometimes."

"That'd be great," she replied, glancing at the photo again before turning and heading out into the courtyard at the front of the pub. No matter how hard she tried to believe that the incident on the moor had been all in her head, she couldn't shake the feeling that the fog had somehow trailed a presence, that for a few brief seconds she'd managed to hear a moment from the past. "Great," she muttered finally, heading across the street in the direction of the Clarendon pub. "I'm losing my mind."

CHAPTER EIGHTEEN

FOR A MOMENT, AS he stepped out of his car and looked up at the old house, Doctor Clarke felt genuinely lost for words. He'd read about the Baxendale house many times, of course, and studied photos on countless occasions, but he'd never actually managed to visit the place until now. Stepping toward the front door, he felt somewhat in awe at the thought that he was in a place with such a strong and terrible history.

He remembered, almost word for word, his first book's account of the Baxendale massacre. On the evening of September the 10th, 1608, Nykolas Freeman and a group of men were said to have arrived at the house and hauled the Baxendale family out for questioning. Having hunted a priest named Darian Kinner for several weeks up until that point, Freeman had no doubt been in the mood for quick answers. The fact that Mr. and Mrs. Baxendale were swiftly executed was no surprise, but word had spread far and wide concerning Freeman's treatment of little Jessica Baxendale. He was said to have beheaded the child in front of her parents, and it was this act more than any other that had cemented his reputation for cruelty. Except that now, Clarke seriously doubted aspects of the Freeman mythology, and was trying to untangle the knots of history so that he might gain a better understanding of what had *really* happened.

As he stood watching the house, lost in thought, the front door suddenly opened and a young woman stepped out, frowning as she saw him.

"Can I help you?" she asked cautiously.

"Are you..." He paused for a moment, feeling as if the journey had been unnecessary after all. Then again, he'd already driven out there, emboldened by several morning pints, and he figured he needed to hear the girl's ridiculous claims firsthand. "Are you, by any chance, Miss Laura Woodley?"

"Why do you want to know?"

"My name is Doctor Alistair Clarke," he continued, stepping toward her and holding out a hand for her to shake. "I'm a historian. I was hoping I might have a word with you about something that happened a few years ago. I believe you're the young lady who claimed to have encountered Nykolas Freeman, are you not?"

From the rush of fear in her eyes, he knew immediately that he was correct.

***

"I don't like talking about it much," Laura muttered, as her fingers tore nervously at a paper tissue. "My therapist says I don't have to, not if it makes me feel bad."

"I understand that," Doctor Clarke replied, taking a sip of tea, "but this is important. I read as much as I could about the incident involving you and your sister, but sometimes the media has a way of blowing these things up out of all proportion. I just wanted to meet you in person so I could find out what triggered your mania."

She glanced at him. "Mania?"

"Well, the delusions that filled your mind."

She narrowed her eyes. "You think they were delusions?"

"You claimed to have encountered Nykolas Freeman in the -"

"I did!" she said firmly, briefly raising her voice. "I did see him," she added, taking a deep breath. "I swear to God."

"My understanding is that you subsequently admitted to your doctors that the -"

"I told the doctors what they wanted to hear," she continued. "If I'd kept telling the truth, I'd still be at Wyvern right now, locked away in a padded cell. They were talking about giving me another round of shock therapy if I didn't show signs of improvement, and for them *improvement* meant changing my story. So I told them that I'd imagined the whole thing, and they let me out. Now I'm studying history in London. I'm all better, can't you tell?" Those last few words came out with a hint of bitterness in her voice, as if she resented her treatment. "I only come back here for holidays and..." Her voice trailed off as she looked around the room, almost as if she expected to see someone watching her. "I come back because I need to prove to myself that I'm strong," she added. "I need to prove that this house hasn't beaten me."

"I imagine -"

"And it hasn't!" she hissed. "I swear!"

"Of course," he replied, trying to remain diplomatic. He watched her for a moment, fully aware that she seemed to be a bundle of nervous energy. She was exhibiting a slight squint in her left eye, and she was unable to maintain eye contact for more than a few seconds at a time. "But do you still believe that you encountered Nykolas Freeman in that church?"

"I know I did!"

He stared at her for a moment longer, struck by the wild intensity of her features. She seemed so fragile and tense, he was worried the wrong question might destroy her, but he knew he had to continue. "Describe him for me. Please, if you don't mind."

She visibly shuddered at the request.

"*Please*," he continued. "I wouldn't be here if it wasn't important." Reaching into his pocket, he pulled out a card with his name and contact details printed on the front, along with the university logo. "This is my area of study," he explained, sliding the card over to her. "I can't rely on what was reported in the media. I need to hear it in your own words."

Picking up the card, she examined it for a

moment.

"You're not a journalist?" she asked cautiously.

He shook his head.

"And you're not from the hospital? You're not trying to trick me."

"I'm a historian," he replied. "I only care about the truth.

She looked at the card for a moment longer, before setting it back down.

"When I saw him in the church," she said finally, "he was rotten, like he'd been buried underground. He was wet, dripping all over the floor, and I could see worms and maggots wriggling through his flesh, burrowing -"

She stopped as soon as she saw Clarke raise a skeptical eyebrow.

"You don't believe me," she stammered. "You're just like the rest of them!"

"I'm sorry," he replied, "please, continue."

"I'd seen him before the church," she admitted cautiously. "I saw him right here in this house, hundreds of years ago, when he came and killed the family who lived here."

"You *saw* that happen?" Doctor Clarke asked, struggling to hide his extreme doubts.

"It was like a kind of time-slip," she replied. "Don't ask me to explain it, because I can't. All I know is that I was there when he..." The words seemed to catch in her throat for a moment. "He beheaded little Jessica Baxendale right in front of me. I saw the blood..." She took a deep breath as tears began to trickle down her cheeks. "I saw her head rolling down onto the ground, I saw her face, she blinked a couple of times after it happened." Closing her eyes, she seemed overcome, and her bottom lip had begun to tremble. "I relive that moment hundreds of times every day. I swear to God, Nykolas Freeman was pure evil. He had a kind of farmhouse, too, with women in cages. He thought they were witches. The things he did to them..."

Doctor Clarke watched as she sat with her eyes closed. After a few seconds she sniffed back more tears, and she seemed close to a breakdown.

"Suzie somehow dealt with it better," she continued, "but I can't get it out of my head."

"What would you say," Clarke replied, "if I told you that Nykolas Freeman never actually existed at all?"

She shook her head.

"I'm afraid it's true," he continued. "Freeman was a bogeyman, he was invented to scare people. He might have been *loosely* modeled on one of the real witch-hunters who lived in this area, but to all intents and purposes he was no more real than Robin Hood or Maid Marian. He was a work of fiction, designed to -"

"I saw him," she said firmly.

"Clearly, living in this house made quite an impression on you."

"I saw him!" she said again, before wiping fresh tears from her eyes with the remains of the tissue she'd been picking apart.

"I'm sure you *think* that's what happened."

"Is that what you came here for?" she asked. "To tell me I'm stupid?"

He sighed. "I can quite understand that you believe you saw these things, but I hope you're a sensible young woman. You must realize that there's simply no way you could have witnessed something that took place four hundred years ago. I know teenagers these days are full of hormones and -"

"I'm not a teenager!"

"Mental illness is a very serious thing," he added. "Miss Woodley, I believe that you are a classic example of someone who allowed a piece of fiction to alter her sense of reality. You were clearly a very impressionable young woman, and when you learned about the history of this house -"

"Get out," she replied, interrupting him.

"I'm only try to help."

"Get out," she said again.

"I'm a historian," he continued. "I've studied Nykolas Freeman extensively, more extensively than anyone else, and I can assure you that despite your emotional response to a set of stimuli, the plain facts -"

Suddenly pushing the table forward, Laura got to her feet. "Get out!"

***

After pulling his car door shut, Doctor Clarke sat back for a moment and watched the house. He could see Laura in one of the windows, but she quickly pulled the curtain shut.

"Poor girl," he muttered with a sigh. "A little arrogant, and certainly delusional."

CHAPTER NINETEEN

SITTING ALONE IN THE silent house, Laura peered through a gap in the curtains and watched as the car disappeared along the driveway. Her eyes were dry now, although tear-tracks on her cheeks still glistened in the morning light.

After a moment, she heard the faintest creaking sound from one of the other rooms. Slowly, she turned and looked toward the doorway. Her bottom lip was trembling, and finally her whole body started shaking with fear as she heard another creak, followed by a bump.

CHAPTER TWENTY

"DOCTOR CLARKE! DOCTOR CLARKE, wait!"

Stopping at the door to the King's Head, Clarke turned and saw Mary hurrying across the courtyard. He forced a smile and prepared to fend off another torrent of poorly-informed optimism.

"Miss Baker, allow me to fetch a drink and then I can spare you a few -"

"I was just at the Clarendon looking for you," she continued, a little breathless as she reached him.

"I took a short drive further afield," he replied.

"Slightly over the limit, perhaps?"

He waved her away.

"You smell of alcohol!" she continued.

"I assure you, I was completely in control of the vehicle at all times," he said firmly. "I simply wanted to see... Well, let's just say that I wanted to see something for myself, and my worst fears were confirmed."

"I'm about to *un-confirm* them," she said firmly.

"We found something at the dig site that you need to see!"

***

"You've heard of John Villiers, I assume?" Mary asked a few minutes later, as they sat in the corner the pub. She watched Doctor Clarke turning the piece of metal around, examining it from all angles, and she couldn't help feeling a flash of relief that he seemed genuinely lost for words. "Please tell me you don't doubt *his* existence too..."

"I do not doubt it for one second," he muttered, clearly lost in thought as he continued to inspect the discovery. "It certainly *appears*, Miss Baker -"

"*Doctor* Baker," she added, interrupting him.

He sighed. "It certainly appears, Doctor Baker, that you have found the long-lost battle standard of Captain Villiers." He paused, as if he couldn't quite believe what he was holding. "As I'm sure you're aware, there has been a great deal of speculation as to where this item ended up. Indeed, as to where Villiers himself ended his days. The historical accounts place him at several key events between 1640 and 1643, but then -"

"But then he vanishes from all the records," she pointed out. "I know. I wrote about Villiers for my undergraduate dissertation. Some people claimed that he might have simply retired from the war, or that he left England on some secret mission for King Charles and never returned, or even that he was killed away from the battlefield and the news was covered up." She paused, enjoying the trace of rapt attention in Clarke's eyes. "Villiers would never have let this standard out of his possession. It had been in his family for several generations, and he would have expected to be buried with it. Even if he'd been killed in battle, his opponents would have granted him the honor of taking his standard with him to the grave."

"Most likely," Clarke muttered.

"So it's clear he fell at the Battle of Sharpeton."

She waited for him to argue with her, for him to tell her she was delusional, but instead he seemed completely lost in his own thoughts as he squinted, taking a closer look at the chunk of metal. After a moment he started scraping a fleck of mud away with his thumbnail.

"I'm right, aren't I?" she asked, unable to hide her excitement. "I know it needs to be officially confirmed, I get that there's a procedure, but basically... We've solved the mystery of Captain John Villiers' last stand."

Clarke paused for a moment, before slowly nodding.

"And it's clear that there was a battle just outside Sharpeton," she continued. "Not just any battle, either. It was one big enough and important enough to draw a man like Villiers to lead a charge, which means Sharpeton must have held some great significance at the time."

"I don't think I can argue with you," Clarke replied, "not now that you've unearthed this remarkable item. Congratulations, Doctor Baker, you have surprised me. Not many people have ever done that."

"The question is *why* was the battle deliberately covered up? That's the part that makes no sense to me."

After setting the piece of metal down, Clarke took a sip from his pint of Guinness before leaning back, letting his ample gut bulge beneath his shirt.

"We have a conundrum here, Doctor Baker," he continued finally. "There is no conceivable explanation for the cover-up of an entire battle, yet we quite clearly have a battlefield of considerable significance. One can only conclude that whatever happened here at Sharpeton, it was quite unlike any other occurrence in England at the time. What could compel two opposing armies to strike an agreement that not only would they cease fighting, but they would pretend the battle had never started in the first place?"

"I can't think of an explanation right now," she admitted.

"Neither can I," he replied, "but I'm sure of one thing. If word of this occurrence had reached the leaders of either the Royalist or Parliamentarian forces, it would never have been allowed to stand. Also, some mention would have been made in the history books. In which case -"

"The armies made the decision themselves," she suggested, interrupting him. "That's my belief, too. For some reason, the armies decided to never mention the battle again, not even to their superiors. God knows how they managed to achieve that. There must have been hundreds of men who survived the carnage, but clearly they never mentioned it either."

"Most of those men would have been rather lowly," he pointed out, "so it's possible that they could still have discussed the incident without it being recorded in texts. Still, I'll grant that it's unlikely such a battle could completely slip by without mention, so I propose that we start searching for any -"

"Already on it," she replied. "I've spoken to a friend at the university this afternoon, and he's going to go through several texts that haven't been digitized yet, specifically to search for any mention whatsoever of Sharpeton in late 1643 or the whole of 1644. I refuse to believe that a battle could be completely removed from every record of the period. Even if it wasn't referenced directly, it has to have left a mark on the surrounding area."

"Your enthusiasm is somewhat chastening," Clarke muttered, taking another sip of Guinness. Glancing at the window, he was just in time to see the street-lamps flickering to life across the road, signaling the arrival of evening gloom. "And rather exhausting, too. It seems that your great victory comes just as I am about to face my failure."

"Are you still talking about Nykolas Freeman?" she asked. "You can't possibly think -"

"Oh, I *know* he never existed," he replied, interrupting her again. "I looked into the eyes of a crazed young woman today, and I saw her madness as she spoke of having encountered Freeman's reanimated corpse. I'm now convinced more than ever before that Nykolas Freeman was a fantasy." He paused for a moment. "It was the ax, in my case."

She waited for him to continue. "What was the ax?"

He sighed. "In all the stories about Freeman, it was said that he carried one particular ax with him. According to legend, he never let that ax out of his sight. The blade was said to be dented but not broken, and the handle was apparently of a very specific, unique design with a serpent etched into the metal, as a reminder of the witches he sought to dispatch." For a moment he seemed lost in thought again. "I always believed that if I could find that ax, it would be the greatest achievement of my career. As time went on, however, I came to see my failure to find that ax as... As a mark of my abject failure."

"It might still be out there," she suggested.

He shook his head.

"It might!"

"It would have been found by now," he continued sadly. "Your miraculous discovery aside, pretty much everything else that *can* be dug up, *has* been dug up. No, my dear, I'm afraid my failure to find Freeman's ax is another nail in the coffin of the whole idea. The ax hasn't been found because Freeman himself wasn't real. That ax, a facsimile of which adorned the cover of my best-selling book, was as illusory as Robin Hood's bow and arrow, or Darth Vader's light-saber. I dare say it shall come to symbolize academic failure throughout the land."

"But -"

"This, on the other hand," he continued, picking up the chunk of metal and gold, "is very real. And I propose that we focus on determining precisely what happened here at Sharpeton." He paused, before glancing at her. "I fear we have a long night ahead of us. I don't know about you, Doctor Baker, but I can't begin to imagine what could have caused every man on this battlefield – from the lowest foot-soldier to the highest commander – to turn around and flee for their lives."

CHAPTER TWENTY-ONE

"BECCA! BECCA, GET THROUGH here!"

Turning to look across the kitchen, Becca listened for a moment to the sound of the TV. Her father was watching another of those reality shows that she hated; although, to be fair, that wasn't *strictly* accurate. It was her mother who'd always hated reality TV, and Becca had simply chosen to copy her mother's tastes. Her mother had loved books, so Becca loved books, constantly reading the paperbacks her mother had left behind, even if she didn't understand half of them. Her mother had also liked old 1960s pop music, so Becca listened to the Beatles and the Rolling Stones whenever she got a chance, despite not really knowing what the singers were going on about. The more she missed her mother, the more she tried to become like her.

"Becca!"

Realizing that her father wasn't going to stop shouting, she made her way to the door and peered through into the front room. The curtains were drawn, and he'd already begun to get drunk. It was only 6pm, but for some reason he always seemed to let himself start on the first beer much earlier on Sundays, and Becca knew she was in for another long, slow night during which he'd get steadily more drunk until, finally, he'd do one of three things.

He'd fall asleep.

He'd get angry and start shouting at her.

Or he'd want to be friends, and he'd make her cuddle more than she wanted.

Whichever of the three happened, however, she had a strategy for dealing with his behavior. Nine times out of ten, she was able to stop him doing whatever he wanted. It had been several weeks since he'd gotten what he wanted from her.

"Becca," he continued, his voice slightly slurred, "why are you boots covered in mud? I saw them in the hallway, it looks like you've been hiking in them!"

"It was muddy out," she replied.

"What about your dress?" He frowned as he stared at her, as if he was seeing double. "The hem's dirty too."

"I didn't go far," she told him. "I didn't go anywhere I wasn't supposed to. I promise."

"Huh." He fell silent for a moment, but he was still watching her intently, as if he was trying to decide what he wanted to do next. These were always the worst moments, when he was only slightly drunk and might still come up with new ideas. "Have you ever tasted wine, Becca?"

She shook her head.

"You wanna?"

Again, she shook her head.

"Why not? Are you scared?"

"I'm too young."

He smiled. "It might loosen you up a little bit."

She shook her head.

"It's good to get started early with wine," he continued. "Toughen your liver up a little, so you're not a lightweight when you get older. How about you come and sit on Daddy's knee, and I'll let you take some sips from my glass? Not much, just enough to give you a little buzz."

"No," she replied, "thank you." She felt a shiver pass through her chest as she realized which type of drunk he was going to be tonight.

The worst type.

The *attentive* type.

"Sometimes you look like your mother," he told her. "Did you know that?"

She allowed herself a faint smile. She *wanted* to look like her mother, and to be like her too. And to find her again, of course. That was the most important thing. More than anything in the world, she wanted to find her mother and go away with her, even though she knew that was impossible. There was always her sister, though...

"Oh God, they're back!" her father bellowed suddenly, leaning back in his chair and letting out a loud hiccup that shook his entire body. Gripping the armrests, he seemed briefly filled with some kind of paralyzing rage, before letting out a long, slow sigh. "TV's shit tonight," he muttered finally. "I don't know what kind of morons they think wanna watch this garbage. The only reason *I* watch it is so I can keep up to date with the decline of civilization. I keep thinking modern Britain is gonna hit rock bottom, but no, there's always worse to come. I truly fear for the world to come, Becca." He hiccuped again as he pointed at the screen. "See that one? She thinks she's a model! Look at her, flouncing around on some reality garbage. She's famous for being famous. Do you know what that's called, Becca? It's a paradox!"

Grabbing the remote control, he started turning the volume up, and the screeching laughter from the TV became louder and louder until Becca wanted to put her hands over her ears. Turning, she began to make her way back to the kitchen.

"Hey!" her father called out. "Get over here! I didn't tell you to leave!"

She flinched, but she knew it was too dangerous to disobey. All she could hope, as she turned and headed over to the side of his chair, was that he'd either pass out quickly or that he'd get drunk enough to forget everything. When she reached the chair, however, she immediately saw that although his eyes were bloodshot and tired, he also seemed wide awake and alert.

"You look like Mummy," he told her again.

She hesitated, not quite knowing what to say. "Thank you," she muttered finally.

"Thank you?" He smiled. "You think that's a compliment?"

"Mummy was pretty," she pointed out.

"She was," he said with a sigh, before pausing again. "You look like your sister, too."

"Thank you."

He chuckled, before letting out another hiccup. "Your sister's a bitch."

She shook her head.

"She left us alone, didn't she?" he continued, his voice filling with indignation. "She buggered off to do whatever she wanted, and she left us here to rot. Your mother had been dead, what, twelve hours before Kerry fucked off? What kind of person does that, eh?"

"She'll come back," Becca replied, holding back tears.

"You think so?" He laughed. "I used to think that too, Becca, but I realized a while ago that the bitch is long gone. Whatever she's doing now, I'm sure she never even thinks about us anymore. Stupid whore." He leaned closer to her, letting her smell the beer and wine on his breath. "I bet she's forgotten she even *has* a little sister named Becca."

She shook her head.

"Of course she has," he continued. "That's the problem with your sister, she never had any sense of responsibility. She's off gallivanting around, probably meeting a different guy each night, opening her legs for them one by one... She doesn't give a shit about either of us, and that ain't ever gonna change! She gets that side from your mother, you know. There was a wild side to your mother, but she had it under control. Not Kerry, though. She lets it spill over." He hiccuped again. "You and me, though, we're very alike."

Again, she shook her head.

"What's wrong?" he asked with a smile. "Don't you wanna take after your old man? I'm a lot more reliable than your mother, that's for sure."

"Mummy loved me," Becca replied, "and Kerry -"

Before she could finish, her father whacked the side of her head, hard enough to knock her to the floor.

"You need to learn how to be grateful, kid," he muttered, taking another sip of wine as Becca sat up. "Your mother's the one who died, not me. I love you. You know that, right?"

He reached out to grab her, but she slipped free and crawled toward the door.

"Becca!" he shouted, stumbling to his feet. "Get back here, you ungrateful little runt!"

CHAPTER TWENTY-TWO

OUT ON THE WILD and lonely moor, a stiff figure marched slowly through the mud. His body, knotted and old, creaked with every step, and in his right hand he held an old, dented ax that glinted in the moonlight.

Ahead, on a far hill, there stood a solitary house, its windows dancing different shades of blue as the light from a TV filled one of the downstairs rooms. Even from this far away, a man's voice could be heard screaming inside the house.

CHAPTER TWENTY-THREE

"BECCA!"

Flinching as soon as she heard her father calling her name again, Becca tried to curl into an even smaller, even tighter ball. She was under the table in the kitchen, waiting for her father to go upstairs so she could make a run for the front door. She knew that if she could just get out of the house, she'd be able to find somewhere safe to hide, and in the morning her father would be hungover but sober, and he wouldn't remember anything from his night of drunkenness. Unfortunately, so far she could only hear him stumbling around in the front room and the hallway, regularly crashing into things.

"Becca!" he yelled again. "Daddy wants you! Get in here!"

A moment later she heard something smashing, and she figured he'd knocked over the vase from the sideboard, or one of the plates from the table.

"Becca!"

She heard his footsteps coming closer, but a moment later she realized he was finally going upstairs. She held her breath, listening to the unmistakable sound of him lumbering up the first few steps. After that, the house fell quiet and she began to wonder whether he'd passed out on the landing. Deep down, she knew she should probably wait a little longer, that it might not be safe to crawl out yet, but she was starting to panic and finally she made her way out from under the table. She paused again, listening for any hint of movement but hearing nothing at all. Getting to her feet, she felt a painful, throbbing ache on the side of her face from where her father had hit her earlier, but she could see the front door now and she knew she just had to get outside.

She waited a moment longer.

The only sound came from the incessant TV, with the reality show still at full volume.

"I didn't nominate you!" a woman on the show shouted. "Don't you go accusing me of nominating people when I didn't, okay? Nominations are supposed to be secret! We're not even allowed to talk about them!"

Becca waited a moment longer, and then she began to make her way as quietly as possible out of the kitchen and over to the door. She constantly glanced around to make sure her father wasn't about to sneak up on her, and then finally she reached the door and -

Stopping suddenly, she saw that the key wasn't in the lock. She reached up and tried the handle, only to find that it was locked. Trying not to panic, she took a step back as she realized she was trapped.

"Looking for something?" her father asked.

Spinning around, she saw him leaning against the wall nearby, grinning as he held the key up for her to see.

"There's nothing out there," he continued. "Just cold and wind, and a dark, forbidding world. Why'd you ever wanna go outside so late at night? There's no -"

Before he could finish, she darted through to the front room. With no time to think properly, she ducked down behind the armchair in the corner, making sure to draw her feet well out of sight. She knew he'd find her soon enough, but all she could hope right now was that she'd be able to buy herself some time. On most nights, she'd have escaped the house by now, but this time she was stuck and she knew exactly what her father wanted. As she listened to him stumbling into the room, she held her breath, too terrified to make a noise. She needed him to fall asleep, but he didn't seem drunk enough yet.

"Becca?" he said finally, his voice filled with a sense of amusement. "Are we playing a game? Is that it? Am I suppose to come find you?"

She heard him stumbling closer.

"What do I get if I win?" he asked. "A kiss? Does Daddy get a kiss?"

She closed her eyes, convinced that he was about to pull the armchair aside and find her. A moment later, however, she heard a loud bang on the front door, followed by two more.

She waited.

The only sound now was the TV, with the reality show still running.

"What the hell?" her father muttered finally.

A moment later, there was another knock, firmer than before.

"What kind of idiot's out this late?" her father said with a sigh. "Jesus Christ, Becca, can you just come out for a minute? I'm gonna have to answer the bloody door, aren't I?"

She waited.

"Becca, I'm not kidding," he continued. "This isn't a joke. Get up! I can't answer it while you're hiding like a fucking child."

Hearing another knock, Becca tried to imagine who could possibly be out there so late. The house was so remote, so far from even the nearest main road, that she never remembered anyone getting so completely lost that they ended up at the door. After a moment, however, she heard her father stumbling through to the hallway, but as the seconds passed she realized he didn't seem to be opening the door. Several more minutes rolled by, and slowly she began to wonder exactly what had happened. There were no more knocks, and her father had fallen silent too. The only sound came from the TV, where a woman was still shrieking about getting nominated for some mindless task.

Finally, Becca began to peer around the side of the chair.

Suddenly the chair was pulled aside and her father lunged down, grabbing her hair and hauling her out onto the carpet. Screaming, she tried to get free, but her father simply tightened his grip.

"Don't worry," he said, leaning down toward her, "whoever it was, they've gone. Anyway, it was probably just the wind. You know how wild things can get round here!"

Grabbing her arm, he dragged her past the coffee table. Becca screamed, trying again to twist away from his grip, but all she could manage was to hook her left foot against the table.

"Oh my God!" shouted a woman on the TV. "I can't *believe* you just said that! They're completely real! Do you want me to prove it?"

"Come on!" Becca's father hissed, pulling the girl around and dragging the coffee table across the room in the process. "I'm taking you up to bed!"

She screamed again.

"Becca -"

He tugged on her arm, finally pulling her closer.

"Relax!" he hissed. "There's no need to be scared. It's just us, Becca. There's not another living soul for miles and -"

Suddenly there was a loud cracking sound from nearby, as if wood was being split apart. Becca and her father both turned, stunned as the front door came crashing down into the hallway. A moment later, a figure stepped into the house, and Becca immediately recognized him as the old homeless man from the underground chamber, holding the battered ax in his right hand. She stared in horror, barely able to believe what she was seeing, and for a moment she felt as if she might pass out.

"What the hell?" her father shouted, as Becca pulled free and scampered across the room, quickly ducking through into the kitchen.

Racing to the back door, she tried desperately to get it open, and then she started looking for the key in one of the pots on the windowsill.

"I don't know who the hell you think you are," she heard her father shouting from the front room, "but -"

His voice cut out suddenly, followed by a series of loud, splitting impacts that filled the house just as a round of applause erupted from the TV. Voices were crying out and cheering, but as Becca frantically searched for the key to the back door she realized she could still hear a steady crunching sound from the front room. Finally she turned and looked over at the doorway, but there was no sign of her father at all. A few seconds earlier he'd been shouting and angry, and now he wasn't saying anything at all.

A moment later, she heard something bumping against the wall in the front room. Instinctively, she ducked down behind the table. Her heart was pounding, but all she could hear now was the TV's studio audience whooping and hollering, and creaking footsteps getting closer.

CHAPTER TWENTY-FOUR

OUT ON THE MOOR, several miles from the house, a woman knelt down and placed her hand on the grass. She waited, and a moment later she felt the faint vibrations she'd been expecting.

"It's too soon," she whispered, with panic in her voice, before turning and looking across the dark moor.

In the distance, she could just about see the lights of town. Turning the other way, she saw a house silhouetted against the stormy night sky.

"They can't come yet," she continued, getting to her feet. "I'm not ready."

CHAPTER TWENTY-FIVE

"OKAY," THE WOMAN ON the TV continued, her voice barely audible over the sound of people clapping and cheering, "let's just calm down, everyone! Let's just calm down, 'cause we're gonna want to hear what Melody says in just a moment. But first, the phone lines are closed now and the people of Britain have spoken. We have the results of tonight's vote and -"

Someone in the crowd shouted a few insults, and everyone clapped.

"People calm down!" the host said firmly. "Do you want to know the results or not? Do you want to know, or do you want to just keep yelling?"

The crowd became a little quieter, although a moment later someone wolf-whistled.

"I've just been handed the final numbers," the host continued, "and..." She paused. "Okay, I can tell you all that I am *officially* surprised by how the members of the British public at home have voted. I think this might be one of the biggest upsets in the show's history, maybe even in the history of British telly, 'cause a pretty huge favorite is going home tonight!"

A gasp erupted from the audience.

Having stayed completely still and silent behind the table for almost an hour now, Becca finally dared to lean out and look across the kitchen. There had been no signs of life in the house for a while now, not since the initial crunching and splitting that she'd heard earlier. Her father hadn't said a word and the homeless guy, whoever he was, didn't seem to be looking around the house, at least not since the initial footsteps had stopped. Swallowing hard, Becca was slowly starting to wonder whether she'd imagined the whole thing, and she began to think that maybe her father was just slumped in his armchair as usual, having passed out in front of another reality show.

Maybe I'm mad, she thought to herself. *Maybe I'm totally crazy.*

"So Calvin hasn't been very popular this week," the woman on the TV continued. "I think everyone remembers those pretty awful comments he made to Belinda on Monday!"

Boos rang out from the audience.

"But Belinda gave back as good as she got!" the woman added. "If you ask me, they're as bad as each other! Come on, Britain! Let everyone know what you think of Calvin and Belinda!"

Lots of clapping.

Slowly, still terrified, Becca began to crawl out from behind the table. She didn't dare get to her feet, and she even worried that her slow, shallow breaths were too loud. Light from the TV was still filling the front room as she made her way, on her hands and knees, toward the open doorway. Glancing into the hall, she saw that the front door was still on the floor, having been broken in half, and she felt a cold breeze blowing in from outside. The hall was brightly lit, leaving the gaping doorway as a pitch-black rectangle.

She froze.

The door really had been broken open.

That part, at least, *must* have happened.

"So what is it with some people?" the woman on the TV asked. "Why, in twenty-first century Britain, do they feel the need to act like complete losers in front of millions of people? I mean, what's that all about?"

A smattering of applause followed.

"We have a special guest," the host continued. "We have Demby589, the viral web sensation, here to give us her thoughts about the events of the past week."

More applause.

Still crawling forward, Becca finally reached the corner and peered through into the front room. She let out a faint gasp as soon as she saw the homeless guy standing next to the sofa. He had his back to her, and he seemed to be staring at the TV as the reality show continued. The results of a phone vote were flashing up on the screen, and the audience whooped and cheered every time another number was announced, but the homeless guy didn't react at all. Instead, he simply stood and stared at the screen, as if he was completely mesmerized by what he was seeing.

In his right hand, he was still holding the ax, with blood smeared across the edge of the blade.

"So Margaret's leaving the house tonight," the woman continued excitedly, "and we've put together a little highlights reel showing some of her best moments over the past couple of weeks. People of Britain, we know you've enjoyed her hijinks, and we know *that* shower scene in particular got a lot of pulses racing. So just remember, we *are* after the watershed here, so some of the shots in this montage might be a little unsafe for work, if you know what I mean." Laughter erupted from the studio audience. "So here she is, in all her glory... The wonderful, unforgettable Miss Margaret Cleopatra!"

Still staring at the homeless man, Becca barely even noticed the images flashes across the TV screen. After a moment, however, she realized she could hear a faint groaning sound from nearby. Turning, she looked across the room, but it took a few seconds before she spotted her father crawling past the sofa. Her eyes widened with horror as she saw that he was bleeding heavily from a series of thick wounds on his chest and neck. One of the wounds, just below the eye-socket on the left side of his face, had left a thick flap of skin torn away, while his other eye had been sliced straight through. Several of his teeth were missing, and a chunk of his upper lip had been mashed into his nose.

"Take the..." her father gasped suddenly, still trying to crawl out of the room. "Just..."

"Here it is, folks!" the woman on the TV shouted. "The most famous shower scene in British television history! Warning, there might be boobs!"

The audience screamed.

"She..." Becca's father stammered. Slowly, he raised a trembling hand and pointed at his daughter. "She's over there," he continued, barely able to get the words out. "If you want her, take her! Just don't hurt me! Please, you can take my daughter, but for God's sake leave me alone!"

Shocked to hear her father betraying her, Becca stared at him for a moment before suddenly realizing that the homeless guy had begun to move. Turning, she looked up in horror and saw his ravaged face staring straight down at her. In the front room's bright light, she could see now that much of the flesh had been worn away from his face, although some still clung to his skull, mainly around the cheeks and mouth. His eyes, which had been so dark and watery in the chamber, now appeared to be much drier, with a small hole in one of the eyeballs, as if something had once chewed its way through.

Becca opened her mouth to scream, but her chest was too tight.

"Don't hurt me," her father whimpered, sobbing on the floor. "Please, leave me alone! Just let me go! Whatever you want, I'll give it to you but I'm not a rich man! All I have is this house, and my daughter, and my cars. Take anything, please, just don't hurt me!"

As her father continued to beg for his life, Becca watched the homeless man stepping across the room. Standing over her father now, the man looked down at him for a moment before slowly raising the ax in his right hand.

"Please!" her father shouted. "Let me -"

Before he could finish, part of his jaw dropped away, leaving his exposed tongue flicking in his mouth. He tried to cry out again, just as the homeless man's ax came swinging down.

Becca turned away just in time, squeezing her eyes tight shut as she heard a sickening thud that abruptly ended her father's sobs. She squeezed her eyes tighter, and a few seconds later she heard a slow cracking sound.

"I am *never* going to wash my eyes again!" the woman on the TV laughed. "Some things, once seen, just cannot be unseen, am I right?"

The audience cheered their support.

"Now Margaret," the woman continued, "tell us, when you took that infamous shower, did you know the cameras were rolling?"

"Were they ever *not* rolling?" another woman squealed, before breaking into a loud, high-pitched howl of laughter.

Trembling with fear, Becca realized she could hear footsteps in the room, heading closer. She squeezed her eyes tighter and tighter shut, so tight that they began to hurt, before finally realizing that she couldn't stay that way forever. She remembered her mother telling her to face her fears, but she couldn't bring herself to look directly at the homeless man, or at whatever had just happened in the front room. At the same time, she told herself that if she was brave, if she looked, she'd probably find that he wasn't so scary. It took a moment, but finally she imagined her mother urging her to make an effort. She knew she had to open her eyes.

Suddenly the kitchen light switched off, plunging the room into darkness. A moment later, with her eyes still shut, Becca realized the light had been turned on again.

Then off.

Then on.

Opening her eyes slowly as the light continued to switch from on to off and back again, Becca stared straight ahead and saw that the ax's blade was just inches from her face. Blood was dribbling from the edge of the blade, and tiny fragments of white bone were stuck to the metal.

And still the kitchen light flicked on and off and on and off again, as Becca's eyes grew wide with fear.

CHAPTER TWENTY-SIX

"I FEEL LIKE I wanna be authentic with my fans," the high-pitched woman said as the TV show continued in the next room. "That means sharing everything with them! Every aspect of my life!"

"Even those, Margaret?" the other woman asked, causing more laughter from the audience.

"Even those!" came the giggling reply.

Although she wanted to beg for mercy, Becca didn't dare say a word. She wasn't even sure she *could* speak, since her throat felt impossibly dry and tight. All she could manage was to stare at the blood as it continued to dribble from the ax. The kitchen light was off again, but a moment later it came back on.

"Pray tell me," a voice said suddenly from above, sounding firm and cold. "What is this witchcraft?"

Silence, and then the light went off again.

Becca could still see the ax in the dark.

Suddenly the light came back on.

"How does it work?" the voice asked. "Is it witchery, devilry or the work of some madman?"

The light switched off, then on again.

"It's the light-switch," Becca stammered.

This time, the light remained on. "It brings illumination," the voice said after a moment, "and it takes it away again. How?"

"I don't really understand it," she continued, "it just... does."

The light went off again, then back on.

"Was that loathsome ruffian your father?" the voice asked.

"My..." She paused, not understanding some of the words, not daring to look up. Her whole body was trembling with fear. "I..."

Still the words wouldn't come. Finally, she simply nodded.

"And tell me, child," he continued, as voices giggled and laughed on the TV, "how did he raise you? In accordance with the royal declarations? What kind of house *is* this?"

Shivering with fear, Becca waited, hoping against hope that the man would go away. Suddenly, however, the table was pulled to one side. She knew that if she looked up, she'd see his old, withered face with patches of bone wearing through the skin. She wanted to run, but she didn't dare move an inch.

In the corner of her eye, she could just about see her father's body in the front room, but she couldn't bring herself to look directly. She could tell, however, that he wasn't moving.

"Are you," the man continued, his voice filled now with contempt, "a child raised within the Catholic faith? Don't lie to me now, girl, for I shall divine the truth one way or another."

She froze, unable to answer, still staring at the ax.

"Are you a Catholic?" the man shouted.

"I don't know!" she stammered. "I don't know what that means."

"You don't know what it -" There was a pause, followed by a sigh. "Are you, then, a heathen child?"

"I don't know what that means either," she replied, with tears in her eyes.

She waited, terrified in case the ax swung closer to her face.

"Tell me," he continued after a moment, "what witchcraft begets that picture? What brings it to life with such noise and color?"

After a moment, the ax swung away as the man made his way back over toward the TV.

"I know witchcraft when I see it, child," he continued. "Someone has bedeviled this image and brought it to life with visions of debauchery and sin. I see women in unfathomable poses, flaunting their wares like common whores. I see fools supporting such devilry. Tell me, who is responsible?"

"It's..." Becca paused, trying to understand what he was asking. Finally daring to look at him, she stared at the back of his head, seeing untidy, matted hair covering his neck. "You mean the... Do you mean the

TV?"

"It is a frightful thing," he muttered, with his back still turned to her as he watched the screen "So loud and displeasing to the eye. Why, even a witch should know better than to bring such horrors to life." He paused, before stepping back and then raising his ax, which he then smashed down against the screen. The TV fell back against the wall, and the man hacked at it several more times until the screen had been completely destroyed and both the image and sound were gone.

Becca stared in shock, still too scared to turn and look over at her father's body, and too terrified to run.

"You screamed earlier," the man said finally, turning slightly until she could see one side of his face. "I note that you are bruised, and cut too. Tell me, did your father beat you?"

She stared up at him. Now that she could see him properly, she realized that he was missing a great deal of flesh, exposing the graying bone of his jaw and cheek. Specks of skin were still visible, dried in a few patches, but part of his eye was bloodshot and swollen.

"Did your father beat you, child?" he asked. "It is a simple enough question."

She paused, before nodding.

"And did he have good reason? Some beatings are well-deserved."

Sniffing back tears, Becca began to sit up. Her heart was pounding and she felt terrified, but she was too scared to run. After a moment, she looked at the man's ax again, and she imagined it crashing down against her father's skull.

"Where is your mother?" the man asked.

She looked up at him again. "She's gone."

"Gone where?"

"She left."

He frowned. "Did she die?"

She paused, before nodding.

"And you have no family at all, now that your father has joined her?"

She hesitated for a moment. "I have a sister," she whispered.

"Speak up!" he shouted, turning and taking a step toward her.

"I have a sister!" she stammered, pulling back as she watched the ax coming closer.

"Then where did *she* go, child? To what other place could a woman possibly travel, when her family is here in such dire straits? Did she go to visit a sick relative?"

"She left us," Becca stammered.

"For what reason?"

"I don't know."

He paused for a moment, towering over her. "Most strange," he said finally. "I have seen enough of the modern world to expect a certain degree of strangeness, but this is beyond even *my* expectation."

"My sister..." Becca took a deep breath, sniffing back more tears. "She left because of my father. I think she went to live in Sharpeton."

"Sharpeton, eh?" he replied, raising an arched eyebrow. "A den of foul revelry, if ever I knew of one, and I am sure it has improved not one bit since I was last there. Pray, what could your sister possibly be doing in such a place? Does she have other family there? Is she married?"

Becca shook her head.

"Perhaps she has become a whore, then," he continued. "There are precious few other ways for a single woman to survive without a husband." He glanced across the room, toward the body by the farthest door. "Your own father seemed a very weak and disagreeable sort, and I cannot fathom why he should have offered you up to me in an attempt to save his own soul. Did the man have no scruples, no honor?"

Unable to hold back her tears any longer, Becca began to sob.

"Why do you make such a loathsome noise?" the man asked. "Do you know who I am, child? In this modern age, does the name Nykolas Freeman no longer instill terror and godliness in the hearts and minds of everyone who hears it?"

He waited for a reply, but Becca was weeping now, her whole body trembling with shock.

"You must quieten your infernal wailing, child," Freeman continued. "It does no good to mourn a man as craven as your father. You waste those tears. What is the point? None, I tell you. Instead, I propose that we set forth for Sharpeton at once and locate your sister, so that she might make clear the manner in which you have been raised. I also wish to learn the identity of whoever bewitched that image that I destroyed a moment ago. Clearly a powerful witch has passed this way, and it is my duty to hunt her down."

Sniffing back more tears, Becca looked up at him.

"How many days' walk is it to Sharpeton from here?" he asked. "Tell me, child."

"It's about an hour by car," she replied, her voice trembling with fear.

"And what is that? Some form of carriage?"

She stared up at him, terrified in case he swung his ax.

"Never mind," he continued. "We must set out at once. If such a powerful witch is on the loose, she must be stopped before she is able to wreak havoc across the entire land. My England must be saved from such debauchery and wickedness. No matter how many heads I must remove, no matter how many suspected witches I must put to the test, I shall not rest until I have wiped such vileness from the world. I have slept long enough, worn down by all that I have seen of this modern England, but now I, Nykolas Freeman, shall ensure that the heart and soul of my beloved homeland shall be saved from the sins that even now overflow as far as the eye can see!" He paused. "Perhaps this is why I was released from that sealed grave."

Becca stared up at him. "Did -"

"And then we shall march on to London," he added, as if he hadn't even heard her. His eyes were almost burning now, filled with passion and determination. "I do not know the state of the modern crown, but if needs be I shall ensure that a godly head rules this fine nation. I swore to protect this land, and as God is my witness, I shall not rest until all sin has been stored away from sight, along with the perversions that labor the land. For this is my home, and my resting place, and I shall fight and slay all those who seek to sully the true nature of this fine and peaceful country!" With the blood-soaked ax still in his right hand, he puffed his chest out proudly, as if he felt certain now of his mission. "Onward! To retake and restore my England!"

Becca paused. She was still terrified, but at the same time this strange man had said the one thing she'd longed for someone, anyone to say for months now; the one thing her father had refused to say, and that she had finally believed would never happen. Despite everything else she'd seen that night, she felt a faint pinprick of hope in her chest.

"Did you say," she whispered finally, as the tears dried on her cheeks, "that you can take me to Sharpeton to find my sister?"

CHAPTER TWENTY-SEVEN

"WHAT IS THIS PLACE?" Freeman asked, his eyes wide with shock as he stopped at the side of the road. Up ahead, the lights of Sharpeton filled the night air, and music could be heard pounding from one of the pubs.

"It's Sharpeton," Becca told him, shivering as a cold gust of wind blew in from across the moors. "Haven't you ever been here before?"

Freeman watched the scene for a moment longer.

"Aye," he admitted finally. "Long ago, I walked these streets plenty. Now that you say it, I *do* recognize the way the houses hug the hill that leads up from the river, although much has changed over the years. That inn has stood since I was a lad, although it was not called the Clarendon back then. It was the Sharpeton Arms, and it served the foulest grog for miles around. Never empty, as I recall, though I never set foot in the place myself." He glanced up at a telegraph pole that stood nearby, and then he looked at the wires that hung high above. "It is clear that a great deal has been done to this town," he muttered. "To the world, even. Since my awakening, I have seen hints of the modern way, but I confess I have not yet been to its heart."

"Were you asleep for long?" Becca asked.

He looked down at her. "It has been some three, almost four centuries, since my birth. I can only assume that the Lord has kept me alive so that I might complete my task and rid the whole of England of the vile heresy that threatens to engulf these shores."

"And you were down in that crack for all that time?"

He shook his head. "A witch sealed me in there with a gold coin," he explained. "I dare say she expected it to keep me down for a while longer."

Becca glanced back the way they'd come. She could no longer see the house in the distance, but she couldn't help thinking about her father's body. She'd carefully avoided looking at him as she and Freeman had headed out, and she'd tried not to think of him too much, yet she could feel her thoughts gradually turning, forcing her to remember the sounds she'd heard while she'd been hiding. At the same time, she knew deep down that although she was *supposed* to be sad, she was actually relieved. No matter how hard she tried to mourn her father, she was unable to do so; instead, she remembered the touch of his trembling hands on her bare skin, and she shivered.

"You think of your father," Freeman said after a moment, "do you not?"

"Did you..." She paused. "Did you really kill him?"

"The man was a vile and worthless pig. You must not waste your thoughts on him."

"He..." Again she paused, thinking back to all the things he'd done to her over the years. Despite her sense of shock, she felt an overwhelming sense of gratitude at the thought that he could never again touch her. She knew that was wrong, of course, and she worried it made her a bad person, but she also knew that she would never again have to spend another night in that wretched house, or stay awake at night, waiting for her bedroom door to creak open. The nightmare was over.

"Your father beat you," Freeman continued. "There is no harm in beating a recalcitrant child, in some cases it can be good for them. I myself was beaten merrily by my father, and in doing so he instilled a sense of resolve in my soul. Still..." He paused. "Some men beat their children for no good reason, or simply to give themselves pleasure, and that is wrong. I fear your father was such a man, was he not?"

Becca looked up at him, before nodding.

"Then waste not one more thought on him, for he is gone and even a river of tears could not drag his soul back from hell."

She paused, before nodding again. She felt certain that anyone else would tell her to mourn her father, but the homeless old man seemed to better understand her feelings.

"And now," he added, "we must find your sister,

and then we must determine the identity of the witch who created that dance of moving pictures in your home. The witch, whoever she is, must be slaughtered at once."

"I don't know where Kerry lives," Becca replied, before looking along the dark street, "but I know someone who might."

"And who, pray, might that be?"

"She had friends here in town. When Mummy got sick, Kerry spent less and less time at Daddy's house. She was here in Sharpeton a lot."

"And you have not seen your sister in some time?"

She shook her head.

"Your family seems exceedingly odd," he replied. "I know that the modern world has changed in many ways, and that I am tied to the old practices. Still, I cannot begin to understand a world in which a family allows itself to be so divided. Come, you must take me at once to meet this sister of yours. If she is trying to make her own way, it is highly likely she has become a whore. So long as she is not a witch, however, I shall let her live."

Stepping forward, Becca looked at the row of dark houses up ahead.

"Does your sister live in one of these abodes?" Freeman asked.

"I don't..." Becca paused. "I don't exactly know," she admitted finally. "She and Daddy didn't talk anymore, not for years, so it's even possible that she moved away. I think she'd have let me know first, though. Kerry and I were close once and -"

Before she could finish, she realized she could hear thumping music in the distance. Looking along a different road, she saw bright lights flashing in the window of a house, and a moment later she realized there were a couple of people hanging around in the doorway drinking beer.

"Kerry always liked parties," Becca said with a frown. "If she still lives in Sharpeton, she's probably in that house right now."

CHAPTER TWENTY-EIGHT

"WOAH, JESUS CHRIST DUDE!" the guy in the doorway exclaimed, almost spitting out his beer as he saw Freeman and Becca approach. "What did you come as? Is that fancy dress?"

"It is far fancier than your attire," Freeman replied contemptuously, stepping past him and making his way into the house. Stopping, he saw flashing disco lights filling the hallway, while the steady beat of loud music was strong enough to make the door's glass panes shudder slightly and the smell of marijuana filled the air. "What in the name of all that is holy..."

"Did someone invite you?" the guy asked. "Dude, everyone's welcome but, like, do you know someone who's already here?"

"He's with me," Becca explained. "We're looking for my sister."

"Your sister?" The guy paused. "Okay, that's cool. Is she in trouble?"

"I don't know," Becca replied. "Her name's Kerry Jameson and she's really pretty. She has black hair, although she changes the color sometimes, and on her shoulder she has a tattoo of a dragon."

"We believe her to be a whore," Freeman added. "Are there whores in this place?"

The guy stared at him for a moment, clearly not sure how to respond. "Um... Well, I don't know everyone who's here tonight, but I guess you can take a look around. If you like." He took a sip of beer. "Dude, I get that you've dressed up as, like, some old-time person from history, but you kind of smell bad. Are you, like, taking the costume to an extreme? Did people really stink back then?"

"If I hear another word from you," Freeman replied, "I shall hang you in the town square at sunrise."

With that, he turned and made his way across the hallway, with the ax still in his right hand. Reaching the open door at the bottom of the stairs, he looked through and saw scores of teenagers dancing to the music, while several others were slouched in chairs and on the sofa, and some were kissing. Empty beer cans had been left all over the floor, along with deflated and burst balloons. Old magazines were piled in the corner, and parts of a game console were spread out nearby, as if someone had started to hook it up to the TV but had somehow wandered off halfway through the job.

"This is some form of madness," Freeman muttered, his eyes widening as he continued to watch the scene. "The modern world has truly lost its mind."

"Maybe you should stay here!" Becca shouted,

tugging on his sleeve. "I'll go look for Kerry!"

"Are these people mentally impaired?" Freeman asked. "Where is the music coming from? Why is it so loud? Is everyone in this room deaf?"

"Not yet," Becca replied, "but they might be soon."

Stepping forward, Freeman made his way across the room, as startled party-goers stood back. Several people made loud, disgusted comments about the smell and, while the music continued to play, no-one was dancing anymore. Freeman looked around at the sea of shocked faces, and finally he spotted a large plasma TV in the far corner, displaying music videos. Frowning, he made his way over, tightening his grip on the ax, until suddenly the music stopped and silence fell upon the room.

"What..." a voice stammered finally from the sofa. "Dude, what's that stench?"

"This thing," Freeman said darkly, still watching the music video's flashing images, "is another form of witchcraft? Are they to be found in every house in the land?"

"No," Becca said, hurrying over to him and grabbing his hand. "It's not witchcraft. It's just a TV."

Freeman looked down at her.

"It's science," she continued. "It's nothing to do with witches. I don't understand how it works, but someone invented it."

"Dude, it's my parents' TV," said the guy on the sofa, getting to his feet. "Who invited you, anyway? You stink like a goddamn trash-heap."

Slowly, Freeman turned to face him.

"Just..." The guy paused, spotting the ax in Freeman's hand. "Is that blood?" he asked.

"Craig, man," one of the other guys called out. "What the fuck, dude? What kind of party *is* this?"

"I feel as if I am in a far-off land," Freeman continued as he looked around the room, "even though I know I am in my England. I am no fool, I understand that many centuries have passed since the time of my birth, and I am capable of recognizing advances in both the sciences and the arts, yet..." He looked over at the bookshelf, and then at the door that led through to the kitchen, and then finally he turned back to face the people on the sofa, who stared back at him with expressions of shock and, in some cases, mild amusement.

"Dude," someone whispered nearby, "should we, like, call the cops or something?"

"We have come here," Freeman continued, "to search out a whore. She is the sister of this young girl, and we have reason to believe she might be plying her trade in this house."

"Dude," said a girl sitting on the arm of a chair, adjusting her shirt to make sure she wasn't showing too much cleavage, "there are no whores here."

"You're getting *way* too into your act," added the guy next to her. "Chill out and go take a shower, for God's sake."

"Is Kerry here?" Becca asked, stepping toward the guy who was standing in front of the sofa. "My sister's name is Kerry Jameson. She's really pretty. Do

173

you know her?"

The guy stared at her, clearly shocked.

"Do you mean Kerry with the dragon tattoo?" a girl asked suddenly.

"Do you know her?" Becca replied, turning to her. "Is she here?"

"I think she, like, moved away about a year ago," the girl explained. "She said she wanted to get out of this crappy little town. I might be wrong, but I have this vague memory that she said she'd got a job somewhere, maybe in a supermarket."

"Where?" Becca asked, stepping toward her.

"I don't know, but..." The girl paused, eying Freeman with suspicion, before pulling her phone from her pocket and getting to her feet. "I have her number. Why don't I give her a call and let her know that you're here, okay?"

Becca watched anxiously as the girl tapped at her phone's screen.

"Voicemail," the girl muttered after a moment, before turning and heading out of the room. "Hey Kerry, it's Julie from Sharpeton. Long time, huh? Listen, this is gonna sound really weird, but your little sister's shown up at a house party at Craig's house, and she's with some heinously stinky old creepy dude..."

As the girl continued to speak, Becca turned and looked around at the other teenagers, most of whom were starting to head for the door. The party seemed to have deflated.

"What is this house of sin and villainy?" Freeman asked, still holding his glistening ax. "Is there any godliness beneath this roof at all, or am I in the presence of heathens?"

"Dude, come back!" Craig shouted, hurrying after the others as they filed out. "The party's not over! We'll kick the stinky guy out! Dude! Everyone, come on!"

A moment later, the front door could be heard slamming shut, and finally Craig returned with a shocked, annoyed expression on his face.

"Thanks a bunch," he said darkly. "Thanks to you and that stench cloud of yours, everyone's gone home. What the hell's wrong with you, coming in and stinking the place up?"

"My name is Nykolas Freeman," Freeman replied, "and I have the authority of the King's warrant. Although I hasted to add that there might be a different face on the throne in this godless age, the warrant has no end and therefore I remain His Majesty's faithful servant."

"We don't have a king," Becca whispered. "We have a queen. Queen Elizabeth."

"A familiar name, to be sure," Freeman muttered, "and not one that is entirely welcome to my ears."

"Okay," Julie said as she hurried back through, "I left a message for your sister, kid, but I don't know when she'll get it. It's pretty late, so she might not call 'til the morning." She eyed Freeman with a hint of suspicion. "So are you, like, her uncle or something?"

"He's just helping me find my sister," Becca explained. "Well, first he..." She looked at the ax's dripping blade for a moment, and she felt a shiver pass through her chest as she remembered the sight of her father's body. At the same time, she was relieved to know that she'd never have to endure another night of the man's drunkenness. Freeman had told her to not waste tears, and somehow, deep down, she felt that he was right.

"My name's Julie," the girl said, forcing a smile as she stepped closer, "and I'm Craig's girlfriend. Well, sort of, anyway. His parents are away this week, so we're kinda using his place to crash and party. We're not doing anything wrong, we're just having fun, you know?" She paused, sniffing the air. "Dude, no offense, but the others were right. You really *do* reek of something foul."

"Did you speak to Kerry?" Becca asked, stepping over to her.

"Like I said, she didn't pick up." Julie paused, still glancing nervously at Freeman, before reaching out and putting a hand on Becca's shoulder. "It's okay, kid. I'm sure your sister'll come as soon as she hears the message I left. Until then, why don't you hang out here?" Again she glanced over at Freeman, and it was clear from the fear in her eyes that she didn't trust him at all. "You don't wanna be out there at night, wandering around with... whoever this guy is."

"This is a foul den of sin," Freeman muttered, looking over at the blinking fairy lights that covered the far wall. "I would weep, that my England has fallen to such depravity. First, however, I must untangle the witchery from the devilry, and treat each with due regard."

"Woah," said Craig, stepping toward him, "watch who you're calling depraved, okay? For a guy who just cleared out someone else's party, you seem kinda brazen."

"And your name, Sir?" Freeman sneered.

"Craig. Craig Donaldson, and you're in my parents' -"

"I have not heard such a name before," Freeman replied, raising his ax. "In this modern world, is the Donaldson family considered worthy? Do you control much land?"

"Do we..." Craig paused, before allowing himself a faint, nervous smile. "Dude, I think you're carrying the cosplay a little too far."

"Tell me the state of the nation," Freeman continued. "It has been a long, long time since I was at the royal court, and I fear I lack an understanding of the situation. I would ride to London immediately, yet I am wise enough to see that the world has changed a great deal around me. It would be better to wait a while and get to know the complexities at play." He paused, before turning to Craig again. "Tell me, boy, what if the faith of England's queen?"

Craig frowned. "What do you mean?"

"What is her faith?" Freeman asked, stepping toward him. "It is a simple enough question, unless you are a simpleton. Or do you have something to hide?"

"I don't know her faith," Craig replied. "Why the hell would I?"

"Church of England," Julie said quickly.

Freeman turned to her.

"I think," she added, a little tentatively. She still had an arm on Becca's shoulder, and now she drew the girl a little closer, as if to protect her. "Yeah, I'm pretty sure. I heard it, like, on TV once."

"Your woman is less ignorant than you," Freeman muttered, turning to Craig. "Does that not shame you?"

"His woman?" Julie asked, raising a skeptical eyebrow.

"And this thing," Freeman continued, stepping over to the TV. He paused, watching the images, before suddenly raising his ax. "It must be destroyed and -"

"No!" Craig shouted, running past and holding his hands out to protect the screen. "Dude, don't wave that thing around in here, even as a joke! This is a widescreen plasma TV, for fuck's sake!"

"Your use of language is crude," Freeman sneered, with the ax still raised. "Are you mentally crippled?"

"Huh?"

Freeman paused for a moment, staring at Craig, before slowly lowering the ax. "I believe I have underestimated the pace of change," he muttered darkly. "You will give me, right now, a summary of the political and social events that have taken place over the past three centuries."

"I..." After pausing for a moment, Craig reached over to grab his laptop.

"Wait!" Freeman shouted, stepping toward him with his ax raised once again. "What is that?"

"I don't exactly have the information to hand,"

Craig replied, eying the ax with a hint of caution. Still convinced that Freeman was a particularly intense cosplayer, he nevertheless was starting to wonder whether the man might be seriously unhinged. "I'm not really into history, okay? If you wanna know what kind stuff's been going on, I have to look it up for you." He muttered something else under his breath, including a few choice curse words.

Freeman stared at the laptop. Still convinced that such devices were a form of witchcraft, he nevertheless was starting to think that it might be wise to act with less haste. After all, it was hard to believe that witchcraft could have spread so far, and could be so widely accepted, so he resolved to wait and at least see whether he could learn a little more about the modern world. In truth, he felt as if he barely recognized his homeland at all.

"Fine," he said after a moment. "Consult whatever oracle you have to hand. I warn you, though, that if I sense witchcraft, I shall have no choice but to end your miserable life."

"Whatever, dude," Craig replied, opening the laptop. "Keep your goddamn pants on. Unless you wanna wash them, 'cause seriously, they smell rank!"

CHAPTER TWENTY-NINE

"OKAY KID, SPILL!" JULIE hissed as soon as she'd managed to get Becca into one of the dark bedrooms upstairs. "Why are you wandering around with some stinky old men who's dressed like a character from the middle ages?"

"I don't know," Becca replied, sniffing back tears, "it just sort of happened. Did my sister call you back yet?"

Julie glanced at her phone. "Not yet, honey," she said as she flicked the light on and led Becca to the bed. Dropping to her knees, she took a closer look at the little girl's face. "You're hurt. Did that asshole downstairs hit you?"

Becca shook her head.

"Then who -"

"Daddy," Becca explained. "I mean..." She frowned, scrunching her nose a little. "My father did it."

"Your father hit you?"

Becca nodded.

"Well, that's..." Pausing for a moment, Julie seemed genuinely lost for words. "That's messed up. My father hit me once, but only once. He didn't like it when I broke his nose in return, and anyway, I never set foot in the house again. My mother wasn't any better. Hell, she was worse, 'cause she saw what he was like and didn't do a damn thing. Where's *your* mother?"

"She's gone," Becca replied, before realizing that she should perhaps be more honest. "She died in the hospital."

Julie opened her mouth to reply, but for a moment she wasn't sure what to say.

"Shit," she muttered finally, "I'm sorry. So the guy downstairs... who is he?"

"I don't really know."

"Well, how did you end up with him?"

"He came to the house while Daddy was... While my father was drunk and hitting me."

"He saved you?"

Becca nodded.

"And where's your father now?"

Becca paused, as a flicker of fear crossed her face. "Mr. Freeman... I mean, he..." She took a deep breath, worried in case telling the truth might get her into trouble. "He killed Daddy."

Julie opened her mouth to reply, but for a moment she seemed too shocked to get any words out. "Okay," she said finally, "when you say *killed*, what exactly do you mean?"

"With his ax," Becca replied, suddenly holding

her right hand up and then miming a chopping action. "Like that!"

"And you saw it happen?"

Becca nodded.

"Jesus Christ," Julie muttered, "I hope you're lying."

"I'm not."

"But if -"

"I think it's because I helped him in the pit," Becca added. "Mr. Freeman was down in a crack in the ground, and I found a gold coin. I think a witch left that there. Anyway, I took some food to Mr. Freeman and..." She paused. "I think he likes me because I helped him. He'd probably still be down there in the pit if I hadn't gone to him. I don't even mind that he did what he did to Daddy. At least Daddy can't hurt me anymore."

"Like hitting you?"

"And other things," Becca whispered, "but I don't want to talk about them."

Julie stared in horror for a moment. "Rough life, huh?" she managed finally, her eyes filled with tears. "So this Freeman guy... He hasn't hurt you, or laid a hand on you, in any way at all?"

Becca shook her head.

"And now he's helping you find your sister?"

Becca nodded. "I don't know why Kerry hasn't come back to see me, but I don't have anyone else now." She paused, with a hint of fear in her eyes. "It's the only idea I've got. If Kerry doesn't want to let me live with her, then I don't know what to do next."

"Jesus," Julie replied, "you're in a pickle, aren't

you?"

"I don't know what that means," Becca said somberly.

"It means we're gonna help you, okay?" Julie continued, forcing a smile. "Whatever the hell's going on here, we're gonna look after you. I'm sure Kerry'll be in touch any minute now, and then we can see about getting you guys back together. And figuring out what's actually going on here." She paused, before pulling the little girl close for a hug.

"Do you have a tattoo?" Becca asked after a moment, spotting the edge of a pattern poking out from beneath Julie's t-shirt.

"Yeah, hun," Julie replied, pulling back and then turning to give her a better view of the fob-watch tattoo on her shoulder.

"Is that from Alice in Wonderland?"

"Sure is." Julie smiled. "It's to remind me that there are better places out there, you know? Better places than this rat-hole, anyway."

Becca nodded, while still staring at the tattoo as if it was the most fascinating thing she'd ever seen in her life. At that moment, she decided that one day she'd like to get a tattoo as well.

"Your poor thing," Julie muttered, reaching out and tucking a loose strand of hair behind Becca's right ear. "I can tell you one thing, there's no way I'm letting you go wandering off with that weird-ass smelly guy. You're staying right here with us until either your sister shows up, or we get the cops to help out. We'll give Kerry a little longer to get in touch before we make any other moves, though. Okay?"

"Okay," Becca replied, her eyes flickering slightly as she relived the moment of her father's death. In her mind's eye, that was suddenly all she could see. The ax, crashing down against the back of his skull and spraying blood across the wall. Over and over and over, as if she could think of nothing else...

CHAPTER THIRTY

"JESUS CHRIST," JULIE WHISPERED a few minutes later as she pulled the bedroom door shut and hurried over to join Craig on the darkened landing. "That little girl is..."

Her voice trailed off as she tried to find the right word.

"Nuts?" Craig suggested.

"Damaged," she continued. "She's exhausted, I finally got her to rest, but..." She glanced over at the door again, to make sure they weren't being overheard, and then she turned to him. "She told me that the smelly guy killed her father. Like, she reckons he hacked his head open with an ax!"

"Gross," Craig replied, his eyes wide with awe. He paused for a moment. "You don't think... I mean, you don't think it's true, do you?"

She shook her head. "It can't be. That kind of stuff just doesn't happen, and she came out with a load of other stuff about a witch and a gold coin, but... It's pretty messed-up that a little girl would even make up a story like that, isn't it? Did you see the look in her eyes? Something definitely isn't right with her. It's like she's really, really..." She tried to think of a better word, but finally she realized there was only one that really described her impression of Becca. "Damaged," she said again. "So, *so* damaged. I just want to hug her and make everything okay."

"Try talking to Captain No-Wash," Craig replied, rolling his eyes. "The man is intense!"

"Still no word from Kerry," Julie muttered, checking her phone. "What do you think we should do? Wait 'til morning and then call social services?"

"Kerry'll be along eventually. Right now, I just wanna hear more from the crazy guy downstairs. I don't know what his deal is, but he's blatantly committed to whatever act he's trying to put on. Like, I think he actually believes some of the stuff he says."

"Like what?"

"About witchcraft and sin and the modern world." He sighed. "Do you know what he's doing right now? I showed him how to use my laptop. It took a little while, 'cause at first he thought it was some kind of sorcery. He'd never used a mouse or a track-pad before, it was like he'd never even seen a screen! But I showed him some stuff and after that he learned kinda fast. Faster than my grandparents, anyway. So I found some websites about history and now he's reading through them. Says he needs to catch up on what's been happening over the past few centuries." He rolled his eyes. "Apart from the smell, he's actually pretty cool to talk to."

Reaching into his pocket, he pulled out a small bag of weed.

"No!" Julie hissed.

"Oh, this is the *perfect* time to smoke," he told her. "Trust me."

"We need to keep clear heads," she continued. "Please, Craig."

Sighing, he stuffed the bag back into his pocket.

"We can't leave Becca alone with him," Julie continued. "There's no way we can let that sweet little girl walk out the door with that... *disgusting* old man!"

He nodded.

"So we need to call someone," she added. "Who?"

"Let's just give Kerry a little longer," he replied. "It's only been an hour since you texted her, maybe she's asleep or at work. Anyway, I kinda want to listen to more of what this Freeman guy's got to say." Pulling his phone from his pocket, he brought up a web-page he'd been checking earlier and showed it to her. "Check this out, though. He's not just using a random name. Nykolas Freeman's supposed to have been this psycho guy who went around killing witches and priests in the seventeenth century. The guy downstairs seems to be cosplaying the hell out of him."

"Freeman..." Julie whispered, staring at the screen. "I've heard that name somewhere else. Wasn't it in the news last year for some reason?"

"No idea," Craig continued, stuffing his phone

away, "but you've gotta admit, the guy has some crazy prosthetic stuff going on. Have you looked closely at his face?"

She shook her head.

"From what I can tell," he explained, "he made up his features like a skull first, and then he added kinda... strips of skin, and he dried them over the fake bone. There are even holes, where it looks like worms were burrowing through at some point, and I guess he's got contact lenses to make his eyes all dark and watery." He paused, clearly in awe of the effect. "I guess the smell is kinda part of the cosplay too. Like, people back then probably *did* smell pretty rank."

Sniffing the air, Julia grimaced slightly. "I can smell it from here. He's starting to fill the entire house."

"He was going on about the state of modern Britain," Craig continued. "He kept referring to it as *my England*, like he's got some kinda personal stake in the whole thing. The crazy thing is, even though he seems totally off his rocker, some of the things he said made sense. Like, he actually had some good points. You wanna come back downstairs and hear him out?"

She paused, before shaking her head.

"I'm gonna go back in and just sit with Becca. I want to make sure she's okay. I feel like..." She paused, with tears in her eyes, before forcing a smile and reaching out to give him a hug. "She reminds me of myself in some ways. Is that wrong?"

"Depends," he replied. "On a scale of one to ten, with ten being the most fucked-up, how crazy do you think the kid is?"

Julie thought for a moment, before deciding that she didn't want to answer. "I'm sure she'll be fine," she continued finally. "Hopefully she isn't permanently damaged. I'm sure she'll be A-OK as soon as her sister comes to get her. She just needs to get her family back."

She headed back into the bedroom, leaving Craig alone on the landing for a moment. Once he was sure she was gone, he took the weed from his pocket and started rolling a cigarette.

"Man," he muttered, looking out the window for a moment and watching as a bunch of vehicles with flashing lights passed the house, "I need *something* to cover up this guy's stench."

CHAPTER THIRTY-ONE

"WHAT?" DANIEL STAMMERED, SITTING up suddenly in the dark room. He paused, genuinely not quite sure what had woken him, before hearing another knock at the door.

Stumbling out of bed, he grabbed his clothes from the floor and started getting dressed.

"Hang on!" he called out. "Who is it?"

"It's me," Mary replied. "Dan, I found something you really need to see."

"I just need to get -"

"It's nothing I haven't seen before," she continued, trying the handle but finding it locked. "Dan, open the door. This is important, I've been up all night!"

"It's almost five in the morning," he muttered, cleaning crust from the corner of his eyes as he wandered over and unlocked the door. A fraction of a second later he stepped back, narrowly avoiding a blow to the head as Mary pushed the door open and hurried in with her laptop balanced on one hand. "I always dreamed of you breaking my door down in a moment of passion," he continued, watching as she sat on the edge of the bed, "but not quite like this."

"I found a reference to the Battle of Sharpeton," she said breathlessly.

Sighing, he made his way over and sat next to her. "That's nice, but -"

"Well, not *exactly* a reference," she continued, clearly too excited to even listen, "but more of... a hole."

"A hole?"

"Where the battle *should* have been mentioned." She scrolled to the top of the web-page that she'd loaded in her browser. "Something about the whole thing began to ring a bell, so I've been trawling through a couple of obscure texts. Finally I found what I was looking for in an old parish survey from 1675, a few decades after the war ended. This particular survey included annotations and comments, and one of those annotations was written by a man named Jonathan Appendon."

"Never heard of him."

"He was just a small-time land-owner," she continued, "but in 1675 he happened to record some comments regarding the recent death of his father, Michael Appendon, who'd passed away a few months earlier. And in those comments, Robert says that his father made vague references to a forgotten battle somewhere near Wyvern. That's barely twenty miles from here! It can't be a coincidence!"

Still not quite awake, Daniel peered at the screen.

"My father spoke on his death-bed," Mary read out-loud, "of his experiences in the war that tore this country apart. I had heard the tales many times before, of course, yet one night he added a little extra detail that had previously gone unmentioned. He described having taken part in the start of a great battle in the vicinity of Wyvern, but he claimed that this battle had been abruptly halted, and that all men concerned had agreed to forget the endeavor and disperse. When I questioned him on this, he seemed to become lost in his own mind for a moment, before denying that the words had left his lips and making me promise to tell not a soul. Yet always have I wondered if there might not have been some truth in the matter. My inquiries on the matter have led to nothing."

She paused, before turning to Daniel.

"Is that it?" he asked.

"Is that *it*?" she replied incredulously. "This passage as good as confirms that something had happened near Sharpeton. Obviously people survived the battle, but it sounds like they preferred to keep the whole thing covered up."

"We still don't know why, though."

"But we know we're not chasing our tails," she continued. "No-one's going to believe us when we start revealing what we've found, so every little piece of information is a bonus that we can use as ammunition. And if I managed to find this reference so easily once I knew what I was looking for, who's to say that there aren't other vague, oblique mentions of the battle in other texts? We're at the beginning of something huge, Dan!

When Doctor Clarke wakes up, he's going to be amazed!"

"I wouldn't expect him to be out and about too early," Daniel muttered. "I'm pretty sure he took a bottle of whiskey to bed."

"He's going through a tough time," she replied, glancing at the window as some flashing lights passed the pub, speeding along the road. A moment later, more lights passed, then more and more. Getting to her feet, she headed over to the window and looked out, only to see that a small convoy of vehicles had just passed through town and was heading out toward the moor.

"You're too buzzed to sleep, aren't you?" Daniel asked.

"I just need to research some other..."

Her voice trailed off as she watched another vehicle speeding past, and this time she spotted some kind of mechanical digger being towed along.

"No," she whispered, as she slowly began to realize what was happening. "Oh no, please no..."

"What's wrong?"

She turned to him, her eyes filled with panic. "Get the jeep! We have to go out to the dig site!"

"Mary..."

"Now!" she shouted, racing out of the room. "Daniel, hurry!"

CHAPTER THIRTY-TWO

"STOP!" MARY SHOUTED AS she raced away from the jeep, stumbling through the mud. "You have to stop right now!"

Up ahead, silhouetted against the brightening morning sky, scores of workers were setting up diggers and loading drilling equipment from trucks. The dig's white tent had already been taken down and moved aside, and cordons were being set up around the perimeter.

"Stop!" Mary yelled again, before stumbling and dropping to her knees. Getting up again, she ran toward the man who was hammering a post into the ground near the spot where the tent had stood. "Who's in charge here?" she stammered, grabbing his arm. "You have to stop what you're doing right now!"

"The boss is over there," the guy muttered, nodding toward the ridge. "I don't think he's gonna want to stop anything, though."

Hurrying past him, Mary made her way toward a set of vans that had been parked nearby.

"Who's in charge?" she shouted. "I demand to speak to whoever's in charge of this!"

Stepping toward her, a gray-suited man with a clipboard offered a cautious smile.

"My name is Edward Carter, and -"

"You have to move all this equipment out of here immediately!" she told him, her eyes wild with panic. Looking down at the mud, she saw tire tracks criss-crossing the ground. "There's no way of telling how much damage you've done already! There are priceless artifacts beneath our feet!"

"M'am," Carter replied, "I don't know who you are, but I can assure you that we're operating in accordance with a permit issued by the local council -"

"This is a site of massive archaeological importance," she continued, interrupting him again as Daniel finally caught up to them. "We're in the process of carrying out a major dig that has already uncovered evidence of military activity in the area!"

"Ah," Carter said cautiously, "then I take it that you are Doctor Mary Baker?"

"You have to leave right now!"

"Your permit to dig expired at midnight last night," he replied. "It was always planned that we'd move in immediately to start checking the ground, ready for the main drilling operation to begin. If you check the documentation attached to the permit, you'll see that we're simply acting in accordance with the original agreement."

"I extended the permit," she told him breathlessly. "I emailed two days ago and explained that we'd made a major discovery!"

"Unfortunately, the extension was denied," he continued. "I'm sorry, Doctor Baker, but the company was extremely generous in the first place. We gave you ample time to explore the area, we even provided funding so you could spend a couple of happy weeks sorting through the dirt, and it *does* seem that you've enjoyed yourselves tremendously." He forced a smile. "If it's any consolation, we have more than thirty additional drill sites lined up for later this year. I'm sure you could go and poke about at some of those."

"You have no idea what we've found here," she replied. "We've discovered evidence of a previously unknown battlefield, as well as potentially the last resting place of Captain John Villiers. We need to secure the entire area and then carry out a major dig, we need to bring up everything that's still waiting to be found."

Carter sighed. "John who?"

"John Villiers!"

He stared at her, clearly with no idea what she was talking about.

"I'll call someone," she continued, slipping her phone from her pocket. "Just give me a chance to call someone, and I'll get them to stop all of this!" Her hands were trembling, but a moment later she heard one of the mechanical diggers being switched on, and she turned to watch in horror as the machine began to roll forward across the mud. "Stop!" she shouted, turning back to Carter. "Just wait five minutes and I'll speak to someone who'll back up everything I've just told you!"

"We're pressed for time, Doctor Baker -"

"I won't let you do this," she continued, bringing up the number for her supervisor at the university. "Invaluable archaeological discovers can't be lost forever just because some company wants to dig around and search for oil!" She waited for her call to be answered, and then she let out a sigh of frustration as she was put straight through to voice-mail. "Just stop the machines!" she hissed, already searching for another number she could try. "Please, for the love of God, you have to understand that you're literally destroying history right now! You're trampling over one of the most remarkable finds for decades!"

Again, Carter sighed.

"Just wait a couple of hours," she stammered, "and -"

"Doctor Baker, please..."

"I'll call someone and -"

"It won't do any good!" he said firmly. "The company has already been extremely generous. Accommodating your request to dig here wasn't easy, especially with the way our schedule has been set up lately. The company has lost money by agreeing to let you do this work, but we felt that in the interests of fostering better relations with the local community -"

"How do you think the local community will react," she continued, interrupting him, "if they find out that your company ransacked a site of historical significance?"

"Frankly?" he replied, with a faint smile. "I

doubt many people will give a damn. If our search for oil is successful, we'll bring actual jobs to the town, and in my experience people value jobs far more than antique curiosities, especially in today's economy. Maybe that's not ideal, but we don't live in an ideal world. Now if you don't mind, I have a dig to supervise."

Mary opened her mouth to argue with him, before spotting a mechanical digger heading straight toward the ridge. Filled with panic, she slipped past Carter and ran across the muddy ground.

"Mary!" Daniel shouted, hurrying after her. "Wait!"

"Stop!" Mary yelled, as she made her way past the digger and stopped in its path, waving her arms and forcing the driver to slow down. "You can't do this! I won't allow it!"

"What are you going to do?" Daniel asked as he reached her. "Sit down in front of the damn thing like some kind of cross between Arthur Dent and Indiana Jones?"

"If I have to," she replied, as she sat on the muddy ground with her legs crossed.

"They'll just drive around you," Daniel said with a sigh, just as the digger turned and began to do exactly that. "Mary, there are better ways to fight this..."

Ignoring him, she got to her feet and ran until she was in front of the digger again, at which point she once again sat on the ground. Even as she did so, however, the digger was already getting ready to try another route, and three more identical machines were approaching different parts of the site.

"We have to stop them!" Mary shouted, close to tears. "Daniel, do the same! We can't let them ruin the site!"

"I need some police officers at the dig site," Carter was saying nearby, clearly irritated as the wireless headset blinked above his ear. "Yes, we have a protester causing an obstruction. She's breaching the peace and costing us a great deal of money." He rolled his eyes. "Absolutely. I want someone to come out here right now and arrest her!"

CHAPTER THIRTY-THREE

"AND DON'T GO BACK up there," the police officer said as he followed Mary and Daniel into the pub. "I'm serious, Doctor Baker. If we're called up to remove you again, I'll have to write a formal incident report and you could be charged with vandalism and trespassing."

"It's public land!" she pointed out, exasperated as she turned to him.

"The council has leased it to the company for six months," he continued. "I get it, you're frustrated, but I'm sure there are other channels you can use."

"It'll be too late by then! You saw the equipment they're using up there! By the time they're finished, anything still in the ground will have been destroyed!"

"I'm sorry," he added, heading back to the door, "but please, don't cause any more trouble up at the dig site." He glanced at her, over his shoulder. "Do I have your word on that?"

She paused, before sighing. "I promise. I won't

go back up there."

"Are you sure?"

"I'm sure."

Once the officer had left, Mary pushed past Daniel and headed to the window. She watched as the police car turned around in the pub's car park and drove away, and then she headed quickly to the door.

"Where are you going?" Daniel asked.

"Back to the site, of course."

"Mary!" Grabbing her arm, he kept her from heading outside. "You heard what he said!"

"I don't care," she continued, slipping free. "Even if it means spending a night in a police cell, I'm going to stop that dig! I can't even imagine how much damage they've caused already, but we can still save some of the artifacts!"

"You'd be better off calling someone at the university," he replied. "What about Professor Carlton? He's liaised with the company before, maybe he can speak to someone who'll overrule that Carter asshole? There are official channels you can use, and they'll be far more productive than storming up there like this!"

She paused, before shaking her head.

"And we have so much already," he continued. "We have more than enough to prove our case."

"Meaning?"

"Meaning..." He sighed. "Meaning that even if we can't get the site back, we can show beyond doubt that there *was* a battle outside Sharpeton, and that this is where John Villiers was killed. It's not perfect, and it's not the granular analysis that we were hoping for when we first made the discovery, but it's still a huge, *huge* achievement. Mary, after this find is announced, you'll be able to take your pick of academic positions all over the world!"

"I don't care about that," she replied. "I care about the irreplaceable artifacts that, even as we speak, are being crushed beneath the tracks of mechanical diggers. And why? Just so some faceless corporation can look for oil. It's obscene, Daniel!"

"It's the way the world works."

"He's right," Doctor Clarke said from the doorway next to the bar. "I'm sorry, I overheard most of your conversation, and I also saw diggers heading up toward the moor. I can well imagine what must have happened. Welcome to the harsh reality of academia, Doctor Baker. There's nothing you can do."

"Help us stop it," Mary replied, hurrying over to him.

He shook his head.

"You have power! Influence!"

"Not enough, I'm afraid," he replied wearily. "I'm flattered that you think I could have any sway at all, but there's nothing I can do. This is just going to have to be a tough lesson for you, my dear. Sometimes we get tantalizingly close to the truth, only for the greedy hands of commerce to snatch everything away from us."

"Not *everything*," Daniel pointed out. "We have lots of items and bones to sort through. We can still get a much bigger picture of what really happened here."

"It's not the same, though," Mary continued, with tears in her eyes. "If they'd just given us one more week, we could have worked around the clock and at least pulled as much as possible out of the ground. God knows what's still down there."

"Let's just focus on what we *have* got," Daniel told her. "Come on, there's so much to sort through and catalog, I don't even know where to start."

CHAPTER THIRTY-FOUR

"ANOTHER FEMUR," DANIEL MUTTERED a few hours later, setting a partially-broken bone on the table. "Clean wound to the lower end, suggesting it was sliced off, probably by a sword."

"Not exactly surprising," Mary replied. "After all, they *were* on a battlefield."

"Look at this," he continued, holding up a skull with an entire section missing from the back. "Whoever this poor guy was, he must have been clobbered from behind. The distribution of damage suggests he would have been wearing a helmet at time, but something still managed to break through and basically crush the back of his head." He paused for a moment, staring into the skull's empty eye-sockets. "At least it would have been quick, I guess."

"Sure," Mary said blandly.

Turning to her, he saw that she was still holding the same damaged helmet she'd first picked up a few minutes ago, but she was staring into space, clearly thinking about something else entirely.

"Don't," he said firmly.

She turned to him. "Don't what?"

"Don't think about what we *didn't* recover. Focus on what's right here in front of us. With any luck, it'll be more than enough to tell the story of the battle."

"But we could have found so much more," she continued. "Now it's all gone. Even if I could get through to the head of the company and somehow persuade him to pull the diggers back, it'd be too late. Most likely they've destroyed what's left. All that history, all those answers, crushed under the tracks of heavy machinery."

"Chin up," Daniel replied.

She forced a smile, but it was clear from her expression that she couldn't stop thinking about the missed opportunity.

"I've got a box of skulls here for you," he continued, grabbing a cardboard box and sliding it toward her.

"Later."

"It needs doing, Mary. Come on, we're professionals. We can lounge about, complaining about what we've lost, but only after we've finished the job that's right in front of us. For now we need to catalog this stuff and prepare it for transport." He watched as she pulled the box closer, but he could see from the look in her eyes that she was still thinking about everything they'd lost. "One day," he added, "we're going to look back on this as a huge success. Plus, we still have to figure out why the battle ended up being forgotten, so it's not like the hard part is over."

Reaching into the box, Mary took out a skull and examined it for a moment. One entire side had been smashed away, and she ran a fingertip against the broken edge.

"I guess *he* died pretty quickly too," Daniel suggested.

"Not if he was wearing a helmet," she replied. "The impact must have been strong enough to cause damage, but the helmet would have held most of the head together at first. He might well have died in the most unimaginable agony." She stared at the remaining eye socket for a moment, before setting the skull fragment aside and reaching into the box to take out another. As she examined the next skull, however, she began to frown. "Look at this," she muttered, holding it up for Daniel to see.

"Pretty small," he pointed out.

"I think it's..." She paused, taking a closer look at the shattered cheekbone and eye-socket. "I think it's a child's skull."

"Is it possible that child soldiers were used in the battle?"

"There are instances of that happening," she replied, "but..." Looking into the box, she pulled out another skull, just as small as the first. "Doesn't it seem unlikely that they'd be among the first we discovered?"

"What are you suggesting?"

After setting the skulls down, Mary got to her feet and headed over to one of the tables, where various discolored old bones had been tagged and laid out. After a moment, she picked up part of a damaged femur.

"I think this was from a child too," she continued. "How did the guys miss this when they were digging these things out of the ground? We need to get it all properly verified, of course, but I'm certain a lot of these bones are from..." Pausing, she stared at another, smaller chunk of bone on the table for a moment, before reaching down and picking it up so she could examine it more closely.

"What've you got there?" Daniel asked.

He waited, but she didn't reply. Instead, she seemed lost in thought, peering at the bone as if she could barely believe what she was seeing.

"Mary?" he continued. "Wanna share?"

"It's part of a knee," she muttered, "but it doesn't make sense." Holding it up for him to see, she tilted the piece of bone until a small metal plate was visible.

"I didn't know they were using that kind of thing back then," Daniel replied, getting to his feet and heading over to join her.

"They weren't," she replied, peering at the plate and seeing that it had been carefully screwed into the bone. "This is way too advanced for the seventeenth century."

"So maybe not all the bodies are from the battle," Daniel suggested.

Grabbing one of the notebooks, Mary flicked through the pages for a moment. "According to the log, these parts were all found together." She turned to him. "It's unlikely that later artifacts would have ended up mixed together with the ones from the battle *before* they were dug up."

"So what are you suggesting?"

Turning the piece of bone over, Mary peered at the metal plate. "There's a serial code on this thing," she said finally, "and a couple of other identifiers. It looks like a plate from some kind of knee surgery, although..." She paused, her mind rushing with thoughts, before slowly she turned to him.

"What?" he asked cautiously. "Mary? I've seen that look on your face before, it means you've got a crazy idea."

"That police officer who brought us back down here," she said after a moment. "Did you happen to catch his name?"

CHAPTER THIRTY-FIVE

"WHAT THE HELL IS going on here?" Carter shouted, as the third police car pulled up at the dig site and more officers stepped out, with Mary and Daniel right behind them. "This is a place of work!"

"Stop the machines," the leading officer told him. "As of right now, this is a crime scene."

"What are you talking about?" Carter blustered, his face reddening with sheer frustration. "I demand to know what you're all doing here!"

"Everyone stop!" the officer shouted, waving at the workmen who were attending to the drilling equipment. "Stop and step away from the machinery immediately! Anyone who doesn't stop will be charged with obstruction!"

"What have you done?" Carter asked, turning to Mary with pure anger in his eyes. "I swear to God, Doctor Baker, I will have you fired for this! Even the slightest delay to our program here will cost millions, and you're putting it all in jeopardy just so you can try to drag more old bones and chunks of metal from the ground! Where are your priorities, woman?"

"That's not it," Mary replied, her voice trembling with shock as she watched the workmen climbing down from the diggers. Half a dozen police officers were already swarming over the site now, leading people away and starting to set up security cordons. "It's..."

Her voice trailed off for a moment.

"This is nothing to do with archeology," Daniel told Carter. "We found something else mixed in with the older specimens. Something the police have been searching for."

"And what might that be?" Carter snapped, already bringing up his boss's number on his phone.

"The children who went missing," Mary replied, turning to him. "Maybe you didn't realize, but a few years ago seventeen children and two teachers vanished near here."

"So?"

"So we think we found some of their bones."

CHAPTER THIRTY-SIX

OPENING HER EYES, JULIE realized that she'd finally managed to get some sleep, and that now morning had arrived. She was on the bed with her arm around Becca, and she waited a moment before sitting up. Taking care to ensure that she didn't wake the girl, she carefully slid off the bed and then headed over to the door. By the time she was out on the landing and had pulled the door shut again, she'd also taken her phone from her pocket to check for a reply from Kerry.

Nothing.

"Hey Kerry," she whispered after calling and being put through to voicemail again, "I don't know if you remember me, but it's Julie from Sharpeton and I'm here with your little sister Becca. Dude, seriously, whatever's going on, you *need* to get your crap together and come back to Sharpeton. Becca needs you, she's..."

She paused, trying to work out how much she should say over the phone. She figured that if she went into too much detail about the smelly old man, she'd sound like she was trying to play a prank.

"Just get here," she added finally. "You have no idea how important this is. I think something weird's happened."

Cutting the call, she leaned back against the wall and sighed, before realizing with a frown that she could hear voices downstairs.

***

"It is not enough," Nykolas Freeman said darkly, as he sat in the armchair next to the broken TV, "for a man to strengthen his own soul. He has a duty, an inalienable *moral* duty, to uphold the fiber of his country, so that lesser man might be emboldened to serve for the betterment of all."

"Kind of like how a rising tide lifts all boats?" Craig asked, sitting cross-legged on the floor and staring up at him.

"The analogy is fitting," Freeman continued. "Witches in all their guises shall attempt to tempt good men, and I have seen some of England's best fall into permanent spiritual decay, all because of the flesh that was put on offer. It is not that all women are witches, but rather that all witches are women, save for a few decadent warlocks."

"And the priests," Craig replied. "Where do they fit into all of this?"

"It is Catholic priests one must destroy," Freeman sneered, "for they seek to undermine this fine country. It would be better for all mankind were Rome to be scrubbed from all maps and burned away, and for the land to then be salted."

"Weird," Craig muttered. "I'm pretty sure everyone loves the Pope these days."

Freeman flinched at those words. "Then the moral decay of the country is clearly set deep. No matter, though." He tightened his grip on the ax. "I have returned at the most opportune moment, and I shall see to it that England's course is set anew, this time for a world where proper thoughts are shared by all good people. And those who delight in witchery, devilry and papacy shall be crushed into the mud! England still needs me!"

"It's really dark in here," Julie said, stopping in the doorway. "And smelly."

"I thought the smell had gone," Craig replied, turning to her. "Maybe I just got used to it."

"I'm hungry," Julie continued, eying Freeman with a hint of caution, "and shock horror but the fridge is totally empty. Becca'll probably be up soon, too. Just listen out for her, okay? I'm gonna pop to the corner-shop and get something for breakfast."

Turning back to Freeman as Julie headed to the door, Craig seemed almost in awe. Having spent the entire night listening to Freeman's sage pronouncements, he was slowly starting to come around to some of the ideas, and he found himself now trying to think of something impressive to say, some way of showing Freeman that he understood.

"So what do you think of modern Britain?" he

asked finally. "Compared to, like, things in your day, is the modern world better or worse?"

"I cannot say as yet," Freeman replied. "I have yet to discern the modern face of witchcraft. I am no fool, and I understand that much has changed over the centuries, but that doesn't mean witchcraft has necessarily faded away. I remain convinced that servants of sin are hiding in the world, waiting for the right time to once again propagate their evil. They are perhaps more skillful at deceit than ever before, but they can still be drawn out. Tell me, boy. Do you know the proper way to divine whether or not a woman is a witch?"

"Not... entirely."

"There are several methods. The woman who were here a moment ago, the one who goes by the name of Julie. Have you tested her?"

"Um, not really."

"Has she shown signs of witchery or devilry?"

Craig considered the question for a moment. "I wouldn't say so. No, not really."

"Yet you cannot be sure?"

"I'm not sure *how* to be sure."

"Do you take her to your bed?"

Craig smiled. "Well... Yeah, of course."

"Yet you do not know that she is pure."

"She's pretty clean. Wait, are we talking about the same thing?"

"If you are not careful," Freeman continued, "you might end up siring a child with a witch. Such a monstrosity would doubtless seek to extend its own power as soon as it became able. You, Sir, have a duty to your country, and you must ensure that witchcraft is not allowed to fester in any corner." He paused, before slowly narrowing his eyes. "Unless you are a supporter of such things, in which case you are an affront to decency and honor, and a traitor to your land! Be you a turncoat, boy?"

"I'm no traitor," Craig replied, "I just... Julie's never struck me as a witch, that's all."

"Does she obey you?"

"Not really."

"Does she speak with a foul mouth?"

"It's been known to happen."

"And her morals? Are they lackadaisical?"

"I don't know what that -"

"Is she morally corrupt?" Freeman roared, suddenly leaning forward and banging his fist on the chair's arm, as if he was a king on a great throne.

Craig flinched, pulling back slightly. "Um... Maybe. Kinda, slightly."

"The human mind is perfectly capable of weakness without witchcraft," Freeman sneered, "but sometimes there *is* witchery involved. If you determine this woman to betray suspect behavior, it is your duty to probe further and discover the truth about her."

"It is?" Craig paused, before nodding. "Yeah. I guess it is."

"Else you would be a traitor to your land," Freeman continued, holding his ax up so that the cuts and dents glinted in the low light, "and I would have to deal with you even before I put the woman to a series of tests."

"I'm definitely not a traitor," Craig told him, eying the ax with a mixture of fear and awe, "so you totally don't need to *deal* with me." He paused, before slowly a faint smile began to spread across his face. "Hypothetically speaking, dude, exactly what kind of tests would you need to carry out, if you were checking whether Julie's a witch. *Strictly* hypothetically, of course. I mean, it kinda sounds like fun."

"I have lost count of how many suspected witches I have encountered. There was a time when I took them all to my farm, where I was able to conduct my investigations without risk of being disturbed. Connaught tended to the pigs while I took my time with the witches, but..." Freeman paused for a moment. "If I could get *back* to my farm, perhaps enough of it is still standing that I might resume my duties. Three centuries and more might have passed since that time, but I pledged long ago to serve my country for as long as I lived, and in some manner I am still here today, which means..."

Craig waited for him to continue.

"Where... Dude, where *is* this farm?" he asked finally.

"It stands near the spot where the forest meets the Kentish road," Freeman replied. "A little way outside the town of Wellington, by the river, but from here it would take three, maybe four days to get there unless we were able to secure horses."

"Horses?" Craig shuffled across the floor and reached up to the table, grabbing a set of keys from a bowl. "Who needs horses, when we've got horse-

power?"

"I do not understand your suggestion."

"I've got a car, dude," he continued. "It's kinda beaten up and crappy, but it's still a car. Plus, I'm always up for a road-trip, so if you wanna go check out Freeman's farm... I mean, *your* farm, then I'm be totally down for that. See a little history, have a little fun, get out of the house for a while..." Getting to his feet, he sniffed the air. "We should definitely get out of the house for a while, at least. And leave the windows open."

"It might help to return to my old home," Freeman muttered. "I confess to not entirely knowing my place in this modern world. I have avoided returning to my farm, but now I see I was in error." Slowly, he rose from the chair, and his body could be heard creaking as he did so. "You will bring the woman Julie back and wake the child, and then we must set off at once! I want to reach the farm by nightfall of the third day!"

"Dude, we can be there in a couple of hours," Craig replied, heading to the desk in the corner and pulling open one of the drawers. He rifled through the contents for a moment before pulling out a clear plastic bag filled with white powder. "We need some fuel, though."

"And what," Freeman asked with a frown, "is *that?*"

"This?" He held the bag up for Freeman to see. "Oh, dude, don't worry. This is just cocaine."

CHAPTER THIRTY-SEVEN

"AND SOME FREE-RANGE EGGS, please," Julie continued, before turning to look out the window as several people hurried past the corner-shop. "Is something going on out there?"

A moment later, as if to answer her question, two police cars drove along the main road. Their lights and sirens were off, but just the sight of two patrol vehicles in Sharpeton was enough to cause concern. Heading over to the door, Julie peered out and saw that a few dozen people had congregated in the courtyard outside the King's Head. Sharpeton was the kind of town where very little of note ever happened, and to see so many people congregating in one place was odd, to say the least.

"What's wrong?" she asked as Mrs. Haggerty made her way past. "Did something happen?"

"They've found them, dear," the old woman replied.

"Found who?"

"The children. That's what people are saying, anyway." She hesitated, with tears in her eyes. "They're saying they've found the poor wee children!"

As Mrs. Haggerty hurried toward the courtyard, Julie stepped out of the shop, open-mouthed with surprise. A moment later, the store-keeper emerged next to her, and they both watched as the police cars stopped next to the pub. For the next couple of minutes, more and more people came out of houses in the nearby streets, as if the entire town had begun to get wind of the news, and Julie couldn't shake a slow, nervous sensation in the pit of her stomach.

"It can't be true, can it?" she asked finally, turning to the store-keeper.

"I..." He paused. "I suppose there was always a chance they'd find them eventually. Do you want those eggs or not?"

After heading back in and buying what she needed for breakfast, Julie stepped back out into the street and made her way over toward the pub. All around, people were chattering with a mix of excitement and trepidation, while the police officers were continually telling everyone that they had no news at the moment. At the same time, Julie spotted the landlord of the King's Head being led over to one of the police cars, and she knew that his son Robert had been one of the missing children. There was a hint of shock in the man's eyes, and he seemed extremely pale.

Figuring that she should get back to the house and check the news online, she turned to head past the courtyard, but suddenly she spotted a woman standing by the far wall, watching the scene with an expression of concern. Sharpeton was a small enough town that strangers were usually noted immediately, but this woman seemed not to be attracting attention as she observed the scene. Heading over, Julie stopped next to her for a moment, and now she was close enough to see tears in her eyes.

"Do you know what happened?" Julie asked finally.

The woman paused, before nodding.

"Did they really find the children?"

"That's just the start of it," the woman replied. Softly-spoken, she seemed to be in her late thirties or early forties, yet there was a hint of great tiredness in her eyes. "I should have known better than to believe these things might stay hidden. Humanity has a habit of digging up the past and trying to find answers. On this occasion, however, it would have been better if everything had stayed hidden, although..." She paused. "I was a fool. This day had to come. It was inevitable."

Julie watched the woman's worried face for a moment, and she considered asking if she was another cosplayer. After a moment, however, she turned and looked over at the courtyard. There was a palpable sense of anticipation in the air, as if the whole town had been holding its breath since the children's disappearance and now, finally, a chance of relief had arrived. In some ways, the loss of so many children had come to define Sharpeton, and Julie had often thought about the fact that if she'd been born just a year earlier, she might have been on that bus herself.

"It's hard to believe we might finally find out what happened," she said finally, before turning to look at the woman again. "It's still so -"

Stopping suddenly, she realized that the woman had completely vanished. She looked around, but there was no sign of her anywhere, although she figured it was possible that she'd simply blended in with the increasingly large crowd that was gathering to wait for news. It seemed as if the entire town had come out, but Julie felt as if she needed to get back to Becca. Deep down, she was worried that something was seriously wrong in the little girl's head.

CHAPTER THIRTY-EIGHT

"A ROAD-TRIP? WHAT THE hell are you talking about? We're not going on a road-trip!"

"Chill, babe," Craig replied, kissing her on the side of the face, only for her to pull away. "Mr. Freeman wants to check out one of his old haunts, and I figured it'd be fun. When was the last time we actually took a trip anywhere?"

"I'm not getting in a car with that freak!" she hissed, lowering her voice so that she wouldn't be overheard. She glanced across the kitchen, looking toward the door that led into the front room, and then she turned back to Craig. "Are you on coke again?"

He shook his head.

"Do you promise?"

He nodded.

"Do you *really* promise?" she continued, her eyes wide with concern. "Craig, after last time -"

"Chill, babe, I -"

"Don't tell me to chill!" she said firmly. "I *hate it* when you tell me to chill!"

"I don't have any coke in my system at all," he replied. "Why? Do *you* want some?"

"I hate that stuff," she reminded him. "I swear to God, Craig, if I ever see you doing coke again, I will walk out and never, ever come back." She paused for a moment, watching his eyes for any hint that he was using drugs. "If you and Sir Stinks-a-Lot want to go for a drive, then I'm not going to stop you. I'll just stay here and look after Becca."

"Becca's coming with us."

"No," she said firmly, with growing exasperation, "she is not!"

"She's already decided," he continued. "She actually *wants* to come, she seems like she doesn't want to be away from Freeman, or whatever his name really is. It's like they're this little duo." He paused for a moment. "You can stay behind if you want, but the three of us are going for a drive to some old farm somewhere. You know what, babe? It might actually be fun." He leaned closer and kissed the side of her neck. "Just unclench and chill, babe."

***

"This mode of transportation is exceedingly strange," Freeman muttered a short while later, as Craig drove the four of them along a country road that led out of town. "I accept your word that there is no witchcraft involved, but still I confess to being a little wary."

"You're doing great, mate," Craig told him with a smile. "See? I told you you'd get used to it. Don't you feel slightly silly for being scared when I started the engine?"

"I was not scared," Freeman replied. "I was simply cautious. This metal carriage moves with great speed. It would be extremely useful for hunting down witches."

"Just think of it as a really high-tech steam engine."

"They didn't have steam engines in the seventeenth century," Julie muttered. "Don't ask him to break character."

"Which way now?" Craig asked, slowing the car as they reached a junction. "Toward Mepley, or toward Wellingham?"

"Wellingham," Freeman explained, "and then toward the river. I only hope that my farm has been left in good hands over the years."

"Yeah, well..." Craig glanced over his shoulder and smiled at Julie and Becca as they waited in the back seat, and then he turned to Freeman. "Let's hope it's still there at all, yeah? It'd be a real bummer to get there and find someone'd built a block of yuppy flats over the damn thing."

***

"Is this it? Mate? Is this your farm?"

Having finally reached a patch of barren scrub-land near the river, the four of them were now out of the car, making their way through the tall grass. A cold wind was ruffling the nearby trees, bringing a constant background hiss to the scene, and Julie had already removed her jacket and given it to Becca so that the little girl wouldn't freeze. Above, the sky was slowly darkening, as if the storm was returning.

"The land has changed a great deal," Freeman said after a moment, stopping to look around. "I barely recognize it at all, yet..." He paused again, as if he was lost in thought. "This is indeed my farm. Or at least, it was."

"What about this?" Craig asked, kicking a low-running section of brickwork that was barely visible in the grass. "Looks like a pile of ruins to me."

"This was once where my barn stood," Freeman explained, with a hint of sadness in his voice. He stepped around the broken section of wall and made his way over to another, smaller pile of bricks. "Here was my kiln. I built it myself, with my own hands, so that it would serve my needs."

"And what needs were those?" Julie asked. "Wait, never mind. I don't think I want to know."

"Burning witches," he replied.

She nodded. "Yep. Pretty much what I thought."

"So was this actually some old farm?" Craig asked, making his way across a patch of open land. "Me and my mates used to come out here sometimes at night. We used to smoke reefers and drink a load of cheap beer. I never really thought about what it used to be."

"How did it come to be left in ruins?" Freeman whispered, reaching out and running a withered, partially skinless hand across some of the bricks. "Was there no-one in England who sought to follow my work? Did nobody in this fair land, upon hearing of my indisposition, seek to come out here and take my place, fighting the good fight against devilry and witchcraft?"

"Doesn't look like it, mate," Craig said with a grin. "I guess you did a lot of research, yeah? Is this where the real Nicky Freeman used to hang out?"

Ignoring him, Freeman made his way over to another ruined section of brickwork.

"My pigs lived here," he muttered, as much to himself as to the others. "Fine animals, finer even than some men. There was nothing they would not eat."

"He's insane," Julie whispered to Craig, as they watched Freeman examining another patch of land. "I don't think he's cosplaying, I think he's really into this, like he truly believes he's this Nykolas Freeman character."

"Cool, huh?" Craig replied.

"It's not cool," she continued, reaching down and putting a reassuring hand on Becca's shoulder. "It's weird, and it's wrong, and we need to get the hell out of here! And then we need to ring the local asylums, 'cause I think one of them's missing a lunatic!"

"What do you think's gonna happen?" he asked. "Take a chill pill, babe, he's some old geezer -"

"An old geezer with an ax," she pointed out. "He never puts that thing down, and I don't like it. I think it's real!"

"It's a prop," he replied. "An authentic, expensive prop. Besides, he's not gonna hurt anyone.

He's a harmless old freak, and obviously he gets his kicks out of this sorta thing. He's probably lonely. Maybe his wife died or something and he's got no family, so he has fun dressing up and wandering around, pretending to be this old-time Freeman guy. We're basically doing him a favor. You always said we should get into charity work and help people out." He shrugged. "Look at us! Keeping some sad old git company."

"Craig -"

"Hey!" he shouted, waving at Freeman as he ran over to join him. "Got any cool stories about this place, bro? I think I'm starting to get interested in history after all! You're really bringing it to life!"

"We'll go home soon," Julie said, rubbing Becca's shoulder. "I promise."

"Did Kerry call you back yet?" the little girl asked.

Checking her phone, Julie saw that she still had no messages or missed calls. "Give her a little longer, sweetie. I'm sure she'll be here as soon as she realizes. In fact, I promise."

"You do?"

She nodded. "We'll get you back to your family. Cross my heart and hope to die."

CHAPTER THIRTY-NINE

"THIS WAS ONCE WHERE I put witches to the test," Freeman muttered, standing by the side of the river and looking down at a set of old red bricks that had once formed a small wall, but which had now mostly collapsed into the water. "A great metal contraption, a type of cage, was in place on this very spot, and I would submerge the suspect witch for several minutes."

"I think I've heard about that sorta thing," Craig replied, rummaging through his pockets before taking out the small bag of white powder. "If they drowned, they were innocent, and if they survived, they were a witch so you executed them. Right?"

"You have the basics, certainly."

"Pretty crazy test, though," Craig continued, opening the bag. "I mean, basically, once a girl was accused, so was screwed, wasn't she? Did you ever test to see if they weighed the same as a duck?"

Freeman frowned and turned to her.

"Monty Python reference," Craig explained. "I guess... After your time, huh?" With a smile, he tipped some of the powder into the palm of his hand and then snorted it up his nose.

"What in the name of all this is holy," Freeman said after a moment, "are you doing?"

"Want some?"

"I do not -"

"It's good coke," he continued, lowering his voice to a conspiratorial hush. Glancing over his shoulder, he saw that Julie and Becca were several hundred feet away, walking across the farthest side of the clearing. "Don't tell the missus, 'cause she freaks out about this sorta thing. She doesn't understand, it's just a way to brighten up the world, start seeing things in a different way." He held the bag out. "Are you *sure* you don't want some? I've got a feeling it'd do you good. I'd love to see you on a coke high."

"Is it a form of tobacco?"

"Never mind," Craig muttered, pouring some more out and taking another snort. Clearing his throat, he wiped his nose and then stuffed the bag back into his pocket. "It's all good, mate. All good." With that, he let out a sudden whinnying noise, sounding for a moment like a backfiring horse. "Jesus, I needed that!"

Freeman's eyes narrowed with disdain.

"Give us a look at that ax, then," Craig continued, taking a step closer. "I've been admiring it all morning, mate. Looks really solid."

"It is an ax," Freeman replied. "It *must* be solid."

"Can I give it a whirl?"

"A whirl?"

"Test it out a bit." He reached out to take the ax, but Freeman moved his hand back, out of the way. "Come on, don't be a spoilsport. Where'd you get it, anyway? Some kinda prop shop? I've always wanted to play with an ax."

"This ax was hand-made by one of the finest smiths in all of England," Freeman said firmly. "It was designed to my specifications, and it has since been used to kill hundreds of witches and priests."

"It's got a lot of dents on the edge," Craig pointed out.

"Every time this ax strikes bone," Freeman replied, "it causes far more damage than it suffers. It has served me well for hundreds of years and..." His voice trailed off for a moment, and he seemed lost in thought as he held the ax up and examined the blade. "Hundreds of years," he said again, as if he could barely believe such a thing was true. "I have been alive for centuries. I was born a mortal man, an *ordinary* man, yet still I am here. How is that possible?"

"Having a mid-life crisis?" Craig asked with a laugh, before reaching out again to take the ax. "Come on, give us a look, I'll only -"

"Silence!" Freeman sneered, raising the ax as if he was about to strike the boy.

"Alright," Craig muttered, rolling his eyes as he took a step back. Pulling the bag of powder from his pocket, he opened it again and took another snort. "Chill, dude. You can keep your crappy little ax, it's no big deal. I only wanted to take a gander, that's all. I've seen bigger."

"I have outlived all other men who were born in my time," Freeman continued, lowering the ax as he turned and looked toward the river. "Why? For what purpose am I still here? Does God see fit to prolong my life for some reason? It cannot be chance." He held up his left hand, slowly forming a fist and watching as his ragged skin stretched over the exposed tendons beneath. "Am I alive, or am I dead? Or am I suspended between the two states, like some kind of..."

"Jesus!" Craig gasped, having taken yet another, longer snort. "Man, I am alive right now! I am smoking!"

"I do not understand this world," Freeman muttered, taking a step closer to the river. "I am out of my own time, and I feel certain that I have barely even *begun* to explore the changes that have taken place. What place is there in the modern world for a man such as myself? Am I to continue my crusade, to hunt down witches and priests wherever I find them, or does God intend for me to take on some other role? It is almost as if witchcraft has been used against me. I await some form of message, some divine interruption that -"

"Let's see the ax," Craig said suddenly, interrupting him. "I'm not kidding now, mate. I wanna see it."

Freeman turned to him, just as Craig reached out and grabbed his wrist.

"I'll give it back, alright? I just wanna hold the ax and swing it around a bit. Nothing wrong with that, is there?"

"Release my hand at once," Freeman said firmly.

"Let me hold the bloody ax," Craig continued, staring at him with wild eyes. "Mate, I thought we were friends, and friends share things. What's wrong, don't you trust me?"

"I -"

"*Don't* you trust me, asshole?" he shouted, shoving Freeman's chest. "After everything I've done for you? After driving you out here to this crap-heap, so you can get all poetic and nostalgic about a pile of bricks? I've done *all* that, and you won't even let me hold your stupid ax?" He sniffed and wiped his nose, brushing away flecks of white powder. "What are you, just some ungrateful old tit who can't reciprocate a spot of solid friendship?" Again he shoved Freeman's chest, this time forcing him to take a step back. "You know what you are? You're nothing but a sad, feeble old man who stinks to high heaven and gets his kicks by -"

Before Craig could finish, Freeman slammed the handle of his ax into his chest, knocking him to the ground with one swift move.

"Jesus!" Craig hissed, wincing with pain as he got to his feet. "I get it! You're an asshole! You're some kind of deviant, you should be on a register somewhere, not wondering around with a little girl. What's going on there, anyway? Is that another way you get your kicks? Have you got wandering fingers, mate?" He took a step back, again wiping his nose, almost as if the action had become a habit. "You know what I reckon? I reckon you're a much bigger pervert than you look. And that's saying something, 'cause you *look* like a goddamn freak!"

Turning, he hurried away, stomping through the grass at the side of the river, leaving Freeman standing alone as, a moment later, Becca approached cautiously.

"Are you okay?" she asked.

Freeman turned to her. "That young man is deeply unsettled in the head," he said after a moment. "I have grave suspicions about his sanity."

"Can I tell you something?" Becca continued, swallowing hard. "I'm scared to, but I think it's important."

Freeman watched for a moment as Craig continued to walk away, and a few seconds later he saw that Julie was running over to catch him.

"I'm glad you did what you did to my father," Becca said suddenly. "I know that's a terrible thing to say, but if he was still alive, I'd just be scared that he might show up. Does that make me a bad person? You were right before when you told me not to get upset. I see that now." She paused, before putting her arms around his waist and hugging him tight. "Thank you."

"The world is turned upside down," Freeman muttered, watching as Craig and Julie made their way along the riverbank. "I feel I have emerged in a different land."

"Like Alice," Becca replied, "when she went to Wonderland. It's okay, I feel the same way."

"I know not of what you speak."

She pulled back, staring up at him, and slowly a faint smile crossed her features. "It's okay," she said after a moment. "I know it off by heart. Do you want me to tell you the story?"

CHAPTER FORTY

"CRAIG!" JULIE CALLED OUT, hurrying after him. "Craig, wait up!"

"That guy's a dick!" he muttered, not slowing or even glancing back toward her. "I reckon we should just dump both of them here, let them walk back to town!"

"Craig!" Grabbing his shoulder, she forced him to stop.

"He wouldn't even let me touch his ax!" he said angrily, turning to her. "Can you believe that? What a selfish idiot! It's probably some cheap prop he picked up on offer somewhere, but he acts like it's the most precious thing in the bloody world!"

"Have you taken coke?" she asked.

He sighed.

"Have you?" With tears in her eyes, she waited for him to answer. "Craig, you promised..."

"It was only to deal with that asshole!" he hissed. "Jesus Christ, the smell alone is enough to drive anyone mad!"

"You promised you'd never use that stuff again," she continued, her voice as tears welled in her eyes.

"Yeah, but come on..." He sighed again. "You knew I didn't really mean it when I said that. You knew it was just something I said to make you feel better. So you can't turn around and get mad now, just 'cause I took a little dash to keep my energy levels up."

"You're an idiot," she replied, sniffing back tears. "You're a lying, hypocritical piece of -"

"Oh, shut it!" he hissed, pulling the clear bag from his pocket. "You'd be a lot less annoying right now if you'd just grow a pair and take some with me! Join in with the fun!"

"What are you doing?" she asked, watching in horror as he tore the bag open. "Craig!"

"Want some?" he replied, holding it out for her. When she tried to snatch it away, he pulled back and then poured the rest of the coke into his hand, quickly holding it up to his nose and taking a deep, long sniff.

"Craig!"

"Better?" he asked, before starting to cough. Dropping the now-empty bag, he doubled over for a moment and started furiously wiping his nose, before standing up straight again and letting out a slow gasp of pleasure. "Man, that was a lot of coke!" he added, before starting to laugh. "I think I'm starting to see whole new colors!"

"I hate you," she replied, taking a step back. "Do you realize that? I really, truly hate you right now! Give me the car keys!"

"Why?"

"You're not driving in this condition!"

"What condition?"

"You're out of your mind!" she hissed, trying to grab the keys from his pocket.

"Chill!" he muttered, pulling away. "You're starting to bore me, bitch. Or are you a witch?"

"I'm not letting you get back in that car," she said firmly, "until you give me the goddamn keys."

"*Everything's* starting to bore me," he continued, looking around with wild, staring eyes. "This whole world is dull! You know what? I reckon Mr. Nykolas Freeman has got the right idea. I'm not talking about the mad old bastard over there, he's just some stinky, incontinent old fart. I'm talking about the real Nykolas Freeman, the one who lived hundreds of years ago! Maybe we should all pretend to be him, huh? Maybe we'd have more fun if we lived according to his ideals!" He took a deep breath. "It's all starting to make sense now. This country has lost its way, and we need to get back on track! Freeman shows the way!"

Sighing, she stared at him, unable to believe what she was hearing.

"I just need that ax, though," he muttered, peering past her. "That'd complete the thing, yeah? The ax is key. Don't ask me why, there's just something about it. Damn, I swear it's almost singing to me! Like the metal is... Like I can hear its atoms vibrating in a way that... vibrates on the same frequency as my own thoughts. That's gotta mean something, right? It has to be, like, cosmically significant!"

"You're out of your mind," Julie replied, still sniffing back tears. "This is going to be just like last time."

Smiling, he tried to push past her, but she grabbed his arm and held him back.

"Where are you going?" she asked.

"Where do you think? We're getting out of here. We'll ditch those two pricks and go home. I think I need to write a manifesto!"

"Give me the keys!" she hissed, trying to shove her hand into his pocket.

"You're eager," he said with a grin, pulling her hand away. "You can get in my pants when we're home, babe." Leaning closer, he licked her neck.

"Don't touch me!" she replied, slipping from his grip.

"Maybe you *are* a witch," he continued, stepping toward her. "Freeman was telling me how to recognize one, you know. He said in his day, a witch was a loud-mouthed woman, one who rattled her tongue off whenever she wanted. He also said witches are pretty freaky in the bedroom, and we both you what you like to get up to, don't we? You're my witchy crazy woman, babe."

"Shut up," she sneered, as tears ran down her face.

"It's all starting to make sense now," he grinned, taking another step closer, forcing her to back away. "Yeah, I see it now, Freeman's right about it all! You're a modern witch, aren't you? Maybe you don't even know it, maybe you've got no idea of your own potential, but trust me, it's pretty obvious now. And the way you tried to look after little Becca was kinda cute, so maybe you figure you can turn *her* into a witch too! All the pieces of the puzzle are starting to make sense!"

"You're off your head!" she replied, as her voice trembled with anger. "You're coked up and you're out of your mind!"

"No, babe, I'm just seeing the truth. It's blindingly obvious when you think about it. I just needed some old-fashioned advice from someone who knows how to see the world properly. God, I need to get stuff down as a manifesto. Nicky Freeman -"

"I'm getting Becca out of here," she said firmly, stepping past him. "I'm taking her back to Sharpeton and finding her sister, and then I never want to see your -"

"Get back here, witch!" he replied, laughing as he grabbed her arm and yanked her closer.

Fumbling to pull her phone from her pocket, Julie tried to slip free.

"Witch!" Craig hissed excitedly in her ear. "Witch! Witch! Who's a witch? Julie's a witch!"

"Don't touch me, asshole," she replied, her eyes getting redder now as tears streamed down her face. She tried to check her phone, only for Craig to knock it from her hand as he tugged her back. "Craig!"

"Witch!"

Again she tried to get free, but this time he yanked her the other way until finally she slipped loose. Unable to stop herself in time, she tripped over the edge of some bricks on the ground and tumbled down the riverbank, landing with a splash in the shallow water and letting out a cry of pain.

"The witch is in the water!" Craig enthused, hurrying down after her.

"Jesus!" she whispered, feeling a pain in her left arm as she tried to sit up. "I think you fractured my -"

"Witch!" he shouted as he jumped down onto her, landing on her chest and shoving her head down into the water. She reached up and fought back, but he was laughing as her flailing arms splashed frantically in the water. After a moment, he let go of her head and allowed her to get a breath of air, but he was still giggling excitedly.

"What the hell are you doing?" she stammered. "Craig, get -"

"Witch!" he shouted again, grabbing her neck and shoving her head underwater again. This time he held her down for a little longer, enjoying the sensation as she desperately tried to push him off. Finally he let her get another breath, but only for a fraction of a second before pushing her back under.

She reached up and tried to push him away, but he simply laughed and waited.

"There's a test they used to run on witches," he explained, as a trickle of blood ran from his nose. "They used to dunk them underwater and see what happened to them. If they died, they weren't a witch and they were pardoned. If they survived, they *were* a witch and had to be executed. Tough life, eh? Then again, there's a kind of logic to it. I'll make sure to mention all of that when I start writing the manifesto." He waited as she continued to struggle. She'd been under for at least a minute and a half, maybe two minutes by now, and he knew he had to let her up eventually.

He just wasn't quite sure when.

Finally he released his hold on her neck by just enough to let her lift her head out of the water. Gasping for air, she simultaneously spat out a torrent of water and started coughing.

"Yeah, maybe you're not a witch," Craig said with a grin, staring down at her as she opened her eyes. He waited as she tried to say something, but she was too busy trying to get air into her lungs. "Then again," he added, "can't be too careful!"

"Craig, you're out of your -"

Before she could finish, he shoved her back underwater harder than ever, until he felt the back of her head hitting the rocky river-bed. Still grinning, he waited for her to fight back, but this time her hands simply rested on his chest for a moment before slipping down into the water. He waited, but as the water became calmer he was able to see her unmoving face beneath the surface, and after a moment he realized that a red cloud was slowly spreading from the back of her head. He hesitated, as his coke-addled mind tried to work out what was happening, and finally he figured that she was just playing some kind of prank. With his hands still around her neck, he waited for a few minutes, convinced that at any moment she'd suddenly burst back up to surprise him.

But she didn't.

After a few more minutes, he started thinking about his manifesto. He imagined himself starting a whole new political revolution, one based on the back-to-basics philosophy of the original Nykolas Freeman. In his mind's eye, he saw the people of England flocking to follow him, embracing the vibe of Freeman's seventeenth century ideas. He knew those ideas would need to be altered a little to fit the modern day, but he figured he was just the right person for the job. Finally, remembering Julie, he let go of her neck and sat back, but she remained beneath the surface, and the bloody red cloud was still spreading through the water.

"Huh," he said finally, shocked but still smiling. "I guess she wasn't a witch after all."

CHAPTER FORTY-ONE

HEARING SOMEONE WHISTLING, BECCA turned just in time to see Craig wandering back toward the clearing. She squinted, waiting to catch sight of Julie, but there was no sign of her new friend at all.

"Continue the story," Freeman said after a moment. "What happened next to this Alice girl?"

Becca turned back to him.

"She was lost in a world that didn't make sense," she explained. "There was a kind of logic to everything, but it wasn't the kind of logic she understood."

"So she was driven mad?"

"I'm not..." Glancing toward Craig again, she saw that he was much closer now. And there was still no sign of Julie.

"When one finds oneself in a strange land," Freeman continued, "one must fight to impose order. Madness cannot persist. Logic and rationality must win out."

"Not always," Becca replied, turning to him. "Sometimes the world you're in is so overwhelming and strange, you have to find your own little path through it all. But you can't change that world or..." She frowned. "At least, that's what my mother told me when she read the story to me. I think I'm remembering it right..."

"So I've got a proposal for you guys," Craig said as he reached them, clapping his hands together as if he was excited about something. "I'm gonna drive you back into town, and then we'll see about getting some food. Sound good? I'm starving my ass off here!"

Becca frowned, before peering past him, still looking for Julie.

"Hey, old guy!" Craig shouted at Freeman, who was lost in thought now. "Do you like Indian food? Why don't we split a curry?"

Slowly, Freeman turned to him, his eyes filled with scorn.

"Or not," Craig continued, holding his hands up and grinning like a Cheshire cat. "Chinese? There's not a lot of choice in Sharpeton. It's basically Indian, Chinese or crap from the pub. I'm gonna be real nice, though, and let you choose! I mean, there's nothing wrong with the crap from the pub, but it's kinda pricey. I don't suppose you could pay, could you? I mean, I shelled out for the gas to get us here so..."

"Where's Julie?" Becca asked.

"Who?"

"Julie," she continued. "You went off with her and now she's gone. Where is she?"

"Forget Julie," he replied dismissively. "The

244

bitch was a witch. Hey, that rhymes!"

"*Why* isn't she coming back?" Becca asked, feeling a flash of panic as she looked across the clearing. "She was going to get in touch with my sister. Hasn't she done that yet?"

"Forget Julie," Craig said again, patting her on the shoulder as he watched Freeman getting to his feet. "We're gonna have fun together, right? You're not the only one who can go after witches and priests, old man. Hell, you know what? I think we should all pretend to be that Nykolas Freeman guy, as a kind of tribute. He had the right ideas! I'm thinking of starting my own political party, the Nykolas Freeman party. We'll wipe the floor with the establishment at the next election!"

Without reply, Freeman started making his way toward them.

"Yeah," Craig continued, nodding as if he was exceptionally pleased with his latest idea, "from now on, I no longer respond to the name Craig. I, too, shall be Nykolas Freeman, famous priest hunter and witch killer! In fact, I might even have killed my first witch, but..." He cupped his hands around his mouth and leaned down to Becca, while lowering his voice to a whisper. "Don't tell anyone about that. It's out little secret. But this Freeman guy is like the Guy Fawkes mask from the internet, except he's real!"

"Where is the woman?" Freeman asked.

"Forget her, she's -"

"Where is she?"

Craig sighed. "Dude -"

"I want Julie to come back," Becca said with a

frown, turning to Freeman. "Make him tell us where she went."

"Yeah," Craig said with a laugh, "like you two freaks can *make* me do anything! I'm the great Nykolas Freeman, or didn't you get the latest memo? We're all Nykolas Freeman, every one of us! And that's not just the coke talking!"

Becca stared at him. "You're not -"

"Yes I am!" he shouted, pushing her aside and stepping toward Freeman. "Everyone can join in the fun! I listened to you last night, old man, and what you said made a lot of sense! It opened my third political eye! The world needs someone like you, someone who sees things for what they really are! You don't pussy-foot around, you don't bend over backwards to lie about everything so people feel better! You say what you think, and you stand up for the morals and principles that are gonna make us great again!"

Freeman frowned.

"You're Nykolas Freeman?" Craig continued as he reached him, staring up into the old man's dark, rotting eyes. Suddenly he prodded his chest with a finger. "Yeah, well join the club. We're all Nykolas Freeman! The revolution starts here, motherfucker!"

"You," Freeman sneered, "are not an honorable man. Where is the woman? Did you -"

Before he could finish, Craig grabbed the ax and wrenched it from his hand. Freeman reached out to grab it back, but Craig slipped away and danced back across the clearing, waving the ax above his head.

"Return that immediately!" Freeman roared.

"Why?" Craig laughed, turning and swiping the ax through the air in several different directions. "Feels good! Feels nimble! I could really use this! Shame I didn't have it when I dealt with that bitch a few minutes ago, but I'm sure I'll find more witches pretty soon!"

"Julie?" Becca shouted, running through the long grass, heading in the direction she'd seen Julie go a few minutes earlier. "Julie, where are you?"

"Return my ax," Freeman said firmly, stepping toward Craig. "You are not fit to hold such a righteous weapon."

"Make me, bitch," Craig replied, holding the ax up, his eyes filled with manic energy. "It's giving me the power of Grayskull! I haven't felt this good in years! Maybe it *is* the coke talking after all, but my thoughts are shooting in every direction like... Well, obviously it's the coke talking, but I'm also really pumped up on ideas right now! I wanna, I wanna, I... I wanna... The possibilities, man! They're making my head explode!"

"Return my ax!" Freeman snarled, lunging for the weapon, only for Craig to once again scamper away.

"It's *my* ax now!" Craig shouted. "I guess that make me the mighty Nykolas Freeman, doesn't it? Whoever holds the ax, gets the name!"

As his anger began to boil over, Freeman once again made his way toward Craig, but the younger man had no trouble slipping away and keeping his distance, while making loud whooshing noises as he sliced the ax through the air several times.

"This thing is really growing on me!" he laughed. "Man, how did I go all my life so far without an ax? It's mental!"

"You will return my ax to me," Freeman said firmly, stepping toward him, "and then you will kneel before me and beg for mercy."

"Or what?" Craig asked with a giggle. "What are you gonna do, old man? Chop off my head? Off with *all* their heads!" With that, he swung the ax down several times, as if he was beheading several imaginary figures.

Freeman took another step closer.

"Anyway," Craig continued, "aren't you forgetting one rather important thing?"

"I am not -"

Before Freeman could finish, Becca's scream rang out in the distance, piercing and horrified. Turning, Freeman realized that the sound was coming from further along the riverbank. As the scream continued, he glanced back at Craig, only to see him running excitedly into the forest, waving the ax above his head and shouting unintelligibly.

CHAPTER FORTY-TWO

"NO, THAT'S WHAT I'M telling you," Mary replied, handing another of the print-outs to Detective Casey, "all those bones were basically found together, or at least within twenty feet of one another. In fact, some of the bones you've identified as having belonged to the children were *beneath* the bones that came from the seventeenth century."

"How's that possible?" Casey asked. "I'm no archaeologist, but shouldn't the newer bones have been higher up?"

"Absolutely," she continued, "but..." She stared at the print-out for a moment before sighing. "I can't explain it. Obviously there has to be a reason, but right now I'm drawing a blank."

"And you're sure these records are accurate? Isn't there a chance someone simply made a mistake?"

"We were working fast and cutting a few corners," she admitted, "but we were still being careful. I could maybe accept the idea that we made a mistake with *one* skull, two at a stretch, but not four!" She paused, still trying to make sense of it all but unable to come up with anything. "Is there any word from the site? Have your men started looking for the remains of the other children? There are thirteen still missing."

"We're securing the location."

"But these bones..." She paused. "We *did* find the missing children, didn't we? There's no doubt about it?"

"No doubt at all," he replied, as his radio crackled to life. "We've got four bodies and we expect to find the rest shortly. Excuse me, Doctor Baker, I have to take this."

As the detective walked away, Mary remained lost in thought, still looking through the print-outs. Completely absorbed in her work, she failed to notice as Daniel and Doctor Clarke came to the door, eager to learn the latest.

"Well?" Daniel asked after a moment. "Is it true?"

"About the children?" She paused for a moment, before nodding. "The metal plate on that knee was traced back to its manufacturer, who confirmed that it had been used on a little boy named Robert Swanson. He was the son of the pub's landlord, and one of the seventeen who disappeared. The police have sealed off the site now and are looking for the rest of the bodies. My bet is that they'll find them pretty quickly."

"But how could they have been up there?" Daniel asked. "How could the bodies of twenty-first century kids be mixed in with bones from the *seventeenth* century?"

"I have no idea."

"They even looked..." He paused, as if he was hesitant about continuing. "I mean, just from a visual inspection, they looked as old and weathered as the rest, as if they'd been down in the ground for hundreds of years."

"I can't explain that," Mary said with a sigh. "I'm sure they have experts in that sort of thing, people who can explain the irregularities." She watched as Doctor Clarke made his way over to the bar and began to pour himself a pint of Guinness. For a moment, she considered asking him to pour another, before realizing that it'd be better to keep a clear head. Besides, Clarke had long ago started down the road of functional alcoholism, and she didn't much fancy going the same way. "I said I'd go up to the site later and offer some advice," she muttered finally. "I don't know, maybe I can help, but... I feel like the whole world makes no sense right now."

"At least this means there's no more drilling going on," Daniel pointed out. "Maybe we can use this to our advantage."

"The children are the priority right now," she replied, still watching Doctor Clarke, who seemed uncharacteristically quiet. She wanted to ask if he was okay, but somehow she felt he wasn't the kind of man who'd appreciate such a question.

"The media's heard all about it," Daniel continued, heading to the window and looking out at the journalists who'd gathered in the car-park. "I guess the story has that perfect mix of intrigue and kids."

Making her way over to join him, Mary looked out at the chaotic scene. After a moment, her gaze settled on one woman in particular, who was standing back as if to observe the others. Somehow this woman seemed different, as if an old soul was staring out from behind a young face. Mary couldn't quite explain the sensation, but a couple of seconds later she was startled when the woman turned and looked at her directly, as if she'd sensed the attention. They maintained eye contact for a moment, before Mary finally forced herself to look away. Somehow certain that the woman was still staring at her, she felt distinctly uncomfortable before finally glancing back, only to see that the woman had disappeared entirely.

"Weird," she muttered.

Suddenly there was the sound of breaking glass. Mary and Daniel both turned to see Guinness slopping across the floor, and Doctor Clarke immediately let out a selection of curse words under his breath as he looked down at his shaking hand, having dropped the glass.

"Are you okay?" Mary asked, before she had time to reconsider the question.

"I'm fine," he huffed, grabbing some tea towels from behind the bar and tossing them onto the large puddle. "I'll clean it up later. Or maybe they have a little woman who comes to do that for them." Clearly frustrated, he grabbed another glass and began to pour a second Guinness, but he was still mumbling away to himself.

"He seems annoyed about something," Daniel whispered.

"Give us a moment alone," Mary replied.

He seemed poised to protest, but after a moment Daniel headed to the door, muttering something about checking the jeep. Once he was gone, Mary made her way over to the pile of tea towels and crouched down, trying to soak up as much of the soaked Guinness as she could manage.

"Leave it," Clarke grumbled. "Let the cleaning lady do it."

"I think the landlord has enough to deal with today," she replied. "He doesn't need more problems."

"I doubt he'll be complaining. Business'll be booming with all those journalists in town."

"His son was one of the children who went missing," she reminded him. "It was actually his son's knee that made us realize what we'd found."

"It was?" Clarke seemed surprised, as if he hadn't really been paying attention. "Well, I'm sure that's... *unpleasant* for the poor fellow."

Picking up the sopping pile of tea towels, Mary carried them behind the bar and tossed them into a laundry basket, before grabbing a mop and bucket.

"I hate jealousy," Clarke said suddenly.

She turned to him. "I'm sorry?"

"I hate it in all its forms," he continued, before taking a sip from his freshly-poured Guinness. "I've always felt that jealousy is the most craven, idiotic of emotions. I despise it."

"Who's jealous?" she asked cautiously.

He opened his mouth to answer, before taking another sip. "I am," he admitted finally.

She paused. "Of what?"

"Of you! Of this!" He sighed. "Just as I'm poised to admit my mistakes regarding Nykolas Freeman, you're on the verge of revealing all about the Battle of Sharpeton, and you've even uncovered the last resting place of Captain Villiers to boot! You'll make your name in the archeology community just as mine is destroyed."

"It's not like that..."

"Oh, it is," he muttered. "Believe me, it's cut-throat out there. There are plenty of people who will delight in my downfall. I'll be metaphorically tied up and roasted on a spit, with an apple in my mouth. It might surprise you to learn this, Miss Baker, but I have a reputation for being somewhat difficult to get along with."

"You do?" she asked innocently.

"Mostly undeserved," he added, "but... not entirely. And I have made a few enemies here and there."

"No-one's going to ridicule you," she told him, setting the bucket in the sink and starting to fill it with water. "Nykolas Freeman isn't the only part of your career. You've done a lot of other good work."

"Freeman was the pillar," he replied. "He was the only truly fresh thing I brought to the table. Now I know he wasn't real, I see that I was nothing special in the academic community. Just another old fool, stirring the pot without adding anything fresh." Before he could continue, his phone started buzzing in his pocket and he slipped it out. "Unknown number," he muttered, before sighing again. "I suppose I should take this. Maybe *I'm* the one who should get a job flipping burgers."

As he headed through to the pub's back room and answered the call, Mary took the bucket over to the mess of Guinness and glass that covered the floor. She felt certain that Doctor Clarke was being too hard on himself and, as she crouched down to start cleaning, she began to think instead about the pile of bones that had been discovered. She still didn't understand how the remains of the children could have ended up mixed in with the bones from the long-forgotten battle, and she felt as if the world around her was no longer behaving the laws of logic.

"I'm down the rabbit-hole," she muttered finally, as she got to work cleaning the mess.

***

"No, I'm a lecturer at the University of Westchester," Doctor Clarke replied as he sat in the pub's empty back room with his pint of Guinness. "I'm sorry, who are you? How did you get this number?"

He waited, but the woman on the other end of the line seemed upset, as if she was sniffing back tears.

"Are you a journalist?" he continued. "If you -"

"I found your card," she said suddenly, her voice trembling with shock. "Your business card, or whatever you call it. Did you... I know this is going to sound strange, but did you come to my house? Maybe to visit my daughter?"

Clarke paused. "If you mean the Baxendale house, and if your daughter is named Laura Woodley, then... Yes, I was there briefly. I'm a historian, I wanted to speak to her about the business that occurred a while ago." He waited for a reply, but the woman seemed to be sobbing more than ever. "Might I ask what this is about?"

"Did she say anything unusual?" the woman asked. "Anything that worried you?"

"She seemed a little emotional."

"What exactly did you talk about?"

"Your daughter claimed to have encountered the undead Nykolas Freeman," he pointed out. "I wanted to hear the story straight from the horse's mouth, so to speak. I must admit, she became a little agitated after a while, so I left. I hope I didn't step on any toes, but I can assure you that my interest is purely academic."

Again he waited. This time, as well as the constant sniffs, he heard what sounded like a paging system in the background, with a voice calling for a doctor.

"When I got home yesterday afternoon," the woman said finally, "I found Laura... She seemed to be doing so well recently, she really seemed to be getting better. I'd stopped worrying about leaving her alone."

"What do you mean, you *found* her?" he asked cautiously, with a sense of fear in his gut.

"It's my fault. I shouldn't have been so slack. I should have known she could relapse and -"

"What happened?" he continued. "Please, just tell me... Is your daughter alright?"

"I found Laura in the bath," she replied, her voice cracking slightly. "She'd cut her wrists open, the water was filling with blood. I pulled her out, she hadn't been in there very long so... They don't know if she'll survive. I'm sitting here waiting for news, I honestly don't know if my daughter is going to live or not. It's just a miracle that I got home when I did."

"Which hospital are you at?"

"Wyvern Lodge. She'll probably be moved back to the psychiatric ward if..." She paused. "If she makes it out of..."

Clarke sat in silence for a moment, listening to the sound of the woman sobbing on the other end of the phone.

"I'm going to come over there," he said finally, even though he knew there wasn't much he could do to help. Somehow, deep down, he felt as if he might be partially responsible for Laura Woodley's situation. "I don't know what I can offer," he stammered, "but I shall be there as soon as possible. Perhaps..."

His voice trailed off, and a moment later he heard another voice over the line, as if a doctor had arrived to provide an update. He tried to hear what was being said, but a moment later the call cut off. For a few seconds, he sat in stunned silence, thinking back to his brief encounter with Laura.

"The car," he stammered finally, getting to his feet and leaving the Guinness behind as he hurried to the door. "Get the car!"

CHAPTER FORTY-THREE

"BUT YOU DON'T ACTUALLY know this girl, do you?" Daniel asked as he took a left turn, following the signs for the hospital at Wyvern Lodge.

"I met her briefly," Doctor Clarke muttered, sitting in the jeep's passenger seat with his suitcase resting on his lap. "I don't know, I feel as if... I worry I might have contributed to some collapse in her recovery. I can't explain it, but I'm compelled to go and see her for myself."

"It's called being human," Daniel told him, "and giving a crap about other people. What's wrong, is it a new sensation for you?"

He waited for a reply, but after a moment he glanced over and saw that Doctor Clarke seemed lost in thought. Having previously written the old man off as a self-absorbed blowhard, he couldn't help but feel shocked by this sudden change. It was as if finally a trace of human concern had broken through and -

Glancing back at the road, he suddenly saw a figure stumbling out from one of the bushes. Slamming his foot on the brakes, Daniel was just about able to bring the jeep to a screeching halt in time, although the figure stumbled a little and bumped against the bonnet.

"What the hell is that youth doing?" Clarke hissed. "Does he *want* to get run over?"

Daniel watched as the guy, who seemed to be in his late teens or early twenties, hurried to the door and tapped on the window with his left hand.

"I don't pick up hitch-hikers!"

"Please, dude," the guy replied, seeming flustered. "You've gotta help me!"

Daniel hesitated for a moment, before winding the window down. "We're in a hurry."

"Just drive!" Clarke muttered darkly.

"Dude," the guy continued, "I'm all alone out here, miles from anywhere! My name's Craig and -" He froze. "No, wait! Ignore that, it's wrong! My name's not Craig! Sorry, I've been out here forming a new political party, my name's not Craig at all, it's actually -"

"Sorry," Daniel replied, reaching out to wind the window back up, "but we really don't have time for -"

Suddenly Craig took his right hand out from behind his back and swung the ax, crunching the blade straight into Daniel's chest. As Daniel gasped, Craig ripped the blade back out and then struck him again, this time in the shoulder, with enough force to break the seat.

Fumbling for the latch, Doctor Clarke pushed the door open on his side and tumbled out of the jeep, landing hard on the ground with his suitcase still clutched in his arms. Hearing the sound of more impacts inside the jeep, he stumbled to his feet, trying not to panic as he looked around and saw that there was no sign of anyone else in the area. On both sides of the road, rolling fields spread to -

Suddenly he heard footsteps coming closer. Spinning around, he saw Craig hurrying toward him with a bloodied ax raised in his right hand. Taking a step back, Clarke stumbled and fell, landing hard on the asphalt.

"Man, that was a rush!" Craig shouted, stopping in front of him. Daniel's blood was dripping from the ax, spattering onto the road. "I feel like... I feel like there's some truth in what I'm doing here today, do you know what I mean? I feel like I've unlocked the infinite knowledge that has been dormant in my soul since I was first spat out from between my dear old mother's legs! All mothers start out as martyrs, don't they?" He paused. "I should write that down. I'm having some profound insights today!"

Scrambling back, too scared to turn his back and run, Doctor Clarke stared in horror at the boy's wild eyes.

"You've gotta believe me," Craig continued, sniffing back blood and briefly wiping his nose, "today has been mental. Brilliantly, overwhelmingly mental. I already killed my first witch and, dude, I think the guy driving this jeep just now might have been some type of warlock! It's insane how clear everything seems suddenly! I think I'm having a vision!"

Pulling the zip open on the side of his suitcase,

Clarke reached inside, pushing his hand through the layers of clothes until he felt the handle of his flintlock pistol.

"What you got in there?" Craig asked with a smile. "Something cool? Let me see!"

Slipping the pistol out, Clarke checked to make sure it was loaded and then he aimed it directly at Craig's head.

"No way!" Craig said excitedly. "That is *so* cool! Is it loaded? Please tell me it's loaded!"

"What did you do to him?" Clarke stammered, glancing at the jeep. Reaching into his pocket, he tried to find his phone. "Daniel! Are you okay in there? Daniel, say something!"

"I don't think he's gonna be saying anything for a while," Craig replied, staring at the pistol. "Probably not ever again, if I'm honest. I'll go and check in a moment. But seriously, dude, can you shoot me in the shoulder?"

Adjusting his finger on the trigger, Doctor Clarke prepared to fire.

"Like, right here," Craig continued, tapping himself at the top of his left arm. "I've always wondered what it'd feel like to get shot! For real, it's kinda been a fantasy of mine, and that's not just the coke talking. Plus, it'd leave a kick-ass scar for when I'm older." He waited breathlessly, still staring at the gun. "What are you waiting for, dude? I promise I won't, like, get mad or anything. Just aim for my shoulder and blast away. I don't even think I can feel pain properly right now, so you'd really be doing me a favor!"

"You're insane," Clarke replied, his voice

trembling with fear. Still on the ground, he looked at the jeep again. "Daniel! If you can hear me, call the police!"

"Come on!" Craig shouted. "Be a pal! Shoot me in the shoulder! Do it!"

Clarke turned to him, his eyes wide with shock.

"Or do I have to *make* you?" Craig asked, taking a step closer and holding the ax up. "I am the great Nykolas Freeman and I have come to rid the world of all its scourges!" He started laughing, and for a moment he couldn't seem to control his giggles. "Man, that cracks me up."

"If you come one step closer," Clarke said firmly, "I will..." Stopping suddenly, he paused for a moment. "Wait... What did you just say?"

"I said it cracks me up! I'm Nykolas Freeman, killer of witches, bitches and priests! And even if I say so myself, so far I seem to be exceptionally good at it!"

"Freeman?" Clarke paused, his mind racing. "What kind of madness is this?" He considered pulling the trigger, but suddenly he spotted the engraving of a snake on the ax's handle, and the sight seemed to transfix him. "Where did you get that?" he asked, his voice filled with a sense of awe.

"This old thing?" Craig looked at the blood-soaked ax for a moment. "To be honest, dude, I nicked it off some stinky old geezer with, like, a rotten body. It seems pretty old."

"It can't be the..." Lowering the pistol a little, Doctor Clarke leaned forward to get a better look. "It can't be, it just can't be..."

"Can't be what, dude?"

"Let me see that item!" Clarke hissed, reaching toward him. "It looks... It looks authentic, but it can't be the real..."

"Dude -"

"Let me see it!" he shouted.

Craig paused for a moment, as if he was genuinely considering the request. His whole body was trembling, and as the drugs moved through his system they were starting to make him sweat profusely.

"Swap," he said finally.

Clarke frowned. "I beg your pardon?"

"I'll give you the ax, just for a moment," Craig continued, "if you let me hold that cool-looking gun. Do we have a deal?"

Clarke looked at the pistol, before slowly turning it around and holding it out toward him. "I must examine that ax," he explained, his voice trembling with fear and anticipation. "I insist! This could be the most important discovery of my entire career!"

Craig hesitated for a moment. After a few seconds, however, he held out the ax, and then he dropped it at Doctor Clarke's feet while simultaneously snatching the pistol from his outstretched hand.

"It can't be the real thing," Clarke stammered, picking up the ax and examining it, almost in a trance. "I must be some kind of highly-detailed facsimile, or..." He ran a fingertip along the handle's edge, feeling the groove of the engraved snake pattern. "It matches the description to a staggering degree, it's just how I always imagined it, and the..." Taking a closer look at the blood-stained blade, he briefly held his breath, as if nothing else in the whole world mattered. "It seems authentic," he said finally. "I can't... I can't quite believe it, but..."

His voice trailed off as he continued to inspect the ax.

"Is this thing loaded?" Craig asked, aiming the pistol at his left eye and peering down the barrel. "It's kinda cool. I've never held a proper gun before."

"Freeman was real," Clarke whispered, still examining the ax. "Nykolas Freeman was..." He paused, before looking up at Craig. "Where did you get this?"

"I told you. Some scabby old dude with, like, a rotten face and serious body odor problems." He paused, frowning slightly with the pistol still aimed at his own face. "You should have seen the special effects make-up, it was unreal. Like, I could actually see holes in his flesh, and bits of bone sticking through. It was kinda gross and..." He fell silent for a moment, with the pistol still in his trembling right hand. "I'm starting to wonder..."

"Take me to him immediately!" Clarke said firmly. "Whoever he is, he must tell me where he found this ax! I was right all along, Nykolas Freeman was real!"

"I'm not taking you to anyone," Craig replied nonchalantly. "No way, dude. I've got things to do, people to see."

"I insist!" Clarke continued, wincing as he started getting to his feet. "This is a staggering discovery, my life's work isn't over at all! It's only just begun, I have to -"

"Nah."

"I insist!"

"Dude, seriously..."

With that Craig aimed the pistol at him and pulled the trigger, blasting Doctor Clarke's head away and sending his lifeless body slumping back down onto the asphalt as birds took flight in shock from nearby trees. Blood and brain matter had been instantly sprayed for several feet, and all that was left of the old man's head was a fragment on the left side of his chin, which hung by a thread of skin from the exposed meat around the top of his spine. More blood was flowing from the meaty wound, spreading across the road.

Reaching down, Craig picked up the ax and held it in his left hand, while admiring the pistol in his right.

"Cool," he said finally. "Ultra, ultra cool."

Nearby, blood was dribbling from the door on the driver's side of the jeep, and Daniel's hand was hanging down almost to the ground.

CHAPTER FORTY-FOUR

"WE'RE GETTING EVERY LAST scrap out of the ground," Detective Casey told Mary as he led her through the cordon at the dig site. Spots of cold rain were falling now, as men in plastic uniforms worked up ahead. "We're going to be here for a few weeks at least. This is a crime scene now, there's absolutely no doubt about that."

"If there's any way I can help," Mary replied, "just let me know."

"Anything that isn't part of our investigation will eventually be released to you," he explained, as they stopped near an area where a forensics team was sifting through patches of soil. "It might take some time for that to happen, but you should get all the bones and other items that you were originally looking for. It'll just take time."

"That almost doesn't seem important now," Mary muttered, shivering as a cold blast of wind passed across the site. "I can't imagine how the parents of those children must be feeling with all the -"

"Why is *she* here?" an angry voice shouted suddenly.

Turning, Mary saw Mr. Carter waving frantically at Detective Casey from behind a police cordon.

"I demand to speak to someone in charge!" Carter continued. "This is outrageous!"

"He's a nice guy," Casey muttered. "He's spent the entire afternoon telling me that he's going to have me fired for doing my job. Seems to have his priorities in order."

"Unfortunately," Mary replied, "the terms of the original contract mean that the company retains ownership of anything we find during the dig. Apart from the more modern items, obviously. If Carter decides to make life difficult for me, he can."

"Then maybe I should go and explain a few things to him," Casey said with a sigh. "I think it's about time Mr. Carter and his company were dealt a dose of reality."

As the detective headed over to speak to Carter, Mary turned her back to the wind and pulled her phone from her pocket. After trying but failing to get through to Daniel, she tried Doctor Clarke's number, but still she had no luck. She figured they should have reached Wyvern Lodge a while back, and that Daniel was probably on his way back by now. As she slipped her phone back into her pocket, however, she happened to glance past one of the police tents, and she was surprised to see that the woman from outside the pub was now watching the dig site. Having been told that members of the public were being kept well away, she frowned for a moment, before heading over to see what the woman wanted.

"It's cold up here," Mary said as she got closer, hoping to start a conversation. "Coldest rain I've ever felt in my life. Almost like ice."

She waited for a reply, but the woman remained silent, watching the police as they continued their work.

"Are you with them?" Mary asked, stopping next to the woman and turning to look back at the site. Again she waited, but after a moment she realized that the woman seemed lost in thought. "Are you with the media?" she continued, hoping to get an answer. "If you are, I don't think you should be up here. The families of the dead children are supposed to be coming soon, to see the site, and I'm not sure how they'd react if -"

"I knew this day would come," the woman said suddenly, her eyes still fixed on the scene ahead. "I tried to hold it off for as long as possible, but I always knew that eventually the tide of fate would be too strong." Her voice trailed off for a moment, and finally she turned to Mary. "If you doubt me, just feel the rain. The colder it gets, the closer we move to a terrible tragedy. The two ends of the battle will meet, and it has always been foretold that this is the first sign of the impending disaster. England shall turn against itself again."

"I..." Pausing, Mary began to wonder if the woman was entirely sane. "I'm really not quite following you..."

"Nykolas Freeman walks upon the world once more," the woman continued. "One day, the girl will go beneath the ground and awaken him yet again. I see now that this is unstoppable. She will not be alone. She will be with others, but she will give them orders. She will be hurt by this point, but she will know what she has to do. Sacrifice will be required, and she will have the necessary strength. Freeman can still be useful to the world, but not yet. He must sleep again before he is called.."

Mary waited, but after a moment she watched as the woman turned to look at the dig site again.

"Well," Mary said finally, "I'm not quite sure what... That all sounds kind of dramatic and, um, I don't know whether..."

Her voice trailed off as she tried to think of something else to say. All around, the freezing rain seemed to be getting a little stronger, and she was starting to wonder whether she should find somewhere to shelter. Before she could do anything, however, she spotted movement in the distance and saw a coach slowly making its way along the dirt road that cut through the moor. With a heavy heart, she realized that the first group of grieving parents was being brought up.

"We should go," she muttered, turning to the woman, only to find that once again she had disappeared. Looking around, she tried to work out how, exactly, the woman had managed to vanish without a trace in just a few seconds.

"This is an outrage!" Carter shouted in the distance, and Mary looked over just in time to see the man stomping back toward his car. After a moment their eyes met, and Mary immediately saw the scorn in his expression. "You!" he yelled, pointing straight at her. "Don't think you've heard the last of this! I wouldn't be surprised if you arranged this entire stunt as some way to protect your precious dig! I will have you fired before the day is through!"

Mary watched as Carter got into his car. As he sped away from the site, he almost collided with the coach, and he used his car horn to express his extreme displeasure as he drove past. The coach, meanwhile, came to a stop nearby, and a moment later its passengers began to step out. The parents of the missing children all looked stunned as they arrived to see the police operation, and Mary noticed that the pub's landlord was among them.

Not wanting to intrude upon their grief, she turned and made her way to one of the police tents, hoping to keep out of sight so that the families could visit – and mourn – in peace. Reaching into her pocket, she pulled out her phone and tried once again to get through to Daniel.

CHAPTER FORTY-FIVE

SHIVERING AS SHE SAT in the long grass, Becca stared straight ahead, reliving the moment over and over in her mind. Her whole body was shaking more and more violently with each passing moment, but all she could think about was the sight of Julie's corpse in the river with a cloud of blood leaking into the water.

"It's not real," she whispered, her lips trembling with shock. "She's okay. She'll come back. She'll -"

Hearing footsteps nearby, she turned and saw Freeman making his way back from the river. As he reached her, he stared down into her eyes for a moment, and she looked up at the rotten flesh that clung to his skull.

"She's okay, isn't she?" she asked after a moment. "Promise she's okay. Tell me she's not hurt."

She waited, but Freeman gave no answer. He simply watched her for a few seconds and then stepped past, finally stopping again and sitting on the edge of a broken wall. His right hand continually clenched and unclenched, as if it missed the feel of the ax.

"She's just..." Becca turned to him with tears in her eyes, desperately hoping that he might tell her not to worry. She remembered all the times her mother had told her to stop being a worrywart, but she felt that for once she might have good reason to feel scared. She wanted Freeman to make everything better, but instead he simply sat and stared down at his empty right hand, as if he was thinking about the ax that Craig had snatched from him.

Above, the gray sky rumbled slightly with a hint of thunder.

"I do not understand this world," Freeman said finally, his voice sounding darker and more gravelly than ever. "I have tried, but I confess now that it seems beyond me. I am from a simpler time, and perhaps it is simply the case that I am incapable of ever knowing this new England. If I cannot divine witches, and if I cannot hunt and kill the Catholic scourge, then I..."

His voice trailed off for a moment.

"Then I see no place for myself," he added after a few seconds. "I am not needed here."

"What do you mean?" Becca asked, crawling over to him and looking up into his rotten eyes. "Is Julie okay? Is she coming back?"

"So long as I held my ax," he continued, "I was able to make myself believe that I had value. The ax was an emblem of my purpose, a symbol of everything for which I stood. Now that the ax has been taken from me, I am forced to recognize the truth. I would do well to simply crawl into a grave somewhere and wait for eternity to pass. Perhaps death will come, if I am lucky." He glanced at Becca. "That is almost what I was doing when you found me. A witch tore the ground open an forced me down there, and she sealed the pit with a gold coin. Now I think she might have been right. She saw that I no longer belong in the world, and she sought to shuffle me away. I am free again now, thanks to you, but what am I to do?"

He paused, as if he could barely get the words out.

"I was scared," he added. "Before the witch caught up to me, I knew I should go to London, to seek out the royal palace and offer my service once again, but when I set out... I get as far as Reading, crossing the countryside because I dared not enter the towns, moving at night so as not to be seen. Past Reading, however, the fear began to grip me with increasing strength, until one night I reached the crest of a hill and saw all of London spread out before me. The lights, the noise, the feeling in the very air itself... There were even lights in the sky, closer and brighter than the stars. At that moment, I knew fear greater than any I had thought possible, and I felt compelled to turn around. So I can back here, to the part of the world in which I feel some semblance of familiarity, but I cannot persist in this state. Hiding away, neglecting my duties... I can hardly call myself Nykolas Freeman any longer if this pitiful fear is all that remains of my soul."

Feeling a few spots of cold rain on her face, Becca waited for him to continue.

"Julie's not coming back, is she?" she asked finally.

"The woman is dead," he replied, "bleeding in the river. Her man appeared gripped by some mania, the likes of which I have never seen before."

"He was on cocaine," Becca explained. "I've never taken it, but I've seen people talk about it on TV."

"You are but a child," he continued, "yet you know more about this world than I."

"I just watched a lot of TV," she told him, before turning to look back across the clearing, toward the river. "I didn't get upset when Daddy died. I was scared of him. But I'm upset about..." She paused, before feeling a tear run down her cheek.

"You should return to your home," Freeman told her, "or find the remaining members of your family, or... I do not know, entirely, but I am sure of one thing. I must find a grave, and I must remain there until the life passes from my body and I slip into death. Perhaps I shall return to the hole in the ground, to the place where you found me. This time, perhaps I will be lucky and the hole will close itself, never to re-open."

Sniffing back tears, Becca looked up at him.

"Aren't you going to help me find my sister?" she asked. "You promised."

"It is a promise I cannot fulfill."

"But you promised!" she said firmly, wiping her eyes.

"There is no more that I -"

"You promised!" she shouted, getting to her feet as she felt a wave of panic in her chest. "First *you* promised, and then *Julie* promised! And now she's dead, so you *have* to do it! You can't break a promise, it's not allowed!"

"Pray, tell me how to find your sister," he replied, "for I know not the means and measures of this world."

"I don't know what you're saying!" she yelled. "You have to help me find Kerry, or I won't ever see them again!"

He stared at her for a moment. "Child, please -"

"You promised!" she said again, more firmly than ever, as she leaned closer to his face. "Please, you have to help me! Alice didn't give up, and neither should we!"

"I do not understand this world," he told her again.

"You understood the light-switch!"

He paused. "What is a... light-switch?"

"The thing you pressed in my house to make the light go on and off. You worked it out all by yourself. If you can do that, you can understand other things too. You're not completely helpless."

He opened his mouth to reply, before hesitating. "The journey alone would take three or four days by foot," he pointed out. "We are far from Sharpeton and -"

"We can drive back," Becca pointed out, turning and looking over at Craig's car. "I know how to make a car go. Daddy used to let me try driving his car on the farm. As long as Craig left the keys, it's easy."

"You can control that metal beast?"

She turned back to him. "It'll be okay as long as

the police don't see. I think maybe if they stopped us, they might have a lot of questions."

"Even if we return to Sharpeton," he replied, "what shall we -"

"We'll find my sister," she reminded him, "and then you can stay with us, if you want! If you don't have any other family, I'm sure Kerry would let you live with us. She probably has a spare room. But please, first you have to help me get back to Sharpeton and then you have to help me find her! Please, I can't do it on my own! You promised! Don't you keep your promises?"

Freeman still seemed hesitant, but finally he got to his feet.

"If this be the very last task I perform in the world," he told her, "then so be it. You are clearly no witch, child, and I know not that you are a Catholic. It would be as well to return you to your family, and this perhaps is one final thing that I can do before I withdraw from existence."

"If he left the keys behind," she explained, as she started leading him toward the car, "it'll be easy to start it. If not, I'm not sure what we'll do." Pulling the door open, she looked inside and immediately saw a set of keys dangling from the ignition.

A few minutes later, once Becca and Freeman were both in the car, the engine started revving and the car lurched forward in a series of stuttering bursts. It took Becca a while to work out how to drive properly, but finally the car started to move a little more smoothly, turning right and heading over to the country lane that led back toward Sharpeton.

Once the car was gone, the scene fell silent for a few minutes, with the only sound coming from the increasingly heavy rain that was starting to fall. Eventually, however, another noise could be heard coming from near the river. Just a few feet from the spot where Julie's body remained in the water, a small buzzing, vibrating sound was ringing out from the grass. Julie's phone, which she'd dropped in the struggle, was lighting up as spots of cold rain fell onto the screen, and the name Kerry was flashing. After a short while, the phone stopped ringing, but it started again just a few seconds later, as someone frantically tried to get through and the name Kerry flashed once again on the screen.

CHAPTER FORTY-SIX

"WHY DIDN'T YOU FIND them before?" a woman shouted angrily, pushing Detective Casey against the side of the tent. "What the hell were all those people doing up here when they were supposed to be searching for our children? Hundreds of cops couldn't find a damn thing, but then a bunch of historians show up and find them right away? How is that even possible?"

"Please calm down," Casey replied, holding his hands up in surrender. "We're still at the beginning of an analysis that we hope -"

"We want answers!" another woman yelled, as the mood of the gathered parents seemed to have soured over the course of just a few minutes. "Our children have been up here, rotting in the cold ground, and we were told that you lot had done everything possible to find them! Why were you lying to us?"

As Casey continued to deal with the angry crowd, Mary spotted the landlord from the King's Head standing a little way apart, watching the police as they continued to work. Heading over to him, she felt as if she should say something, although she knew she couldn't really help. As she reached him, however, she saw that he was holding the framed photo that had previously hung in the pub, and she looked down at the image of seventeen smiling schoolchildren standing next to their bus.

"Do you have children, Doctor Baker?" he asked after a moment.

She shook her head.

"Don't want them, or..."

"It's complicated," she told him. Better that than to admit the truth and have to talk about clinics, examinations and cold steel on flesh.

"My ex-wife's coming to town tomorrow," he continued, still watching the police. "It sounded like she was having a breakdown over the phone. I told her there's no need for her to be here, it's not like she can do anything for Robert now, but I suppose people just like to have a little closure, don't they?"

"I can't even imagine what you're going through," she told him.

"Have they found the rest of him yet, or is it just the knee?"

"The knee is the only part that's been positively identified so far," she replied, "but..."

Her voice trailed off.

"I'm sure the police are doing the best they can," he said after a moment. "They said it was your lot who made the first discovery."

"We were looking for something very old," she replied. "I've been on lots of digs over the years, and I never flinched when I found bodies in the ground. But this time, learning that some of those bones were..." She paused for a moment. "I can't quite get my head around it."

"How did no-one find them before?" he asked.

"I have no idea."

"I heard someone saying they were deep down. Like, mixed in with the stuff you found from some battle?"

She nodded.

"How's that possible?" he continued. "Shouldn't they have been higher up, closer to the surface?"

"They should," she told him. "There are a lot of question marks still hanging over this site. We don't even know why the Battle of Sharpeton was hidden from the history books. I've got to be honest with you, Mr. Monkton, it doesn't make any sense to me at all. I can only assume that some kind of weird geological phenomenon somehow sucked the modern bones down until they reached the..." Her voice trailed off as she realized how ridiculous that idea sounded, although to be fair it was the only answer so far that was at least partially grounded in science. "This isn't really my area of study," she added finally. "Hopefully someone will come in and find an explanation. It'll get figured out eventually."

"Unless they ended up back there somehow," he suggested.

She frowned. "I'm not sure that I follow..."

"What kind of injuries did they have?"

"I'm really not -"

"What if they died in the battle?" he continued.

She opened her mouth to reply, but the words caught in her throat. "The Battle of Sharpeton took place around three hundred and fifty years ago, so..."

"But what if they ended up back there?" he asked. "I know it sounds crazy, but then none of this really makes sense, does it? What if somehow the children fell through a hole in time and ended up right in the middle of the battle, and that's why their bones were down there with the rest?"

"That's simply not possible," she replied, feeling a little sorry for him. He was clearly clutching at straws, trying to come up with any explanation that brought him answers, no matter how absurd they might seem. "We just have to be patient and let the investigators do their jobs. I know that must be extremely hard for you, but I think it's better than leaping to wild conclusions."

"The fog isn't right in this part of the world," he continued. "Everyone in Sharpeton knows it."

"I'm sorry?"

"People don't talk about it much, they're scared, but it's true. When the really thick fog comes rolling in across the moor, it brings something with it." He paused for a moment. "There was fog that morning, when they disappeared. The same kind you get from time to time, the kind that comes on quickly and brings..." Again he paused, as if he was worried about saying too much. He glanced over his shoulder, watching as the other parents continued to angrily confront Detective Casey, and then he turned back to Mary. "There are lots of people around here who've heard voices in the fog. What if there's more to it *just* voices?"

Mary hesitated for a moment, wondering whether she should mention her own strange encounter, the time when she'd heard voices calling out on a foggy day. Those voices had sounded so real, and she'd heard at least one name that was linked to the disappearance of the children, but she still didn't feel ready to start believing in something so insane. She'd always been a firm believed in rational explanations, and talking about mysterious fog would make her feel almost like a different person.

"I think the fog took them," the landlord continued, "and I think it put them back down in the battle. There, I said it. You can think I'm crazy, if you want, but..."

His voice trailed off.

"I'm pretty sure there'd be a record of something like that happening," she pointed out, before realizing that since the battle itself had been covered up, no such record would exist. In fact, the more she thought about it, the more she felt as if the sudden appearance of seventeen children in the middle of the battlefield might explain a lot more about the situation. If the Royalists and Parliamentarians had suddenly slaughtered those children, perhaps they could have been too shocked to continue the fight. She knew the suggestion was a huge leap, but at the same time it came closer to making sense than any of her other theories. All she had to do was accept the idea of time-traveling fog, and everything else slipped into place.

She sighed.

"There'll be another explanation," she said finally. "There has to be."

"Ask around," the landlord replied. "There are a few people who dismiss talk of the fog, but the rest... If someone lives in Sharpeton for long enough, and if they come out onto the moor when there's fog about, they'll tell you about the voices." Spotting some of the other parents heading to the coach, he took a step back. "Mark my words, they'll never properly explain what happened here. My ex-wife told me I was crazy, but the fog on the moor is more than *just* fog. Everyone knows it. They know about the witch, too!"

"Witch?" Mary replied. "What witch?"

"Some say her name's Kate," he continued. "Some say she's Black Annis herself. Either way, she's been seen plenty of times over the years. She knows about the fog. She knows what's happening here, and she always appears when something's wrong. If I'm right about what happened, people'll start seeing her around. I'm sure of it!"

"What does she look like?" Mary asked, thinking back to the strange woman she'd encountered a couple of times during the day.

"I've never seen her myself," he replied. "There are plenty who have, though. It's said she watches over the moor and tries to protect the people as best she can. They say she doesn't always succeed, though. Some powers are too strong for anyone to hold them back."

With that, he turned and headed toward the

coach. Tempted to call after him and ask him what he meant, Mary finally realized she could wait until she got to the pub later in the evening. The landlord seemed to have developed something of a melodramatic streak, but she figured he was in shock after finally learning that his son's body had been found. If the poor guy wanted to retreat into some kind of fantasy world about haunted fog and witches on the moor, she didn't have the heart to argue with him, and she *definitely* didn't want to get sucked into contemplating such wild ideas.

Although, as she looked around, she couldn't help checking to see if there was any sign of the strange woman from earlier. She was under no illusion that the woman had been a witch, of course, but she still felt as if her presence had been unusual.

"Mary!" Detective Casey called out, waving at her. "I need your help with something!"

Nodding, she set off to join him. It felt good to be working, because at least then her mind couldn't start straying onto other subjects. Checking her phone, however, she couldn't help but wonder why Daniel still hadn't returned.

CHAPTER FORTY-SEVEN

"I NEED A RIDE!" Craig shouted, running along the road as the car screeched to a halt. Once again almost clattering into the vehicle, he nevertheless managed to race around to the passenger-side door and knock frantically on the window. "Give me a ride into town, yeah?"

Rolling her window down, the woman inside seemed shocked.

"Craig?" she said cautiously. "Is that you?"

"The name's Freeman," he replied, taking a step back. "Nykolas Freeman. Scourge of the entire country! I got a lift from a bird a while ago, but she chucked me out after a couple of miles. Please, if you don't help me, I'll have to walk the rest of the way across the moor! It's gonna start pissing it down soon."

"Where's Julie?" she asked. "Craig, I've been trying to call her all afternoon! She sent me a message, something about my sister! Do you know what's going on?"

He frowned. "And who might you be, my dear?"

"Craig, you know me!" she hissed, opening the car door and stepping out to join him. "Kerry, remember? I used to live around here!"

"Why do you persist in calling me by that foul name?" he asked. "I am not Craig! I am -"

"Are you on coke again?"

He hesitated. "It's possible, but only because it helped me to reach this higher state of understanding. Do you want some?"

"I have to find Julie," Kerry replied. "It sounded like something was really wrong with Becca. I can give you a lift, Craig, but we need to get -"

"What are you wearing?" he asked, interrupting her.

"It's my uniform from work," she told him. "I was pulling a double-shift at the factory, that's why I didn't answer the bloody phone sooner. Craig, seriously, I need to find my sister! If she's not -"

Before she could say another word, Craig raised Doctor Clarke's pistol at her face and pulled the trigger, but the only result was a dull clicking sound.

"What the hell is *that*?" Kerry asked cautiously.

"I guess it's out of ammo," he muttered, examining the pistol for a moment before shrugging and tossing it aside. Smiling, he held up the ax. "Good thing I've still got this baby, huh?"

With that, he lunged at her, swinging the ax down toward her face. She ducked out of the way at the last moment, leaving the blade to slam into the car's roof.

"Craig!" she yelled. "What the hell are you doing?"

Letting out a cry of anger, he swung at her again, this time shattering one of the windows on the side of the car.

"Jesus Christ!" Kerry shouted, stepping back.

"I'm *better* than Jesus!" he yelled, his eyes filled with excitement. "I'm Nykolas Freeman, and I'm going to lead this country to a new age of glory! England expects!"

Swinging the ax several times, he narrowly missed Kerry's face as she took a couple of steps back.

"Mad skills, yeah?" he continued. "You should've seen the sorry old bastard I took this from. The guy stank like you'd never believe. He was really into the role, but he was just wasting this thing. I've already slain one witch and two warlocks, and when I get back to town I intend to gather some acolytes who'll hang on my every word and let me lead them to the promised land! I'm gonna set up a new political party and we're gonna sweep the Tories and Labour aside. Everyone'll love us, 'cause we're gonna follow the teachings of the great Nykolas Freeman and make England strong again!"

"You owe me for a new window," she said firmly. "Craig, I don't have time for your coked-up rubbish! I have to find my sister in case she ends up in some kind of -"

She ducked just as he swung the ax at her head, and this time she hit back, punching him hard on the nose. As he staggered away, she stepped toward him and hit him again, this time sending him sprawling to the ground. As he landed in a heap, he dropped the ax, which skated across the asphalt and into the weeds at the side of the road.

"You're still a complete dick then, I see," she muttered, stepping over his unconscious body. She hesitated for a moment, figuring she should find the ax and confiscate it so he couldn't hurt anyone, but she wasn't entirely sure where it had landed and she felt more than ever that she had to get to town and find her sister.

Climbing into the car, she floored the throttle, heading off in a cloud of smoke. As she disappeared into the distance, Craig slowly began to wake up, still dazed after having been momentarily knocked out.

CHAPTER FORTY-EIGHT

"LAURA'S SHOWING SIGNS OF improvement,"
Doctor Carlisle explained in the hospital corridor, "but
we're going to keep her here tonight for observation and
then tomorrow we'll most likely transfer her back to the
psychiatric ward. I'm sorry, Mrs. Woodley, but for some
reason Laura seems to have suffered a real setback. I
remain hopeful, though, and -"

Suddenly a scream rang out from one of the
nearby rooms. Mrs. Woodley and Doctor Carlisle
immediately ran through and found a nurse trying to
subdue Laura, who'd woken suddenly and had begun
desperately crying out.

"Sedate her!" Doctor Carlisle shouted, rushing
into the room.

"They're coming!" Laura screamed. "They're
back! Can't you tell? They're coming!"

Her eyes filled with tears, Mrs. Woodley stared
as a needle was pushed into her daughter's arm,

delivering some kind of sedative. Unable to watch any longer, she turned and headed out into the corridor, but a moment later she saw a woman standing over by the doors at the far end. The woman seemed troubled by something, but then – before Mrs. Woodley could ask anything – she vanished in the blink of an eye.

"They're coming!" Laura shouted, although her voice sounded slurred now as the sedative began to take effect. "They're coming," she continued, starting to whisper now as she slumped against the bed. "It's not just him! They're coming, they're *all* coming! They're going to see them again!"

Once she was unconscious, Doctor Carlisle took a step back, clearly shocked.

"I don't understand," he muttered, "she was doing so well just a week ago. Now she seems worse than ever."

CHAPTER FORTY-NINE

RAIN WAS FALLING FASTER and harder than ever now, crashing down from the darkening sky as rumbles of thunder could be heard in the distance. A couple of police vans were bumping across the muddy ground, ferrying the forensics team back to town after a long day's work, while a series of arc lights stood nearby, casting light across the site.

"That's everyone," Detective Casey told Mary as he joined her in the tent's doorway. "We're the last two up here right now. I can't leave yet, not until the night crew have shown up to guard the place, but it's fine if you want to head back, get something to eat."

"I'd rather keep working," she told him, even though she felt exhausted. Checking her phone again, she saw that there was *still* no word from Daniel. "You haven't heard about any accidents or major delays on the road between here and Wyvern, have you?"

"No. Why do you ask?"

"My friend was supposed to get back hours ago." She tried Daniel's number again, then Doctor Clarke's, but there was no answer from either of them. "He's probably just caught up with Alistair Clarke. God knows what they're up to, but..." Glancing back into the tent, she saw her laptop waiting for her, complete with various thumb-drives filled with data from the dig. "I think I just want to stick around while you're still here," she told Casey. "It feels good to get on with work and keep my mind off other things."

"I'm sorry I can't give you all the data you requested," he replied. "Some of it just can't be shared yet."

She nodded. "I understand, just -"

Before she could finish, another rumble of thunder filled the darkening sky, and a gust of wind blew rain through the tent's entrance, briefly catching them both and forcing them to take a step back.

"You're from around here, right?" she asked.

"Born and raised in Mepley."

"Have you ever heard stories about the fog on these moors? Or about..." She sighed. "This is going to sound really dumb, but about some kind of witch?"

"Only old wives' tales," he replied. "People like to invent mythologies about the places they live. Off the top of my head, I can think of the White Woman of Mepley Common, the ghost of St. Martin's cemetery, the hangman of Swirren's Road and about a dozen other supposed ghosts in the area. Trust me, when your story about some lost battlefield goes public, they'll roll that right into it. It wouldn't surprise me if some of the locals start pretending they've seen ghostly English Civil War soldiers wandering the moors for decades. The scary thing is, I think after a while they start to believe their own crazy tales."

"But there *have* been stories about the fog?" she asked, keen not to admit too much about her own experience.

"There are two types of people who hear voices in the fog around here," he continued with a smile. "Liars and nut-cases." Zipping his jacket shut, he pulled the hood up and stepped out into the rain. "I'm going to go check on the covers, just to make sure the site is rain-proofed. Everything's been kinda rushed today, so maybe a few corners were cut."

Once he'd headed out into the storm, Mary made her way over to the laptop and plugged the first thumb-drive into the side. After setting up the data transfer, she looked over at a clear plastic box on one of the tables, filled with some of the first bones that had been discovered at the site. Those, at least, were certainly from soldiers who'd fought in the battle, but as she wandered over to take a closer look, she couldn't help thinking about the landlord's crazy theory. She knew there was no way the schoolchildren could have been magically transported back to the time of the battle, but she had to admit that the idea made the pieces of the puzzle fit together somewhat neatly.

For a moment, she imagined the shocked soldiers standing around a pile of bloodied bodies. If they'd slaughtered a group of children, might that have been enough for them to have stopped the battle and then pretended it never happened in the first place? The idea was a stretch, but at the same time it made some degree of sense, even if she felt that something else, something even more horrific, would have been necessary. She even -

Suddenly a flash of lightning filled the sky outside, lighting up the tent's wall and briefly showing the silhouette of a figure making its way toward the door. Surprised that Casey would be back so soon, Mary waited for him to step inside, but after a moment she realized there was no sign of him. Heading over, she leaned out into the rain and looked around, and finally she spotted him a couple of hundred feet away, working with a section of tarpaulin next to one of the arc lights.

She glanced around, before telling herself that the silhouetted figure must have been a trick of the light. After all, she'd only seen it for a fraction of a second, and she was way past the point of exhaustion. She waited a moment longer, just to make sure that none of the relief officers had shown up yet to guard the site overnight, and then she headed back to her laptop and saw with relief that the data had finally finished transferring.

It was time to get back to work, and to put crazy theories out of her mind. As she peered at the screen, she failed to notice that nearby the floor of the tent was moving slightly, as if something was pushing up from beneath the fabric.

**

"Captain John Villiers," she muttered a short while later, as she clicked the mouse to magnify the picture on her screen. She was examining a photo of the chunk of metal that had been recovered during one of the previous days, and she couldn't help but marvel at the idea that she'd located Villiers' final resting place.

At the end of the day, it was the history that mattered. She told herself the same thing over and over, trying to put all other concerns out of her mind. Between Villiers and the Battle of Sharpeton, she figured she had enough discoveries from this one dig to fill thirty academic papers, maybe even several books. The cold, hard truth was already fascinating enough, without the need to add a bunch of crazy stories.

Grabbing her phone, she brought up Daniel's number and tried yet again to get through. For the umpteenth time she was put through to voice-mail, and this time she decided to leave a message.

"Hey," she said, unable to hide the exhaustion in her voice, "it's me. I don't know where you are, but I'm at the dig site and I'm about to head into town so I can -"

Suddenly a huge rumble of thunder shook the tent, causing the lights in the corner to briefly flicker. Mary looked around, feeling a little spooked, but as the rumble faded she heard the sound of rain once again.

Detective Casey, she realized, had been outside for a long time now.

"I'm going back to the King's Head," she continued with a sigh, "to get some food and a wash, and then I'll see if I can sleep. Fat chance with this storm brewing, but I guess I'll meet you back there or something. Just... Call me when you get this, okay? I'm starting to wonder whether you've disappeared off the face of the planet."

She paused, wondering if she should add something else, before realizing that the line was dead. Checking the screen, she saw that her signal had dropped out, which she figured must be due to the storm. Sighing, she set the phone down and then closed the lid of her laptop. As she did so, she heard a rustling sound nearby, and she turned just in time to see the tent's far wall billowing inward a little, almost as if something solid had bumped into it from outside.

Sighing again, she got to her feet and headed over to the door. When she pulled the flap open, she saw vast torrents of rain still crashing down, hammering the already muddy ground. A couple of arc lights were still running over by the nearest dig site, providing the only illumination on a cloudy, moonless night, but she could hear a constant flurry of rainwater dripping down not only from the roof of the tent, but also from the equipment coverings nearby. She paused for a moment, waiting for some sign of Detective Casey, before checking her watch.

Almost midnight, which meant it had been ninety minutes since he'd headed out to check the covers. His car was still parked over by the dirt track, so she knew he hadn't left. She considered calling out his name, before realizing that the rain was too loud, so instead she grabbed a rainproof coat from the pile and slipped it over her jacket, then she pulled the hood up, took a flashlight from the box, and stepped out into the storm.

High winds immediately buffeted her, and her feet sank into the muddy ground with every step she took. Several days' worth of bad weather had turned the moorland into a swampy mess. Her socks were quickly soaked, but she waded around the side of the tent and began to make her way toward the arc lights.

"Detective Casey?" she called out, hoping he might be close enough to hear. Switching the flashlight on, she shone the beam straight ahead toward the generators. "Detective -"

Suddenly she felt something brushing against her left ankle. Instinctively stepping away, she turned and shone the flashlight down at the mud, but all she saw were puddles of water. Still, she was certain that something had moved, almost as if fingers had tried to grab her foot from down in the mud, although she knew that was impossible.

"Detective Casey?" she shouted, trying not to sound worried but still raising her voice a notch. "Are you still here?"

She asked the question as a half-joke, but as she stood and listened to the howling storm, she couldn't shake the growing feeling that maybe he *had* somehow abandoned her. Again, she knew that was impossible, since his car was still parked nearby, but as she turned and shone the flashlight all around, the entire site seemed so desolate, as if -

Suddenly she felt it again, something clawing at her ankle, and she took a couple of steps back. Shining the flashlight down, she saw a patch of mud briefly churning, as if something was moving just beneath the surface. This time she was certain that the sensation hadn't been imagined but, as she felt her heart racing, she told herself that there were probably rats around or...

Taking a deep breath, she tried to work out whether rats would really be swimming around in the mud. The idea seemed ludicrous, but there was no other explanation.

"Detective Casey?" she called out, turning to look around. "Where are you?"

She waited, but all she heard was the rain.

And then she saw him.

She was certain he hadn't been there a moment ago, but now he was over by one of the arc lights, about twenty or thirty feet away. Squinting slightly, she realized that something about his posture seemed strange, as if he was kneeling on the ground right in front of the tripod, staring straight up into the blisteringly bright electric light above. She waited for him to move, but slowly she began to realize that he seemed somehow locked in place, as if maybe he'd found something startling in the mud. Either that, or he was praying.

"Detective Casey!"

Trudging through the mud, struggling at times to pull her feet out of the thick, boggy pools of rainwater, Mary made her way toward him as quickly as possible. After a couple of minutes she was only halfway, and she had to stop for a moment to catch her breath since wading through the mud was so exhausting. She looked around for a moment at the dig site, and she couldn't help noticing that in some places the ground seemed almost to be churning as rain continued to fall. Resuming her trek, she battled through the wind and rain until she came up behind Casey, who was still on his knees, still staring up at the arc light.

"What are you doing?" she asked, holding a hand up to shield her eyes against the blinding light. As she began to step around him, she couldn't understand how he could be staring directly into the heart of the light, although after a moment she noticed that he seemed to be leaning back on something. Stopping, she shone the flashlight toward his back, which allowed her to see a long wooden pole that seemed to have been used to prop him up. She paused, feeling a growing, unsettling sense of concern in the pit of her belly, before shining the light toward his face.

She froze as she saw that a thick, bloody chunk had been hacked out of his neck and chest. His eyes, meanwhile, had begun to burn as they stared up directly at the arc light. After a moment, Mary realized that parts of his eyes were discolored and thick, as if the burning light was cooking them in their sockets.

Taking a step back, Mary stumbled and fell, dropping the flashlight. She continued to stare at Detective Casey's corpse, which remained propped against the pole, and then she fumbled to grab the flashlight again, turning and -

Suddenly she spotted a figure running past through the darkness, giggling in the rain and quickly disappearing into the gloom. She shone the flashlight after the figure, but it was gone now. A moment later, one of the other arc lights suddenly switched off. She turned, just as it came back on again, then off, then on, as if someone was constantly flicking the switch.

Her mind racing, she stumbled to her feet and looked back at Casey. She half expected to find that she was wrong, that she'd suffered some kind of mental break, but once again she saw his dead face, with his eyes smoldering and slowly cooking as they stared up at the intense arc light.

Turning, Mary shone the flashlight all around and then began to hurry through the mud, heading toward Casey's car over by the top of the dirt-road. She almost fell a couple of times, but she pushed onward even though her ankles were aching and her chest was filled with panic. Finally, however, she tripped and fell, landing hard against the mud. As she spluttered and tried to get up, she felt something brushing against her neck and she pulled away, shining the flashlight down and seeing a dark shape slipping out of sight beneath the muddy surface.

She froze for a moment, before getting to her feet and trying to run toward the car. After just a couple of steps, however, she spotted movement up ahead, and when she shone the flashlight forward she realized she could see a figure trying to pull the car's door open. Seemingly oblivious to the fact that he was being picked out by a beam of light, the figure took a step back and then raised an ax above his head, bringing the blade crashing down against the window, which shattered instantly.

Suddenly the figure turned and stared straight at Mary, his eyes widening as he looked directly into the flashlight.

Panicking, Mary turned and scrambled through the mud until she reached the tent, where she threw herself through the doorway and then turned, quickly zipping the entrance shut. Covered in mud and trembling with fear, she shone the light all around, but there was no-one else inside. Just the table, the boxes of bones from the original dig, and her laptop. She could hear rain crashing down outside, however, and she felt certain that the figure next to the car must be coming closer. A moment later, she felt something bumping against her leg. When she looked down, she realized that the tent's canvas floor was bulging slightly, as if some kind of object was reaching up through the mud beneath and trying to break through the fabric. She watched in horror as the faint shape of a hand pushed harder and harder, scraping furiously as it tried to get to her.

Above, another huge rumble of thunder filled the night sky.

CHAPTER FIFTY

THUNDER RUMBLED ABOVE AS the car crawled to a halt on a dark country lane. A light was flashing on the dashboard, causing a repetitive beeping sound, and finally the car rolled to a stop.

"What is the meaning of this?" Freeman asked dourly.

"I think it's out of petrol," Becca replied, leaning forward and peering through the steering wheel as she tried to make sense of the dials. "We can't go any further without petrol."

"And is this petrol difficult to acquire?"

She turned to him. "We need -"

Suddenly she flinched as a crack of lighting burst across the sky, followed a moment later by another deep rumble of thunder.

"I think we're nearly home," she continued, trying not to let him see that she was terrified. Rain was pounding down, hitting the car's roof and trickling onto the windshield, and the wipers were barely able to keep the view clear. "We could sit here, or we could walk the rest of the way. Maybe we should stay here for a while and hope the rain stops."

She waited for a reply, but after a moment she realized that Freeman seemed to be staring forward, as if he'd spotted something on the road up ahead.

Turning, Mary frowned as she saw a figure in the distance, at the edge of the pool of light that had been cast by the car's headlamps.

"Who's that?" she whispered, watching as the woman's long, dark dress was buffeted by the wind and rain. "Why's she just standing there? Isn't she cold?"

Without answering, Freeman reached out and opened the door, before stepping out of the car and making his way through the storm. Although she briefly considered going after him, Becca felt a twinge of fear and instead she remained in the car's driving seat, watching through the windscreen wipers as she saw Freeman approaching the crazy woman in the middle of the road.

Instinctively, Becca reached out to make sure that the car's doors were all locked.

***

"Where's your ax, old man?" Kate asked calmly, watching as Freeman stepped toward her. "I never expected you to let that thing out of your sight. After all, we both know you're powerless without it."

Silhouetted now against the lights of the car,

Freeman appeared almost to be falling apart, as the scraps of his centuries-old clothing fluttered in the wind. Bowed and crooked, he walked stiffly, and stray strands of skin had begun to peel from his skull. He stopped just a few feet from the woman, as thunder rumbled in the dark sky above.

"I told you this day would come," she continued. "Remember the stories we heard all those years ago, about the Battle of Sharpeton? When I understood the truth about why that battle was abandoned, I wept for days on end. Now we're doomed to see the tragedy from the other end. The poor children who fell back to that day were just part of what happened. The rest..." She paused, with tears in her eyes. "I don't think I can bear to watch again."

"What do you want with me, witch?" he sneered.

"Aren't you curious about your role in all of this?" she asked. "Who let you out of that hole in the ground, anyway? I'd rather hoped it would contain you for a little while longer. Until you were needed."

Receiving no answer, she peered past him and looked at the car. Despite the windscreen wipers constantly moving back and forth across the rain-soaked glass, she was just about able to see Becca's wide-open, terrified eyes staring back.

"A child?" Kate said with a faint shiver. She turned back to Freeman. "Why haven't you cut her head off by now? That's what you do to children, isn't it? I don't believe for one moment that you've developed a conscience, so why have you let her live?"

"She is no witch," he replied darkly, "nor do I

believe her to be a Catholic. She seeks her family -"

"So you're *helping* her?" Kate asked incredulously.

"I have no other purpose in this world," he continued. "My time has passed."

"Oh, you have a purpose," she replied, "but it has nothing to do with that child. You must simply wait until..." She paused suddenly, staring at the car for a moment longer. "Unless that is the child who will one day grow up to lead others. Yes, I see it now. Perhaps she is the one who will finally wake you when your time has come. I have witnessed that moment already, Freeman. Tell me, do you think the little girl would make a good soldier?"

"Leave her alone," he sneered. "I seek merely to reunite her with her sister."

"Seriously?" At this, Kate seemed genuinely shocked for a moment. "You surprise me, Freeman. I must admit, it never occurred to me that you might be capable of change. I thought you were locked forever in that desperate spiral of hate and venom. Or does some hidden part of your heart still seek redemption for what you did to children during the old days? Is the great witch-hunter, the scourge of Catholic priests, finally changing his ways?"

"Remove any man sufficiently from his time and place," Freeman replied, "and give him no hope of ever returning, and he shall doubtless become a *new* man. In part, at least. I wish merely to return the child to her family and then I have no further role to play. I am too tired and too old to rejoin the battle against sin. This world makes no sense to me, I cannot begin to fathom its madness."

"You will understand it one day," she replied, "but for now you have another role to play. You know *why* the Battle of Sharpeton was hidden away, do you not?"

He nodded. "I do."

"There are certain qualities of this land that beget great tragedy," she continued. "The Battle of Sharpeton should have remained forgotten forever, but humans possess a remarkable talent for digging through the dirt and hauling up their own past. As soon as the first bones were removed from the Sharpeton battlefield, it was inevitable that the rest would rise to join them, and that has begun to happen now, not more than half a mile from here. The two ends of the paradox must meet, it seems."

"This need not concern me," Freeman muttered darkly.

"I despise you," she sneered, stepping closer to him, "and I know full well that the feeling is mutual. I would have consigned you forever to death, had a man named Hodges been able to follow instructions all those years ago. He was supposed to kill you with your own ax, but instead he used another weapon, and thus you were left trapped between life and death. I can do nothing to change that now, but I swear, Freeman, you can at least still be useful!"

"There is nothing I can do here," he replied. "The Battle of Sharpeton -"

"A madman has your ax," she pointed out,

interrupting him. "Even now he assumes your name and claims to be the great Nykolas Freeman. He has killed several times today, and he will most assuredly kill again. Meanwhile, the soldiers of Sharpeton are rising from their graves and they must be stopped before they march across the land. The coin that was supposed to condemn you to an eternal grave... Do you still have it?"

Freeman stared at her for a moment, before reaching into his pocket and taking out the gold coin that Becca had given to him several days earlier.

"You know what you must do," Kate told him. "The soldiers of Sharpeton do not belong in the modern world, at least not today. They must be consigned to a grave, one that will not be discovered until the time is right. If I do the deed, I will destroy the entire town and half the county in the process. You, on the other hand, can lead them to another grave, one that will cause less suffering to the rest of the world." Again she looked past him, toward the car where Becca still watched with fearful eyes. "If the soldiers run free, it is the children they will seek to kill first. And this child in particular must live, so that she can play her part in a later tragedy."

Still looking down at the coin in the palm of his hand, Freeman seemed lost in thought for a moment. Thunder rumbled above, and finally, slowly, he nodded.

"Seal them in with you," Kate continued. "If you don't, then you know what will happen to your precious England. No matter which way you turn, you can never avoid your destiny."

Freeman turned and looked back toward the car,

staring at Becca for a few seconds, before turning again and looking toward the moor. In the distance, flashes of lightning seemed to be congregating in one particular part of the sky, as if drawn to a patch of land. Finally, after closing his fist around the gold coin, Freeman began to walk away, trampling through the undergrowth at the side of the road and then making his way across the moor.

"This is how it always had to be," Kate whispered, as she watched him leave. "Now I finally understand why such a cruel man was fated to survive." She paused, before turning to look at the car and seeing Becca's terrified face staring back at her from behind the rain-soaked windshield.

CHAPTER FIFTY-ONE

"PLEASE WORK," MARY STAMMERED, frantically trying her phone again and again, only to find that she still had no signal. "Come on, why can't you just -"

Suddenly she heard a tearing sound, and she turned to see that the tent's floor was starting to become shredded in one spot near the door. Muddy water was leaking inside, and something was trying to force its way through. After a moment, she saw a skeletal hand reaching up from the ground beneath, but a fraction of a second later the tent's lights failed, plunging the scene into darkness.

The only light came from her phone's screen now, but as she tried yet again to get through to the police, she began to feel increasingly desperate. All around, she could hear rain battering the tent, and then a moment later another flash of lightning briefly lit the scene. Out of the corner of her eyes, Mary saw – for just a fraction of a second – that an entire rotten arm had reached up from the hole in the floor.

Freezing for a moment in the darkness, Mary listened for a moment to the sound of the raging storm. Slowly, she realized she could hear another sound, too; a creaking, tearing hint of movement. At the same time, she felt the tent's fabric tightening beneath her feet, as if it was being tugged upon.

Another flash of lightning flashed through the air, and Mary gasped as she saw that the rotten arm was reaching toward her, with stringy trails of flesh hanging from its bones. Part of the shoulder was also inside the tent now, as the creature continued to crawl through the hole in the floor.

Pulling back as darkness returned, Mary stayed completely still for a few seconds, not know what to do. Finally she reached out and grabbed the fabric wall, and then she made her way around the very edge of the tent's interior, hoping to get to the door without going anywhere near the emerging creature. Another flutter of lightning lit the room, and she saw a rotten, skeletal face rising up through the hole in the floor.

Trying not to panic, Mary finally got to the tent's door. Fumbling with the zipper, she was able to get it open, but suddenly something pushed back at her, sending her tumbling to the ground. Looking up, she saw the silhouette of a man standing in the doorway, holding an ax and grinning at her wildly.

"I am the great Nykolas Freeman!" he yelled. "I have come to save England from devilry and witchcraft!"

With that, he brought the ax crashing down

toward Mary's face.

CHAPTER FIFTY-TWO

"WHAT THE HELL'S GOING on in here?" Doctor Carlisle shouted as he ran into the hospital room. Machines next to the bed were frantically beeping, while two nurses were trying to hold down Laura's shivering, convulsing body.

"She kept saying that something was about to rise through the ground," one of the nurses said breathlessly, "and then she started shaking like this!"

"There's nothing *physically* wrong with her," the doctor muttered as he checked the machines. "It's all in her head, unless she's managed to work herself up into such a state that she -"

He stopped suddenly as he saw several readings that made no sense. It took a moment before he finally realized what was wrong, at which point he turned and looked down at Laura.

"She's in cardiac arrest," he stammered, before racing around the bed and checking her pulse. "Get the paddles! She's having a heart attack! She's -"

"They're coming!" Laura gasped, grabbing his arm and squeezing tight, digging her fingers into his flesh until her nails scratched bone. Her eyes, filled with fear, stared up at him. "You have to stop them!" she hissed. "They're coming back! All of them!"

CHAPTER FIFTY-THREE

BECCA SAT IN THE car, watching with a sense of mounting horror as the strange woman approached. She'd already locked all the doors, so she knew the woman couldn't get inside, but she still felt terrified. Finally the woman leaned down and peered in at her, before tapping gently on the window just as another burst of thunder rumbled overhead.

Shaking her head, Becca waited for the woman to leave.

"Please!" the woman said firmly. "It's important!"

Becca shook her head again, but a moment later she heard the car's locking mechanism being activated, and to her shock she watched as the woman swung the door open.

"How did you do that?" she shouted.

"Come with me," the woman said, crouching down and smiling at her. "Your name is Rebecca, isn't it? There's no need to worry, Rebecca. Everything is going to be okay, and I can help you find your family. You have a role to play in all of this, but not yet. Not for many, many years. My name is Kate, or... Well, that's one of my names. You could called me Annis, if you prefer, or Azael, or any one of a thousand others." She paused, before reaching in to touch Becca's arm. "If you just -"

"Where is he?" Becca shouted, pulling away and clambering onto the passenger seat. The woman had a kind, friendly face, but deep down Becca couldn't shake the feeling that something was wrong.

"Nykolas Freeman is not of this time," the woman replied with a smile. She leaned a little closer, and now her face was easier to see thanks to the lights inside the car. She *was* pretty, with the most beautiful brown eyes, but still Becca couldn't ignore the fear in her gut. "It was a mistake for Freeman to be here today," the woman continued. "It was a mistake for you to be here, too. You both have parts to play in what happens to this country, but you've met far too soon. I should have anticipated that, but I'm afraid I was distracted. Let me help you, and you can live a full life until the day comes when -"

"Where is he?" Becca shouted again, interrupting the woman and trying not to panic as she heard thunder in the distance. Looking toward the dark moor, she felt a shiver at the thought of Freeman out there all alone. Despite everything she'd seen and experienced, she felt bad for the old man, and she felt certain that he was the only one who'd actually help her in her quest to find her sister. "He'll be cold," she stammered, "and wet. And all by himself, with no-one to talk to."

"That man *deserves* to be alone," Kate replied. "Think of him no more, he's just -"

"No!" Becca yelled. "He's going to help me find my sister!"

"Sweetheart, he can't possibly do that." She leaned closer and tried to grab Becca's arm, but the girl pulled away again. "Don't be foolish, petal. You have to come with me, and I'll make sure everything's okay. You trust me, don't you?"

Although she knew it was rude not to answer, Becca still just stared at the woman's smooth, smiling face. She desperately wanted to find her sister, but at the same time she felt nauseous at the thought of going anywhere with the woman, who seemed to unsettle every fiber in her body.

Above, thunder rumbled again.

"Come, petal," the woman continued, leaning close again and reaching out to her. "Don't be silly, now. You simply have to trust me."

Suddenly a flash of lightning filled the air all around the car, and for a fraction of a second Becca saw the woman's face change from beautiful to haggard, from smooth to old and rotten. It was as if the flash of light briefly revealed her true face, and when it was over the woman's appearance returned to normal.

"What's wrong?" the woman asked, leaning ever closer. "Are you scared?"

Another flicker of lightning lit her face for a

half-second, once again revealing the rotten ugliness. Translucent flesh was hanging from her skull, and her eyes were shriveled and dry.

Screaming, Becca opened the car's door, quickly stumbling out into the rain just as the woman tried to grab her shoulder. She ran around to the other side, making sure to keep away from the woman, and then she began to hurry through the darkness, heading off after Freeman. She wasn't sure *exactly* where he'd gone, but she knew he'd stumbled toward the moor's eastern slopes. Ahead, she saw a swirl of thunder and lightning in the sky, and she felt certain that Freeman had gone in that direction.

"Wait!" Kate shouted. "Leave him alone! He can't help you! He has a role to play! I'm the only one who can get you back to your parents!"

Ignoring her, Becca hurried through the undergrowth. She tripped and fell as soon as she reached the edge of the muddy moor, and she looked over her shoulder just as another flash of lightning lit the scene. For a moment, she saw the woman stepping after her, her whole body rotten and skeletal, with strands of old flesh hanging from her bones. Once the lightning had passed, the roadside fell back to darkness and Becca wasted no time in getting to her feet. Turning, she began to run through the mud, desperately trying to catch up to Freeman so that he wouldn't be alone.

Another flash of lighting briefly lit the moor, allowing Becca to see Freeman's silhouette in the distance, at the crest of the hill as rain came crashing down all around.

"Wait!" she screamed, even though she knew he wouldn't be able to hear her. "I'm coming! Wait for me!"

CHAPTER FIFTY-FOUR

"COME ON," CRAIG SHOUTED, "it'll be fun!"

Dragging Mary out of the tent, he shoved her down into the mud and then stepped around her, still holding the ax in his right hand. He'd missed her head by inches a moment ago, but this time he was taking a moment to aim properly.

"My name, dear maiden," he continued, as rain crashed down all around them, "is Nykolas Freeman. You might have heard of me, since I have rather a notorious reputation that stretches back for several hundred years." Tightening his grip on the ax, he smiled as she tried to sit up, and he quickly kicked her in the chest, sending her crashing back down. "What is wrong, fair lady? Does something about my person cause you to quiver with fear? I must tell you, I have had an exceedingly fruitful day. I have already dispatched one witch and three warlocks, and I mean to add to my tally before sunrise. The question is... Are you a witch?"

Gasping, Mary tried to turn and crawl away, only for Craig to grab the back of her collar and haul her up.

"There are many ways to test your true nature," he whispered into her ear, as he pressed the ax's jagged edge against the small of her back. "I must admit, the logic of the situation rather escapes me, but I'm sure we'll have fun along the way."

With that, he slammed her face-first down into the mud, before pushing on the back of her head to make sure that she couldn't sit up. Unable to breathe, she tried desperately to get free, but Craig's grip was too strong and he waited almost a full minute before lifting her up again and grinning as she gasped desperately for air. Rain was washing most of the mud from her terrified face, although she'd swallowed several mouthful of dirty water and now she started bringing them back up, spewing mud across the ground.

"Gross," Craig muttered with a frown. "Methinks it is time, dear lady, to -"

Suddenly he felt something clawing at his ankle. Letting go of Mary for a moment, he looked down at the mud, but there wasn't enough light for him to see anything. Still, he could feel fingers digging into his flesh, so he headed back into the tent and grabbed one of the flashlights. He failed to notice as a rotten arm reached out to him from the darkness, almost catching his elbow. Stepping back outside, he aimed a beam of light at the ground, and finally he saw another rotten, skeletal hand poking up.

"Huh," he said after a moment, tilting his head

slightly. He continued to watch the hand for a moment longer, as it slipped a little further from the mud, revealing a muddy arm. Rainwater was already washing the bone, causing it to glisten in the flashlight's beam, but Craig simply watched for a moment longer before finally raising the ax and then bringing it crashing down, smashing the arm and pushing it back down into the mud.

He waited, but there was no sign of any more movement, and after a few seconds he turned to see that Mary was desperately trying to crawl toward the parked car nearby.

"Seriously?" Craig muttered, stepping after her. "Don't you wanna come to my -"

Before he could finish, he felt something else grabbing his ankle. He pulled away and shone the torch down, but all he saw now was a patch of mud.

"You guys are really getting on my tits," he said with a sigh, before turning and following Mary. She'd almost reached the car now, but he grabbed her arm as she reached out toward the door. Pulling her back and around, he grinned into her sobbing, mud-covered face and held the ax up for her to see, just as another streak of lightning flashed across the sky.

In that brief moment, Mary's terrified eyes saw what appeared to be several arms reaching up from the ground near the tent, as if figures were trying to haul themselves from the mud. She also saw something lumbering out from inside the tent, although she was unable to look at it properly before the light faded and the site was plunged back into darkness.

"Come on!" Craig yelled, pulling her up and then shoving her against the side of the car, slamming her face against the metal. "You know your problem? You're ungrateful! It was the same with that guy a minute ago, he went on about how he was a cop and how I'm not allowed to be up here. Just yakking on, blah blah blah, loving the sound of his own voice." He sniffed, as if he was trying to draw any lingering cocaine further into his nose. "People don't appreciate history these days, do they? They think it's all dusty and unimportant. There's no respect for the good old days. Well, I'm gonna bring that back, aren't I? I'm Nykolas Freeman, and I've got what the crappy modern world needs! Tonight, a new era is born!"

Raising the ax high above his head, he swung it toward Mary. She ducked out of the way just in time, crawling around the side of the car as the blade crunched against the windscreen. Moving as fast as she could manage, she felt herself sinking into the mud, and for a moment she was sure there were other hands under there, reaching up and trying to grab her. Ignoring the sensation, she reached the other side of the car and slumped back for a moment, desperately trying to get her breath as rain continued to pour down. A couple of seconds later, however, Craig stepped into view again, with the ax still in his right hand.

Mary turned to crawl away again, but suddenly she cried out as Craig sliced the ax down against her right leg, cutting through her mud-soaked jeans and into her flesh, striking bone. She felt the ax pulling out again, as warm blood rushed from the wound. Looking down, she couldn't see the damage, but when she fumbled with her right hand she felt a long, jagged tear in her trousers.

Craig was saying something, but his voice could barely be heard at all above the sound of rain crashing down against the ground.

Unable to get to her feet and run, Mary leaned back on her elbows and stared up breathlessly at the dark figure above her. She could see the ax's outline, with rain hitting the metal, and she knew it was only a matter of time before the maniac struck her again. A moment later, however, another flash of lightning briefly lit the scene, and to her horror Mary saw that whereas earlier there had been arms reaching up from the muddy ground, now there were whole torsos, struggling desperately to climb up from beneath the surface. In just that split second of light, she'd seen twenty or thirty bodies rising from their muddy graves.

"Madness," she stammered. "I'm losing my mind..."

"Are you listening to me at all?" Craig shouted.

She saw him stepping closer. Raising her arms across her face, she cried out, but a moment later she felt the ax crashing into her right ankle. She let out a cry of pain as the blade scraped against bone, and when she looked down at her legs she was just about able to see that her right foot was hanging by scraps of flesh and muscle, having been almost completely severed.

"Say my name!" Craig yelled through the rain.

Staring at her damaged foot, Mary felt an immense pressure in her chest, as if pure panic was flooding her body.

"Say my name!" Craig screamed.

She flinched as he smashed the ax against the side of the car.

"Say my name!"

With that, he stamped on her damaged ankle, causing her to scream.

Another streak of lightning crackled across the sky. Mary's eyes widened in horror as she saw that some of the figures behind Craig was almost free of the mud, but she also saw a separate, taller figure making its way closer. Somehow this figure seemed different to the others, and in the brief flash of light she was just about to catch sight of his face. Rotten, skeletal and old, with eyes fixed firmly on Craig, the figure almost reminded her of -

Suddenly something grabbed Craig from behind, slamming him into the side of the car and then sending him splashing down into the mud.

Mary began to crawl away, as she heard screams and shouts. She had no idea what was happening, but she knew she had to hide. Detective Casey had mentioned more officers coming up to the site to watch it overnight, and she could only hope that they'd show up soon and deal with whatever madness was unfolding. Finally, seeing nowhere else to go, she began to wriggle under the car, as Craig's cries rang out through the rain. Above her, the car was starting to shudder with the force of several large impacts.

CHAPTER FIFTY-FIVE

"SAY MY NAME!" CRAIG screamed, swinging the ax toward Freeman but missing by several inches and instead hitting the car. Almost losing his balance, he stumbled backward, breathlessly watching as Freeman came closer. "Just say it! I'm Nykolas -"

Before he could finish, Freeman reached for the ax again. Craig lunged at him, flailing with the weapon and striking Freeman's shoulder. Losing his footing in the mud, Craig briefly dropped to his knees before getting to his feet and running back toward the car. He reached into his pocket, hoping to find more cocaine, but all that remained was a torn plastic bag. He took a moment to search frantically for more grains, before turning and seeing that Freeman was calmly coming closer.

"Don't you ever give up, old man?" Craig sneered, even though he could feel himself flagging now. The immense energy and excitement he'd felt earlier was fading, but he knew he couldn't give up, not yet. His rational mind was starting to creep back past his coke-fueled madness, but the two sides were starting to tear his thoughts apart as they fought one another for dominance. "Fine!" he shouted. "You wanna cosplay as some old dude from the English Civil War? Go ahead, I really couldn't give a -"

Stopping suddenly, he remembered the moment next to the river, when he'd held Julie's head under the surface. His rational mind raced and he tried to think of ways she might be alright, but after a moment he thought of her hands desperately trying to force him back. There had been times in the past when he'd hit her during his coke binges, but she'd always forgiven him.

"She'll forgive me this time, too," he stammered, stepping back as Freeman came closer. For a moment, he felt as if there were two voices in his head, screaming at each other to stop. "She has to forgive me," he stammered. "She *always* forgives me! I didn't kill her, I just... She'll be fine, she..."

He froze, thinking of her face beneath the water, and finally he let out an agonized scream as he realized the truth. For a moment, he looked down at the ax and considered driving the blade into his own chest, but his thoughts quickly moved on to the fact that there'd be police at the river, and that he could be arrested for murder. A sense of panic swelled in his chest, as if his entire body was about to be torn apart at the seams.

"I can fix it," he whispered, barely even aware now that Freeman had almost reached him. "What have I done? What the hell have I done? I can hide the body.

It's sad, but it's not fair for me to go to prison just because -"

Suddenly spotting Freeman nearby, he swung wildly with the ax and then staggered back around the car.

"I can't go to prison!" he shouted. "I'd never survive! They'd kill me in there, they'd ruin me for life! I'm too fragile and pretty for prison!" Stepping back, he felt as if his mind was falling apart, as if all his thoughts were disconnecting from one another, replaced by a pure, pounding rush of blood. After a moment, he let out a slow groan of pain.

Feeling something brushing against his shoulder, he spun around just as another flash of lightning lit the scene, and he found himself face-to-face with a face more rotten than Freeman's, with several others watching from nearby. Stepping back, he realized that more and more figures had risen from the ground. He swung the ax at the darkness ahead, and this time he felt the blade crunching into a rotten chest. When he tried to pull the ax free, the blade caught against something, and another burst of lightning allowed him to see that the weapon was embedded in the ribs of a skeletal figure that was reaching out toward him.

Pulling the ax free, Craig scrambled around the car until he saw Freeman again.

"What are they?" he yelled, his voice filled with panic. "What the hell is going on up here?"

"The warriors of Sharpeton have risen from their grave," Freeman replied darkly. "They were always destined to return once the first of their number had been disturbed."

Freezing for a moment in the rain, Craig tried to make sense of everything. Finally, however, he realized that there was only one possible explanation. The coke he'd taken earlier must have been laced with something else, he told himself, maybe with LSD or something even crazier. He knew he'd be fine, he knew everything would be good in the morning, but right now he felt an overwhelming sense of fear rising through his chest. Hearing a gasping sound over his shoulder, he turned and saw several dark silhouettes stumbling closer, so he waved the ax at the figures and then stumbled back, before turning again as he realized Freeman was just a few feet away.

"Make them stop!" he screamed. "I don't care what you want, but make them stop!"

He waited, but Freeman simply stared at him darkly.

"This is *your* fault," Craig sneered, strengthening his grip on the ax. In his addled mind, he'd come to the conclusion that Freeman was somehow responsible for all the madness, and that getting rid of Freeman would solve the problem. He took a step closer, still breathless but determined to end the insanity. "Everything went wrong when you showed up," he continued. "That's when Julie..."

He paused, hating the sound of her name.

"You're just... You're a monster!" he yelled, raising the ax high above his head, ready to bring it crashing down against Freeman's chest. "You're -"

"Stop!" a voice screamed, and Craig saw a dark

figure rush forward through the rain, stopping in front of Freeman with its arms out.

It took a moment before he realized that he'd seen this figure before.

"Don't hurt him!" Becca shouted. "He's just -"

Bringing the ax swinging down in a moment of blind panic, Craig drove the blade straight through the side of Becca's head, crunching into her skull. The blade sliced out through her eyes and cheek, and the momentum of the strike caused Craig to slump against the car. Turning, he saw what was left of Becca's mangled head, which had been split open down to the neck. The little girl took a single step forward and reached up, feeling her wounds with trembling hands. Her heart was still furiously pumping blood around her body, but the fluid was simply slopping out through the hole in her neck in brief bursts until finally she slumped to the ground.

"Well that..." Craig paused, staring at Becca's corpse before looking at Freeman again. "That was unfortunate," he continued, forcing a smile. The last of his rational mind was retreating now. "I mean, she was just a kid, right? It's not my fault there was a goddamn kid in the way! And I'm... I'm the great Nykolas Freeman! That's what he used to do, right? He used to kill kids, women, anyone who got in his way! That kid was probably a witch anyway, like all the rest and -"

Another flash of lightning filled the sky, and Craig briefly saw not only Freeman's face but also the faces of rotten soldiers all around. A moment later, he felt sharp, bony hands clawing at his shoulders from behind. He spun around and swung the ax, slicing through the chest of one figure and sending it crashing to the ground.

"What are these things?" he screamed as he bumped against the side of the car. His mind was in pieces now, as he saw dark shapes shuffling closer through the rain. "Get back!" he yelled, pushing past Freeman. Spotting more and more of the dark figures, he waved the ax at them, desperately trying to scare them away. "I'm Nykolas Freeman!" he shouted wildly. "Fear me! I am the great -"

Suddenly he felt a hand grab his throat, pulling him back. Turning, he looked into Freeman's rotten eyes, and a moment later he felt the ax being wrenched from his hand. He tried to pull away, before the ax's blade was crunched into the base of his spine, causing him to cry out.

"The child was searching for her family," Freeman sneered angrily, dragging Craig through the mud, away from the car and toward the tent in the distance. After a moment he shoved him to the ground, before pulling the ax from his back. "She should not have been involved in this."

Craig gasped with pain as he tried to crawl away, only to find that the wound to his spine had left him unable to use his legs. He reached out, trying to drag himself through the mud, but he quickly felt other hands grabbing his torso, scratching their bony, skinless fingers into his flesh. Now that they were closer, he could hear the hisses and sighs of the undead soldiers, and he screamed as several of them started pulling him in different directions. Although he could no longer feel his legs, he could still hear the sound of his skin and muscle being torn away, as the soldiers began to rip him apart. He screamed, looking up at the stormy sky as rain came crashing down. One final cry of pain erupted from his lips, followed by a burst of blood, before a pair of bony hands tore his head from his neck.

Further down his body, his ribs were being snapped away as hungry soldiers tried to get to his heart and lungs.

Another burst of lightning crashed through the sky as Freeman watched Craig's corpse being ripped to shreds. Nearby, fog was starting to drift closer.

"I can't watch what happens next," Kate said, standing nearby and staring at the scene with a sense of great sadness in her eyes. "Whatever these soldiers were once, they're certainly not fit to live in the modern world. They have to be led away."

"Not before they perform one final task," Freeman muttered.

In the distance, from beyond the fog, voices were already crying out, and the muddy ground was starting to rumble with the force of hundreds and hundreds of men, heading closer. Slowly, the rotten soldiers turned to face the fog, as if they sensed what was coming.

"You have the coin," she continued. "You know what you must do with it, when this is over?"

Turning to her, Freeman saw thick fog approaching across the moor from the other direction too. There were more cries, as another army advanced through the storm. Angry voices filled the air, and the ground was rumbling as a vast storm of men began to appear in the distance. They were just silhouettes in the fog now, with weapons raised, but with each passing second they came closer and closer.

"I do," he said darkly, watching as the rotten soldiers picked their swords from the mud and turned, ready to battle the approaching silhouettes.

"I saw this tragedy from the other side," Kate explained, "in 1644. Now I am seeing it from *this* side. From today. I fear it shall be no less -"

Before she could finish, the seventeenth century Royalist army stormed through the fog, screaming as they launched the first wave of the Battle of Sharpeton. At the same time, the Parliamentarians attacked from the other side of the moor. Stuck in the middle, between the two armies, the rotten soldiers raised their swords and cried out as they joined the battle.

CHAPTER FIFTY-SIX

"PLEASE BE OKAY!" MARY stammered as she pulled Becca's body under the car. She rolled the little girl closer, searching for a pulse, before realizing that she could feel thick blood caked around the child's neck. There wasn't enough light to see the extent of the girl's injuries, but her fingers moved up the side of Becca's face until she felt the deep groove that had been cut by the ax, with blood oozing from the wound.

She instantly pulled her hand away, but her fingertips were wet with blood.

Beyond the car, screams were ringing out through the fog. Mary turned and looked, and with a growing sense of horror she realized she could see pair of legs everywhere, and she could hear the sound of swords striking one another. Men cried out in pain, and figures slumped down into the mud with terrible injuries. Turning, she looked around, but the scene was the same in every direction. It was as if a great battle had suddenly broken out in the fog, but she told herself that such a thing couldn't possibly have happened, even as the screams became louder.

Suddenly a body slammed to the ground just a few feet away, with half its face missing. Mary stared at the corpse and realized that it was wearing the full battle dress of a Parliamentarian soldier. She instinctively moved to crawl out and take a closer look, before suddenly the flash of a nearby sword forced her back. A man screamed behind her, his voice filled with agony, and a body slumped against the other side of the car. As she pulled back, Mary saw blood dribbling down into the mud, as the sounds of battle became louder still.

A moment later, something grabbed her shoulder from behind, clawing at her flesh. Turning, she saw more hands grabbing her, this time bursting up from the mud beneath her body and taking hold of her arms. She quickly realized she was being dragged down into the sodden ground, and this time she couldn't fight back. Taking in big gulps of muddy water, she screamed for help as she was pulled deeper into the mud. She reached up and grabbed the underside of the car, desperate to find some kind of anchor, but more and more hands were dragging her into the depths.

Suddenly another hand grabbed her arm and began to pull her out from under the car. She struggled, but when she looked up she saw that it was Kate, the woman from earlier, who was dragging her free, and this time one of the car's doors had been opened.

"Get in!" Kate shouted.

"But -"

"Get in! It's the only place that's safe!"

Even as more hands reached up from the mud to grab her, Mary stumbled to her feet. She was about to climb into the car, when she remembered the little girl. She turned, pulling her body too from under the vehicle.

"Hurry!" Kate hissed. "There's still time for her!"

As she bundled Becca into the car, Mary suddenly heard the scream of another child nearby. She turned and looked through the fog, seeing the soldiers fighting, but a moment later there was another scream.

"Nanny!" a little boy's voice shouted. "Help!"

"It's the children," Mary whispered, limping forward.

"Don't!" Kate said firmly, grabbing her arm. "They're already lost! Get in the car, it's the only place that's safe right now!"

Opening her mouth to reply, Mary suddenly realized she could see a couple of children stumbling through the fog, ducking to avoid the swords of the soldiers all around them.

"We can't leave them out here!" she stammered. "They'll die!"

"They're already dead," Kate replied. "They died years ago, when they vanished from the moor. This is where they ended up, but their destiny is to die on the battlefield!"

"I'm not leaving them," Mary said firmly, pulling free from Kate's grip and hurrying toward the children.

"You'll die with them!" Kate called after her.

"You're an idiot!"

Barely noticed at all by the soldiers, who were busy fighting the rotten warriors, Mary was able to limp across the muddy battlefield until she reached the children. There were five of them, wandering lost and terrified with tears in their eyes.

"Come with me!" she shouted, grabbing the arm of the nearest child. "This way!"

"Where are we?" one of the girls sobbed. "Where's the bus? Where are Nanny and Mr. Bronson?"

"Just come with me!" Mary hissed. "There's no time to -"

Before she could finish, she heard the sound of musket-fire. A fraction of a second later, one of the children shuddered and fell back, and Mary looked down to see that his head and chest had been blasted apart.

"This way!" she shouted, grabbing the four remaining children and ushering them through the fog, heading back to the car. "Hurry!"

"Where's everyone else?" one of the boys asked.

"I don't know," she replied, reaching the car and starting to shove them in one by one, "but -"

Suddenly she heard an agonized scream. Turning, she saw another child in the mud, reaching out toward her. She paused for a moment, before realizing that she recognized him from the photo.

The landlord's son.

"Robert," she whispered, turning and hurrying toward him. "Robert wait, I -"

Before she could finish, two fighting soldiers crashed into her, sending her slamming down into the mud. She felt a sharp pain in her ankle, but she forced herself up and half-ran, half-staggered across the battlefield until she reached the boy. As soon as she was close enough, she saw to her horror that his right leg had been severed just above the knee, and blood was pouring from the wound.

"Are there any more of you?" she asked, kneeling next to him as musket-fire blasted overhead.

"They're dead," he stammered, his eyes filled with shock. "I saw... I saw them..."

"It's okay," she replied, reaching out and grabbing him before slowly getting to her feet. With the boy in her arms, she limped as fast as she could manage back toward the car. She had to change course a couple of times, to avoid the soldiers who were still fighting all around, but finally she got to the vehicle and carefully placed Robert in the front passenger seat. "Are you sure there's no-one else out there?" she asked. "Have you seen any of the other children from your class?"

"They're dead," he sobbed, before slumping back unconscious as more blood flowed from his severed leg.

Climbing in with him, Mary pulled the door shut and then pulled her shirt off, using the fabric to tie a crude tourniquet around the wound.

"You could have been killed," Kate told her from the back-seat, where she was holding Becca's lifeless body while four other children, crammed into the car's narrow space, shivered with terror. "As far as the world is concerned, these children are dead! Their bones were found!"

"Only some of them," Mary replied as she finished tying the tourniquet. "I'm not going to leave them out there to die just because you tell me it's fate!" Looking down at Robert's bloodied leg, she thought back to the knee she'd discovered with the metal plate. She turned and looked back out at the battlefield, quickly realizing that the leg must be out there now, waiting to sink into the mud so it could be dug up hundreds of years later.

"The children slipped back in time to the battle!" Kate shouted. "They should have stayed there! Only Becca matters, because only Becca has an important role to play in the future!"

"How is this happening?" Mary stammered, looking out through the windshield and seeing scores of men fighting with swords. She'd seen historical re-enactments of English Civil War battles, but the brutality of the real thing was beyond anything she'd witnessed before, and blood was running down the window, mixed with rain. Everywhere she looked, she saw men being cut down, their bodies hacked to pieces by the rotten soldiers which now attacked Royalists and Parliamentarians alike. "What is this?" she whispered.

"What do you *think* it is?" Kate asked. "It's the Battle of Sharpeton."

"The Battle of Sharpeton took place over three hundred years ago," Mary pointed out, watching as a man was run through with a sword. A little further off, another man was beheaded.

"Three hundred years ago," Kate replied, "*and* today."

Mary turned to her.

"The fog is responsible," Kate continued. "The fog allows separate time periods to meet. It took the children from 2010 and sent them back to the battle, and now it has briefly brought the battle to the present day. The Battle of Sharpeton began in 1644 when the Royalists and Parliamentarians came face to face on this land. But when they began to fight in the fog, they found themselves up against another threat, something from the twenty-first century. They found themselves facing a third army of dead, rotten soldiers that had risen from the mud. Like zombiefied versions of their own corpses."

Mary shook her head.

"You might not understand it," Kate hissed, "but the proof is right outside this car!"

Staring out the window, Mary realized it was true. The dead soldiers, covered in mud and with most of their flesh missing, were fighting with more vigor than any of the living men, carving their way through the ranks on both sides. Royalists and Parliamentarians, sworn enemies for so long, now helped one another up from the mud as the rotten soldiers advanced.

"But the dead soldiers..." she stammered. "I mean, they're... The dead soldiers *died* in the Battle of Sharpeton. That's *why* they're dead!"

"And then they rotted in the ground for three and a half centuries," Kate continued, "until they rose up tonight to rejoin the battle from the other side of the split in time. Even now, men from the seventeenth century are charging into the fog, only to find themselves fighting their own dead, future selves. Men are being cut down and slaughtered by their own corpses."

Mary watched as one man raced past the car only to stop a moment later as a rotten soldier turned toward him. With a slow sense of realization, she realized that the man was facing his own corpse, which quickly snarled as it cut him down with a strike from its sword. As the dying man slumped down into the mud, his future self was already stepping over him, pushing him down into the mud as it set off in search of a fresh victim.

"This isn't possible," she whispered.

"It's a paradox," Kate explained. "One side couldn't exist without the other, yet they each exist *because* of the other. Such is the nature of the fog on this moor. Two periods in time, momentarily fused together. The result is chaos."

Mary turned to her.

"It's the same hole in time that the children fell into," Kate continued. "They ended up at this moment too."

"Please," one of the boys stammered, staring out at the horrific scenes. "I want to go home."

Next to him, two of the girls were hugging one another, their bodies shivering with fear.

All around, more and more soldiers – both Royalist and Parliamentarian – were being cut down by their own rotten, future selves. Mary wanted to look away, to hide her face and ignore the screams, but she couldn't bring herself to even blink. Even when dead bodies slammed into the side of the car, she barely reacted at all, watching instead as more and more soldiers came charging onto the battlefield from either side, only to be quickly cut down by the army of dead men at the center. Finally, however, she noticed that some of the soldiers were stopping a little further away, as if they were seeing the horrific truth.

A moment later, she saw soldiers from both the Royalist and Parliamentarian side starting to run for their lives.

"Run men!" a voice cried out nearby. "It's some form of witchcraft!"

Even now, the army of the undead refused to yield, still claiming as many lives as possible. Over the next few minutes, however, the fighting outside the car began to die down. The rotten soldiers still cut down a few more victims, but finally the battlefield was clear of all but the undead, who waited in the fog for more victims to arrive. The fog itself, however, was starting to fade away, leaving the undead warriors with no-one left to fight.

"It's over," Kate said after a moment. "I was there in 1644 when the battle first took place, and now I have witnessed it from the other side of the time-split. As I always knew I must."

"Those men," Mary stammered, turning to her, "were killed by their own future selves?"

"Some of them, yes. They also cut down the children who vanished on the moor a few years ago, who found themselves transported to the heart of the battlefield."

"So that's why the Battle of Sharpeton was

forgotten?" Mary asked. "Because men faced their own dead selves on the battlefield and turned back?"

"In some ways, the ones who died were the lucky ones. The rest had to live the rest of their lives, remembering such a horrific scene. Imagine charging into battle, only to face your own rotten corpse coming at you, with your own rusty sword raised. Of the soldiers who ran today and escaped back to the seventeenth century, I imagine most died in the corners of dark pubs, trying to drink their nightmares away."

Staring out the window, Mary saw that the fog had begun to recede, leaving the undead soldiers still standing on the battlefield. The saved schoolchildren were whimpering and sobbing in the car's back seat, but Mary was too stunned to comfort them. Instead, she stared at the rotten soldiers, horrified by the sight of ragged flesh hanging from their bones.

"How can this be real?" she whispered. "How can two moments in time meet like this? How can men face *themselves* in battle?"

"It will happen again," Kate said darkly. "This is just a taste of the greater tragedy to come in this country."

Mary turned to her. "What do you mean? What tragedy?"

Before Kate could answer, the car door opened and a figure stopped outside, waiting.

"The girl must go with him," Kate said, starting to gather Becca's dead body in her arms. "Becca can't be allowed to die. She has a role to play when she's older, and there's still time to set her destiny back on course."

"A role?" Mary asked. "What role?"

"There's no time to explain!"

Opening her mouth to argue, Mary suddenly saw the true horror of Becca's injuries, which had left the girl's face carved open all the way from the top of her head down to her neck. There was clearly no hope of reviving her, so Mary simply watched as Kate carried her out of the car and placed her in Freeman's arms. Wisps of fog still curled through the air, drifting around the little girl's dead body.

"You know what you must happen next," Kate said firmly.

"I do," Freeman replied, "but the girl -"

"Don't fight this!" Kate continued. "Your country will need you again one day, but until then there is nothing for you to do here. I put you beneath the ground once, and you broke free. This time, you must stay there until you're called." She paused, before placing a hand on Becca's dead shoulder. "Until *she* calls you. Soldier to soldier."

"I understand," Freeman muttered. "But she is -"

"You know what to do," Kate told him.

"Aye," he replied, "that I do."

"Perhaps this is how it was always meant to be," Kate continued. "I see the broad strokes of future history, but rarely the details. You are a dark and cruel man, Nykolas Freeman, but I sense that this girl has lightened you a little. I pray that such a change will hold."

"The modern world is too different to my own," Freeman replied. "I know not my place in it, but I see full well that the rules of the past no longer apply. I can only trust that if I am woken again one day, I will have a better understanding of what I must do."

"You will," Kate told him. "That, I promise you. And next time, you will have an army at your side."

Left alone in the car for a moment, Mary finally crawled across the blood-soaked seat and climbed out, only to see that Freeman had dropped his ax and was now carrying Becca away into the last of the fog. The rotten soldiers, meanwhile, were slowly starting to follow him. Scores and scores of undead figures stumbled past, ignoring Mary completely as they made their way into the fog. Finally, she watched as their shadows faded into the distance, as if the fog was swallowing them up.

She turned, filled with a thousand more questions, but Kate had vanished too.

"Can we go home?" one of the schoolchildren asked, her voice trembling as she sat in the back seat with her classmates. "I want to go home."

"Where are the others?" added one of the boys. "Where are Nanny and Mr. Bronson?"

Mary turned to them, and then she looked at the landlord's son, who was pale and unconscious but still breathing. The tourniquet seemed to have done the job, at least for now, but fresh blood was already soaking through the fabric.

"I..." Pausing, Mary tried to find the words, but her mind was racing and she couldn't believe what she'd seen.

Shivering in the rain, barely able to register the

pain in her leg and ankle, she turned and looked around at the fog, terrified in case another figure was about to come stumbling toward her, but finally she realized that they were truly gone. She tried to take a step forward, but the agony in her right leg was too much and she dropped back down against the side of the car, breathless and cold. She waited, but she knew she lacked the energy to move. Finally she began to ease herself down to the ground, where puddles of blood were already soaking into the muddy battlefield. Exhausted and barely able to think straight, she stared ahead into the receding fog and realized there was no way to rationalize everything she'd witnessed. Either soldiers had traveled forward in time to fight their undead selves, or she'd completely lost her mind. Behind her, the other children were starting to crawl forward, as if they finally dared come out of the car.

A moment later, Mary heard footsteps running closer.

Looking around, filled with fear, she suddenly saw that a figure was approaching through the last of the lingering fog. Bracing herself for another of the undead creatures to arrive, she realized after a few seconds that this figure was smaller somehow. She watched in horror, until finally she saw that the figure was another child. A moment later, Becca came into view. The little girl quickly dropped down and wrapped her arms around Mary's shoulders, hugging her tight.

"What are you doing?" Mary stammered. "Where did you come from? How are you even -"

Pulling back, she stared into the girl's face.

"How are you alive?"

"He saved me," Becca replied, with all her injuries having faded away. She paused, before turning to look back at the receding fog, just as the last wisps faded into the night air. "A crack in the ground opened up and he led them all down there. He took me with them, deep into the ground, into the darkness, and then he placed a gold coin on the ground. He said that would seal them all in, at least until they were needed, and then..." Reaching up, she felt her own face for a moment, as if she couldn't quite believe that her wounds were gone. "He told me he was giving me his life force. He said he'd have to take it back one day, when England needed him again, but that for now it could be mine. He told me I didn't belong with the dead, and he said I had to run." Shivering, she turned back to Mary. "And then the crack in the ground closed again, as soon as I was out."

"Who was he?" Mary asked.

"His name was Nykolas Freeman."

"Freeman?"

Becca nodded.

"No," Mary continued, "Nykolas Freeman lived a long, long time ago. That man can't possibly have been him."

"He told me my sister would be here soon," Becca added. "He said I just have to wait a little longer."

Mary paused for a few seconds, unable to believe what the little girl was saying, but a moment later she looked at the child's face and saw that all the wounds from the ax really *had* been taken away. She reached out, running her fingertips against the girl's smooth flesh, marveling at the fact that such deep, horrific injuries could have vanished in the space of just a few minutes. She told herself that it was impossible, but at the same time the proof was right in front of her. So many impossible things had happened, in fact, that she felt she could never be certain about anything again.

"I..."

She paused.

"I just... It can't... That can't have been Nykolas Freeman, it just can't. Even after -"

Stopping suddenly, she saw something glinting in the mud. Reaching out with a trembling hand, she picked up the battered ax that the dark figure had dropped a few minutes earlier. Even before she turned it over to examine the handle, she knew what she was holding, and she understood that somehow the ax of the great Nykolas Freeman had finally been unearthed. The lights of approaching police cars could be seen in the distance now, but Mary didn't even notice them. Instead, all she could do was stare at the ax as slowly she began to realize that the impossible really *had* happened.

And she was holding the proof in her hands.

CHAPTER FIFTY-SEVEN

"SHE'S STABLE FOR NOW," Doctor Carlisle muttered as he adjusted a couple of settings on the machine next to Laura's hospital bed. "Whatever was causing her cardiac problems, it seems to have passed as quickly as it started. Frankly, I'm at a loss."

"It's coming," Laura whispered for the hundredth time, as her fevered face twitched slightly. Her eyes opened briefly, just for a second, before slipping shut again. "Now the pain starts."

"We should just let her rest," the doctor continued. "I'm sure she'll start to recover soon."

"But the things she's been saying," Laura's mother replied. "About pain, and about something that's going to happen -"

"Just the ravings of a sick mind," he said firmly, interrupting her. He stepped closer and patted her on the shoulder, as if to offer a sliver of comfort, before heading to the door. "Don't pay too much attention.

Laura's very troubled. Whatever comes out of her mouth right now, it's just going to be gibberish. We're going to need to restart her therapy."

"He'll be needed one day," Laura whispered, as her mother took a seat next to her bed and began to stroke her hair. "The rain's going to get colder and colder. There'll be so many battlefields..."

EPILOGUE

"EXTRAORDINARY SCENES HERE AT Wyvern Lodge this morning," the reporter continued, addressing a camera as he stood in the hospital's parking lot. "We don't know the exact circumstances, but sources have confirmed that five of the missing Sharpeton children have been found alive and well. Unfortunately, police also say that a number of bodies have been discovered on the moor, so it looks like there won't be a happy ending for all the families involved."

***

Mary stood at the window of the hospital room and watched the car park below. Bright afternoon sun was shining as Becca ran toward Kerry, finally embracing her sister after so long apart. Having already met Kerry briefly during the morning, Mary knew that Becca would be going to live with her now. Their family, or what was left of it, had finally been reunited.

Hearing a gasp of pain nearby, Mary turned and saw that Daniel was trying to sit up in the bed. Covered in bandages and hooked to a series of machines, he looked as if he'd been almost hacked apart, but somehow he'd managed to hang on until the police had discovered him in the jeep. Limping over to him, Mary winced at the pain in her ankle, but finally she managed to sit on the edge of the bed.

"Don't try to move too much," she told him. "Remember what the doctor said."

He tried to reply, but the effort was too much and he let out another frustrated gasp.

"I spoke to some people at the university earlier," she continued. "As soon as we get out of here, they want us to start heading up a new exhibition. They also have some research funding they're going to divert our way, so we can establish a multi-year program. I told them our first job should be to organize an exhibition in Doctor Clarke's memory, with that ax as the main draw. The whole thing is going to focus on Nykolas Freeman, now that we have absolute cast-iron proof that he was a real figure. Something tells me that Doctor Clarke's books are going to sell like crazy. I've been thinking about the different angles we can use, and maybe -"

"What are you doing?" he asked suddenly.

She paused. "I'm... planning the next phase of our work."

He began to laugh, before wincing as the stitches pulled on his wounds. "Can't you shut off the academic side of your brain for five minutes?" he gasped.

"I just want to hit the ground running," she told him. "Nykolas Freeman -"

"Freeman..." Daniel replied, pushing through the pain. "Forget Freeman. We should be focusing on the Battle of Sharpeton."

Mary shook her head.

"The Battle of Sharpeton is more important than Freeman," Daniel continued. "We still have to figure out why it was covered up."

"I think I know why it was covered up," she told him, with a hint of sadness in her eyes. "I saw things last night, Daniel. Things that couldn't be real, things that defy all logic, but at the same time they were right in front of me. I can't even begin to describe what it was like in that car, or running out across the battlefield to rescue the children, but you just have to trust me. The stories about that moor are true. Men from the past fought their future, dead selves. I don't blame them for running, but I sure as hell don't know how to tell their story in an academic paper." She paused. "Do you know about Laura Woodley?"

"That mad girl who thought she met Freeman?"

"She wasn't mad. And part of her story was that she'd somehow slipped back in time to the seventeenth century. I don't know what it is about that fog, but it seems to link two periods in time. I think something similar happened to the schoolchildren. Somehow they ended up on the battlefield. Most of them were quickly slaughtered, they didn't stand a chance, and that's why their bones were buried so deep."

She paused for a moment.

"But five of them survived," she added finally, with a faint smile. "Robert lost his knee, but I saw the pub's landlord earlier, he came in to be reunited with his son. If anyone doubts what happened, those five surviving children are here today as proof. And the bones of the other twelve, and their two teachers, will be identified soon, I'm sure of it." She immediately saw the hint of incredulity in his eyes. "You don't believe me?"

He stared at her. "You're talking about some kind of time travel," he pointed out. "Mary, that's completely insane."

"The children are here," she replied. "They're in this hospital, getting checked over. Robert lost his leg, but the rest of them are more or less fine. From their perspective, they were only gone for a few minutes."

"But..." He hesitated. "It's too much, Mary. I can't get my head around it all."

"I'm pretty sure most people will think the same thing," she continued, "which is why we can't really publish any papers on the subject. At least, not any that put forward the truth about what happened. So the Battle of Sharpeton is something we can wait to study. Who knows? Maybe we'll come up with another explanation, one that's more believable and that'll be more palatable to the people who peer-review our work. I doubt it, though. For now we'll focus on Freeman."

"But the bodies," he replied. "We have hundreds of bodies that we dug up from the site!"

She shook her head.

"What do you mean?" he asked. "Did the company take them?"

"Most of them are gone," she explained. "They got up and walked away. They followed Nykolas Freeman deep into the ground. The only ones left behind are, most likely, the remaining schoolchildren. We actually have very little proof of the battle at all, although we still have Captain Villiers' standard."

Daniel paused, as if he still didn't quite believe everything she was telling him.

"Are you serious?" he asked finally. "Mary, you're the most level-headed person I've ever met in my life. You care about facts! And proof! You've never entertained a ghost story, you laugh at people who believe in that sort of thing!"

"Because I'd never seen any proof that they could be real," she replied, thinking back for a moment to the sight of the soldiers rising up from the mud. "Now I *have*, so I'm sticking to my usual rule. If I see something right in front of my eyes, then I have to accept that it's real, even if I don't quite understand it yet." She forced a smile, although the effort caused the stitches in her belly to hurt a little. "Of course, the police aren't going to accept that explanation. They want to talk to me later. I guess they still need to figure out an explanation for the fact that the bones of the children seem so old, and the fact that Robert and the others don't seem to have aged over the past few years. They'll probably come up with some theory to satisfy their curiosity and calm the parents' questions, but I don't think they'll ever explain it properly. They're already tying themselves in knots about that Craig guy, and how he fits into everything."

Watching Daniel for a moment, she realized he was staring at her with an expression of concern.

"What?" she asked.

"Nothing."

"You're looking at me like I'm crazy."

"Well, you..." He paused. "You know what? Never mind. When I get out of here, we'll have plenty of time to discuss it while we're working on the Nykolas Freeman study."

"Until then," she replied, slowly getting to her feet, "you need to rest."

"I'll be out in a day or two."

"Hardly. You were damn-near hacked to death. It's a miracle you survived at all." She paused, before leaning down and kissing his bandaged forehead. "I just wish Doctor Clarke had lived to know what we'd found. Can you imagine how he'd have felt if he'd seen Freeman's ax taking pride of place in an exhibition?"

"His smugness would've gone off the charts," Daniel pointed out. "Rest in peace and all that, obviously."

Shuffling toward the door, Mary tried not to let it show that she was in so much pain.

"Do you *really* believe Nykolas Freeman came back to life and was roaming the moor over the past few days?" Daniel asked suddenly.

She turned to him.

"I mean deep down," he continued, "after everything you've seen and experienced, are you really going to accept that something like that might have happened? That it *could* happen?"

She paused for a moment, feeling as if she'd be ridiculed for answering honestly.

"I think we have some research to plan," she told him finally, "and an exhibition to set up, and an ax to study in great detail. We'll stick to the facts, and we'll let them guide us. If a logical, rational study of the situation proves that Freeman somehow came back, then... We can't ignore those facts, can we? I just wish we could have saved *all* the children."

Stepping out into the corridor, she was just in time to see the pub's landlord wheeling Robert into the elevator. They exchanged a glance for a moment, before the landlord mouthed "Thank you" and then headed through the doors.

"Doctor Baker?"

Turning, Mary saw two police detectives heading toward her.

"I don't really know where to start," one of them said cautiously, "but... Can we go and talk somewhere? We kinda have a lot of questions about what happened last night."

***

A few lingering strands of mist drifted across the moor. Afternoon sunlight had begun to dry the huge puddles of muddy water left behind after the storm, although it would take many days, even weeks, for the land to become dry again. The storm had been monumental, one of the strongest for centuries, and in some places the very shape of the moor had been altered by such a long and sustained onslaught.

In one valley, not far from the dig site, a long scar had been left in the ground, as if the moor itself had briefly opened up and had then slammed shut again. The soil on the surface was twisted and damaged, yet somehow it wasn't loose and muddy like the rest of the surrounding land. Instead something seemed to be binding the scar shut from beneath, as if there was an invisible force that insisted on keeping its secrets locked away tight. Already, fresh grass was starting to grow over the scar, far more quickly than should ordinarily be the case. At such an accelerated rate, the scar would most likely be completely covered in a matter of days, and eventually the land would become smooth again, with nothing to indicate that it had ever been torn apart.

Standing nearby, Kate watched the damaged earth. She knew what was down there, and she also knew that one day it would be called upon to return to the surface. Although she would try desperately to stall the inevitable, she had come to accept that her powers were not enough to keep the rampant danger from tearing the land apart. When she'd witnessed the Battle of Sharpeton in 1644, she'd realized that she would witness it again from the other side, and that once that day arrived she would be unable to forestall the inevitable. A terrible conflict was coming to the land, and it would bring more madness and pain that she would be forced to observe. Just as she had observed so many tragedies during her centuries of life.

Feeling ice-cold rain starting to fall, Kate turned and walked away.

Deep down beneath her feet, several hundred meters beneath the surface of the moor, hundreds of rotten soldiers lay wedged in the soil, frozen in place and unable to move. Buried deeper than ever before, they were still aware of their surroundings, but most of them were lost in memories, thinking of the horrific day when they'd faced their own faces on the battlefield. They had endured the battle once as living men, and then as the undead. None of the soldiers really understood what had happened, but their minds had been wrecked by the horror of fighting themselves. Some of them still tried to dig themselves free, to rise from the earth, but they could only get so far before they were forced back down. The gold coin, embedded once again in the ground, served as a barrier.

Beneath them all, in a pocket of air, there sat a lone figure. Hunched and still, he stared ahead into darkness. He knew that one day he would be called to rise again and rejoin to the world above, but for now Nykolas Freeman was content to rest and reflect upon the horrors he had witnessed.

Waiting until the day he would be needed again.

BATTLEFIELD

Also by Amy Cross

The Curse of Wetherley House

"If you walk through that door, Evil Mary will get you."

When she agrees to visit a supposedly haunted house with an old friend, Rosie assumes she'll encounter nothing more scary than a few creaks and bumps in the night. Even the legend of Evil Mary doesn't put her off. After all, she knows ghosts aren't real. But when Mary makes her first appearance, Rosie realizes she might already be trapped.

For more than a century, Wetherley House has been cursed. A horrific encounter on a remote road in the late 1800's has already caused a chain of misery and pain for all those who live at the house. Wetherley House was abandoned long ago, after a terrible discovery in the basement, something has remained undetected within its room. And even the local children know that Evil Mary waits in the house for anyone foolish enough to walk through the front door.

Before long, Rosie realizes that her entire life has been defined by the spirit of a woman who died in agony. Can she become the first person to escape Evil Mary, or will she fall victim to the same fate as the house's other occupants?

Also by Amy Cross

A House in London

"You'll love our little Ivan. He's such an easy boy to look after."

Short of money after moving to London, Jennifer Griffith accepts a job babysitting for a wealthy couple. When she arrives at their house, however, she quickly learns that this particular baby isn't quite what he seems.

Although she agrees to go through with the job for one night, it doesn't take long before she starts to regret her choice. Something dark lurks in the shadows of the house, something that wants something from Jennifer. Something that won't let go, not even after she heads home...

A House in London is a horror novella about a girl who always dreamed of a house in London, and who finally discovers a nightmare waiting in the shadows.

Also by Amy Cross

The Bride of Ashbyrn House

In the English countryside, miles from the nearest town, there stands an old stone house. Nobody has set foot in the house for years. Nobody has dared. For it is said that even though the lady of the house is long dead, a face can sometimes be seen at one of the windows. A pale, dead face that waits patiently behind a silk wedding veil.

Seeking an escape from his life in London, Owen Stone purchases Ashbyrn House without waiting to find out about its history. As far as Owen is concerned, ghosts aren't real and his only company in the house will be the thin-legged spiders that lurk on the walls. Even after he moves in, and after he starts hearing strange noises in the night, Owen insists that Ashbyrn House can't possibly be haunted.

But Owen knows nothing about the ghostly figure that is said to haunt the house. Or about the mysterious church bells that ring out across the lawn at night. Or about the terrible fate that befell the house's previous inhabitants when they dared defy the bride.

The Bride of Ashbyrn House is a ghost story about a man who believes the past can't hurt him, and about a woman whose search for a husband has survived even her own tragic death.

Also by Amy Cross

The Ghost of Longthorn Manor

A woman watches from a high window as her brother approaches the house...

A little girl realizes that her family's new home is trying to warn her about something...

A teenager with a debilitating mental health problem starts hearing a scratching sound, coming from the attic...

The Ghost of Longthorn Manor and Other Stories is a collection of short horror stories by Amy Cross. From families looking to start over in a new house, to people trying to scrape a living in a harsh world, all the characters in these stories have one thing in common. They're all about to find that death isn't necessarily the end, and that some houses harbor the most terrifying secrets.

The Ghost of Longthorn Manor and Other Stories contains the new stories *The Ghost of Longthorn Manor, Black Pages, Isn't This the House..., Touched, My Father's House, The Swimming Pool* and *The House Speaks*, plus a completely new version of *The Writer*. This book contains scenes of violence, as well as strong language.

Also by Amy Cross

Laura

"You don't think this could be about Laura, do you?"

Ten years ago, they were all friends. Ten years ago, something terrible happened. Ten years ago, they agreed to take the truth about Laura to their graves. All they had to do was forget, and keep their mouths shut.

But when a hidden force starts cutting them down one by one, in a series of increasingly horrific incidents, the remaining friends are forced to face the truth.

Somehow, Laura has come back.

Laura is a horror story about six people who thought they could hide the truth, and about the girl who returns from the grave to make them all pay.

Also by Amy Cross

The Devil, the Witch and the Whore

When a horrific discovery is made at the edge of town, Sheriff James Kopperud realizes the answers he seeks might be waiting beyond in the vast forest. But everybody in the town of Deal knows that there's something out there in the forest, something that should never be disturbed. A deal was made long ago, a deal that was supposed to keep the town safe. And if he insists on investigating the murder of a local girl, James is going to have to break that deal and head out into the wilderness.

Meanwhile, James has no idea that his estranged daughter Ramsey has returned to town. Ramsey is running from something, and she thinks she can find safety in the vast tunnel system that runs beneath the forest. Before long, however, Ramsey finds herself coming face to face with creatures that hide in the shadows. Soon, she's offered a terrible deal, one that could save or destroy the entire town, and maybe even the world.

The Devil, the Witch and the Whore is the first book in a trilogy about a town and its demons, and about the consequences of making a deal with the devil. Contains scenes of horror and violence.

Also by Amy Cross

The Farm

One farm. Two tragedies, thirty years apart. And a tortured figure whose presence connects both incidents...

In 1979, the Bondalen family farm in Norway is home to three young girls. As winter fades to spring, Elizabeth, Kari and Sara each come to face the secrets of the barn, and they each emerge with their own injuries. But someone else is lurking nearby, a man who claims to be Death incarnate, and for these three girls the spring of 1979 is set to end in tragedy.

Today, the farm has finally been sold to a new family. Dragged from London by her widowed father, Paula Ridley hates the idea of rural life. Soon, however, she starts to realize that her new home retains hints of its horrific past, while the darkness of the barn still awaits anyone who dares venture inside.

Set over the course of several decades, *The Farm* is a horror novel about people who live with no idea of the terror in their midst, and about a girl who finally has to confront a creature that has been feeding on the farm's inhabitants for generations...

Also by Amy Cross

B&B

A girl on the run, hiding from a terrible crime.

An old B&B in a snowy city.

A hidden figure lurking in the streets, waiting for his next victim.

When Bobbie takes a room at the rundown Castle Crown B&B, all she wants is to get some sleep and make a tough decision about her future. Unfortunately, the B&B's other guests won't give her any peace, and Bobbie soon realizes that she's stumbled into a world with its own rules. Who is the mysterious bandaged woman? Why is there a dead man in the bathtub? And is something deadly lurking in the basement?

Before she can leave, however, Bobbie learns that the city of Canterbury is being terrorized by a mysterious figure. Every time snow comes, the Snowman claims another victim, leaving their blood sinking into the ice. If Bobbie leaves the B&B and ventures out into the empty streets, she risks becoming his next target. But if she stays, her soul might be condemned forever.

B&B is a horror story about a girl with a secret, and a building with a past.

Also by Amy Cross

The Ghosts of Hexley Airport

Ten years ago, more than two hundred people died in a horrific plane crash at Hexley Airport.

Today, some say their ghosts still haunt the terminal building.

When she starts her new job at the airport, working a night shift as part of the security team, Casey assumes the stories about the place can't be true. Even when she has a strange encounter in a deserted part of the departure hall, she's certain that ghosts aren't real.

Soon, however, she's forced to face the truth. Not only is there something haunting the airport's buildings and tarmac, but a sinister force is working behind the scenes to replicate the circumstances of the original accident. And as a snowstorm moves in, Hexley Airport looks set to witness yet another disaster.

Printed in Poland
by Amazon Fulfillment
Poland Sp. z o.o., Wrocław